"I'm not the enemy."

Liam willed her to believe him, knowing she wouldn't. "I'm here to help."

Danielle shoved her hair back from her face. "You can't. Don't you get it?"

"Yes, I can. Because I know things you don't." About Titan. His handiwork. His trail of devastation. "I have resources you can't begin to fathom."

"I don't want your resources," Danielle shot back. "Why can't you understand that?"

"Because you're scared," he told her, even though he didn't understand. Bringing down Titan was all he'd thought about, wanted, for three long years. "Because I stood in the shadows watching you for over an hour." And had seen her shaking, shivering. "And because I'm your best chance." He grabbed her arm. "You need me, Danielle. You need me in ways you can't even begin to imagine."

And, God help him, *he* needed *her* even more.

Dear Reader,

Welcome to another month of excitingly romantic reading from Silhouette Intimate Moments. Ruth Langan starts things off with a bang in *Vendetta,* the third of her four DEVIL'S COVE titles. Blair Colby came back to town looking for a quiet summer. Instead he found danger, mystery—and love.

Fans of Sara Orwig's STALLION PASS miniseries will be glad to see it continued in *Bring On The Night,* part of STALLION PASS: TEXAS KNIGHTS, also a fixture in Silhouette Desire. Mix one tough agent, the ex-wife he's never forgotten and the son he never knew existed, and you have a recipe for high emotion. Whether you experienced our FAMILY SECRETS continuity or are new to it now, you won't want to miss our six FAMILY SECRETS: THE NEXT GENERATION titles, starting with Jenna Mills' *A Cry In The Dark.* Ana Leigh's *Face of Deception* is the first of her BISHOP'S HEROES stories, and your heart will beat faster with every step of Mike Bishop's mission to rescue Ann Hamilton and her adopted son from danger. Are you a fan of the paranormal? Don't miss *One Eye Open,* popular author Karen Whiddon's first book for the line, which features a shape-shifting heroine and a hero who's all man. Finally, go *To The Limit* with new author Virginia Kelly, who really knows how to write heart-pounding romantic adventure.

And come back next month, for more of the best and most exciting romance reading around, right here in Silhouette Intimate Moments.

Yours,

Leslie J. Wainger
Executive Editor

Please address questions and book requests to:
Silhouette Reader Service
U.S.: 3010 Walden Ave., P.O. Box 1325, Buffalo, NY 14269
Canadian: P.O. Box 609, Fort Erie, Ont. L2A 5X3

A Cry in the Dark
JENNA MILLS

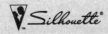

INTIMATE MOMENTS™

Published by Silhouette Books

America's Publisher of Contemporary Romance

A special thanks to my fellow FAMILY SECRETS: THE NEXT GENERATION authors—Marie Ferrarella, Candace Irvin, Linda Winstead Jones, Kylie Brant and Ingrid Weaver. You ladies define class, talent and professionalism—working with you was an absolute joy.

For Stephanie Maurer and Leslie Wainger—thanks for inviting me to participate in such a wonderful project. Developing these characters and this story was a terrific experience.

For Susan Litman—thanks for being such a gem to work with!! Thanks also for all your guidance and input as Danielle and Liam came to life. You're awesome!

And for little Ellie, thanks for allowing me to finish this book before you made your big arrival!

Special thanks and acknowledgment are given to Jenna Mills for her contribution to the FAMILY SECRETS: THE NEXT GENERATION series.

SILHOUETTE BOOKS

ISBN 0-373-27369-X

A CRY IN THE DARK

Visit Silhouette Books at www.eHarlequin.com

Printed in U.S.A.

Books by Jenna Mills

Silhouette Intimate Moments

Smoke and Mirrors #1146
When Night Falls #1170
The Cop Next Door #1181
A Kiss in the Dark #1199
The Perfect Target #1212
Crossfire #1275
Shock Waves #1287
A Cry in the Dark #1299

Silhouette Books

Family Secrets

A Verdict of Love

JENNA MILLS

grew up in south Louisiana, amidst romantic plantation ruins, haunting swamps and timeless legends. It's not surprising, then, that she wrote her first romance at the ripe old age of six! Three years later, this librarian's daughter turned to romantic suspense with *Jacquie and the Swamp,* a harrowing tale of a young woman on the run in the swamp and the dashing hero who helps her find her way home. Since then her stories have grown in complexity, but her affinity for adventurous women and dangerous men has remained constant. She loves writing about strong characters torn between duty and desire, conscious choice and destiny.

When not writing award-winning stories brimming with deep emotion, steamy passion and page-turning suspense, Jenna spends her time with her husband, two cats, two dogs and a menagerie of plants in their Dallas, Texas, home. Jenna loves to hear from her readers. She can be reached via e-mail at writejennamills@aol.com, or via snail mail at P.O. Box 768, Coppell, Texas 75019.

FAMILY SECRETS: THE NEXT GENERATION

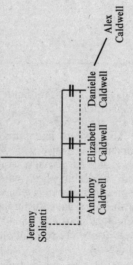

Henry Bloomfield (d.) ~ Deanna Payne

Jeremy
Solienti

Anthony
Caldwell

Elizabeth
Caldwell

Danielle
Caldwell

Alex
Caldwell

Key:
— Birth Family
- - - Adoptive Family
m. Married
d. Deceased
═ Triplets

Prologue

The cry ripped through the late-afternoon silence.

Gretchen Miller stopped folding her daughter's pink-and-white play outfit and looked up abruptly. She held herself very still, listening intently, as only a mother could.

Violet.

Her heart kicked hard. She sprang to her feet and ran across the hardwood floor of her suburban Boston home, toward the staircase leading upstairs, where her daughter napped.

"Sweetheart?"

She heard her husband's voice but didn't slow. Couldn't. Not when her daughter needed her. After years of longing for a child and believing the miracle would never come her way, Gretchen had dedicated herself to motherhood with a ferocity that even she had never imagined. Gone was the woman whose life had once consisted solely of ancient writings and academic pursuits. In her place lived a mother who thrived on art projects and play dates.

"Violet?" she called, reaching the top of the stairs. She tried to strip the concern from her voice, but adrenaline drowned out her effort. The cry had been sudden and intense, drenched in distress and fear. If her little girl was hurt—

Wide blue eyes greeted Gretchen the second she raced into the pink room with the white canopy bed. Sandy-blond hair framed her daughter's pixie face. She sat in a small chair in front of the art table. In front of her, crayons lay scattered across a sheet of drawing paper.

Gretchen drank in the scene—the beautifully, perfectly normal scene—and tried to regain her equilibrium.

"Whatcha drawing?" she asked, moving to squat beside her little girl. With a hand she fought to steady, she brushed the hair back from Violet's pale face.

Her little girl gazed up at her, her eyes darker than usual, her pupils dilated, almost trancelike. It took a moment for Gretchen to realize the child was still mostly asleep.

"Come, now," she cooed, lifting her daughter into her arms and carrying her back to bed. She deposited her among the messy sheets and stretched out beside her. "How about we nap together?"

"Everything okay?"

The soft Texas drawl had her glancing toward the doorway. She and Kurt had been married for three years now, but his rugged handsomeness still stole her breath. "I thought I heard something," she said. "A cry."

With a gentle smile he strolled to the bed and leaned down, kissed her softly on the lips. "Looks like everything's okay now."

Emotion swarmed the back of her throat. Fighting tears she didn't understand, she looked at her little girl, sleeping now, her breathing deep and rhythmic, as though five minutes before she'd not sat with crayon in hand. "I hope so," she whispered.

But deep inside, an innate sense warned otherwise.

The cry drowned out the gentle strains of the lullaby.
Lieutenant Marcus Evans, celebrated U.S. Navy SEAL,

man of steel, staggered against the chipped Formica counter. For a brutal, heart-stopping moment he was back on the Navy frigate that had failed miserably trying to tiptoe through a minefield. The impact rocked him hard, jump-started his heart.

Samantha.

On a violent rush of adrenaline he ran from the kitchen of the rented Naples, Florida, beach house, to the sprawling, sun-dappled room beyond, where his wife sat in a rocking chair, their five-month-old daughter, Honor, at her breast, their two-year-old son, Henry, tinkering with a building set at her feet.

The serenity of the scene stopped him cold. Through a curtain of flaming-red hair, Samantha, esteemed ambassador to the small country of Delmonico by day and gloriously creative wife by night, looked up and smiled. "Something wrong?"

His mouth went dry. "That's what I was going to ask you."

"Is it time yet?" Little Hank, as they called him, an astonishing combination of his mother's refined, classic beauty and his father's rough edges, bounded to his feet and raced across the room. "You promised we could go in the ocean," he said, sounding far older than most children his age. Enhanced genetics, they'd learned, could be passed from generation to generation. "I want you to teach me how to be a seal, like you."

Marcus hoisted his son into his arms, all the while his heart threatened to burst out of his chest. His son. His and Samantha's. Sometimes he still couldn't believe it. "Give me five, champ," he said, ruffling the boy's dark hair. "Why don't you go put your trunks on."

The second Hank's feet hit the sandy tile floor, he was racing toward his room in a flurry of energy that stunned even Marcus.

Samantha shifted Honor from one breast to another. "You've got that look," she observed.

"What look?"

Her mouth twisted into a wry smile. "The superhero look," she said. "Like you think there's someone you need to be saving."

He wanted to laugh. He tried to laugh. He knew that was the right response. But God help him, he could find no laughter, not when his pulse still pounded. A Navy SEAL, he'd learned to trust his sixth sense. Not only trust it, worship it. The tingling at the back of his neck, the churn to his gut—without these warnings Samantha would have died one horrible day three years before, and he would not be standing here staring at her in the rocking chair, with the sun streaming down on her face and his daughter suckling greedily at her breast.

"Just a feeling," he muttered, trying to scrape away the nasty sense of unease. His family was fine. He could see that for himself. There was no more danger stalking them. No more shadows. No more deception. That had all ended years ago, in what seemed like another lifetime.

But the cry had been so real. So panicked and incessant. A small cry. A child's cry.

"Reddy?" Hank asked in his two-year-old voice, skidding into the room. He'd stripped off his tattered "Property of the United States Navy" T-shirt and pulled on a pair of khaki swim trunks. No water wings for his boy. His son had inherited his love of, comfort with, water.

"You bet." Already bare-chested and in trunks himself, Marcus indulged one last, lingering look at his wife and daughter. Then he grinned at his son. "Last one to the water is a rotten egg," he taunted.

"Hoo-wah!" Grinning, the little boy took off toward the door, threw it open and raced outside. Laughing, Marcus charged after him, into the warm breeze of a lazy, sunny Florida afternoon.

But deep inside, the chill, the uncertainty, lingered.
Something was wrong. Very wrong.

The cry stopped him cold.

Outside the temperature soared near one hundred degrees, but the chill went through Jake Ingram like a frozen knife. He held himself very still for all of one punishing heartbeat, then he ran. Through the sunny foyer of his Dallas home, up the stairs, toward the master bedroom.

"Mariah!" Fear gripped him. Just yesterday the doctor had pronounced his wife in perfect health. Their unborn baby was thriving. Jake had seen the image on the sonogram screen, the heart beating strong, the little legs and arms wiggling. It was as though his son or daughter had been waving hello, dancing madly.

But now Mariah was home three hours early.

And he'd heard the cry.

"Honey—" He stopped abruptly, stared.

She emerged from the bathroom with her dark hair streaming down her back and a smile curving her lips. "What do you think? Do I look fat?"

The breath left his body on a painful rush. He told himself to move, to speak, to do something, anything, but all he could do was stare at his wife, standing beneath the skylight in a skimpy red bikini, with the most beautiful pouch in the world just starting to round her belly.

She frowned. "That bad?"

"No." The word almost shot out of him. And then he was across the room, tugging her into his arms, loving the feel of their child nudging against his abdomen. "You look perfect," he murmured, burying his face in her hair and drawing in the fresh, clean scent that was Mariah. After all this time, the intensity of his love for her still staggered him. "I just…" How to explain? "I thought I heard you cry out."

She pulled back and gazed up at him, amusement dancing

in her sharp, intelligent eyes. "I think maybe you're taking this visualization a little too far."

He forced a smile. "Maybe." From the moment they'd learned they were finally pregnant, Mariah had teased him incessantly, telling him it was time to start preparing for the sleep deprivation sure to come. She'd suggested he begin visualizing himself with a crying baby in his arms, pacing the dark halls of the house late at night.

"How about a swim?"

Again he let his gaze dip over his wife's body, more lush now in her fourth month of pregnancy, more feminine. He loved being in the pool with her, slippery flesh sliding, legs twining, especially late at night when she had a fondness for skinny-dipping. "Sounds great."

She pushed up on her toes and brushed a kiss over his lips. "Hurry down," she said, then swept out of the room, leaving him staring after her.

She was fine. He'd seen that for himself. Happy. Radiant. Glowing. Nothing was wrong. There was no one or nothing sinister lurking in the shadows. Not anymore. Their lives had returned to normal. The threat to him and his brothers and sisters had long since been neutralized.

Jake walked to the window, looked down through the thick canopies of a cluster of post oaks and saw his wife stepping into the black-bottom, lagoon-shaped pool. She dipped beneath the water, came up seconds later with her hair wet and slicked back from her face, water cascading down her body. Normally the sight fed his soul.

But standing there in his sunny bedroom, next to the big king-size bed that his tough, gutsy, FBI-agent wife insisted upon cluttering with an array of girlie throw-pillows, he couldn't push back the slippery edge of darkness. He'd heard the cry, damn it. He'd heard it. Loud. Panicked. Urgent. Like a summons, a plea. And deep in his gut, he knew the truth.

Something was very wrong.

Chapter 1

The remnants of the cry echoed, low, soft, deceptively benign, like the distant rumble of thunder from a passing summer storm.

Standing behind the reception desk of one of Chicago's elite hotels, the Stirling Manor, Danielle Caldwell ignored the unsettling sensation, concentrating instead on the collection of sun-dappled roses and fragrant lilies on the reception desk. Once, she would have been urgently seeking out the source of the disturbance, crafting a way to help. Once, she would have risked everything.

Once, she had.

Now she hummed softly as she slid a yellow and pink-splashed rose into the vase beside the snow-white lilies. Her brother would have accused her of trying to drown out her destiny, but Danielle no longer believed in such nonsense. Destiny, chance, did not rule her world. There were no such things as lucky or unlucky stars. You created your own fate, made your own choices.

Never again would she chase shadows. Never again would she splurge on instinct.

But the disturbance lingered at the back of her mind, dark and unsettling, choppy like the waters of Lake Michigan on a storm-shrouded day.

She knew better than to look. She knew better than to indulge. But she glanced around the richly paneled lobby, anyway, toward the collection of formal sofas and wing chairs situated next to a stone fireplace. A large Aubusson rug stretched leisurely across the hardwood floor. A huge mahogany bookcase held leather-bound books.

The scene was perfectly normal, a few lingering guests, a woman curled up with a book, almost a carbon copy of a hundred other afternoons since she'd joined the hotel's staff. And yet, something was off. Something was different. It was like a movie playing at the wrong speed, motion slowed just a fraction, elongated, jerky. Not quite real.

Because of the man.

He sat in a wing chair near the fireplace, impeccably dressed. His button-down shirt was dark gray, open at the throat, and his jeans were black. In his hands he held a newspaper—the same section he'd been holding for close to an hour.

She'd never seen someone sit so very, very still for so very, very long.

The disturbing current pulsed deeper. She knew she should look away, quit staring, but the whisper of fascination was too strong. He was tall. Too tall, too broad in the shoulder, to fade into anonymity. She'd noticed him, felt the ripple of his presence, the second he'd walked into the lobby. He carried an aura of authority like so many of the powerful patrons of the hotel, but the shadows were different. They were thick and they were dark, and they swirled around him like flashing warning signs.

Just like they did her brother, Anthony.

Look away, she told herself again, but then the man's eyes

were on hers, and for a fractured second it was all she could do to breathe. They were a deep brown like his hair, yet the darkness eddying in their depths defied color.

His expression never changed. There was no amusement at catching her staring, no quick swell of masculine triumph, no discomfort, no irritation, just the cool, impassive gaze of a man who saw everything but felt nothing.

It was a look she'd never seen before, and it scorched clear to the bone.

Frowning, humming louder, refusing to let the man affect her one second longer, she grabbed another rose, this one a pure deep yellow with a long, dark-green stem, and debated where to place it for maximum impact. Until she'd come to work at the hotel styled after an English manor house, she'd never imagined something as simple as a vase could cost more than she earned in a month. Granted, it was lead crystal and made in Ireland, but still. She'd always found old mason jars and chipped drinking glasses worked just fine.

"The lights are on, but apparently nobody is home."

Danielle looked up to find Ruth Sun, one of the hotel's long-time assistant managers, smiling at her. "Pardon?"

The woman's dark eyes twinkled. "You haven't heard a word I've said, have you?"

Danielle's heart beat a little faster. Everyone in the hotel knew Ruth had the boss's ear. She'd been around forever. One bad word from her, and all Danielle's hard work could be for nothing.

"You know how I get when the flowers arrive," she said lightly. "Everything else—"

"—falls to the background," Ruth finished for her. "I noticed." Her smile faded abruptly, and she reached out to grab Danielle's wrist. "Dear, you're bleeding."

Danielle stared at the trail of dark-red blood running against the pale skin of her arm. "I…" Focused on the unsettling man, she hadn't felt a thing. "It's just a prick."

Ruth made a maternal clucking noise, one that should have

comforted Danielle, but instead unleashed a sharp curl of longing for the mother taken from her life over a quarter of a century before. "You need to get that cleaned up."

Danielle nodded but didn't move. "Did you need something?" she asked. "Before?" When she'd been oblivious to everything but the echo of the cry that had ripped the fabric of the quiet June afternoon, and the man with the disturbing eyes.

"Not really." Ruth reached into a cabinet behind the long reception desk and came up with antiseptic and cotton. "Just thought you'd want to know someone was asking about you."

"About me?"

Ruth poured antiseptic onto the cotton. "What your name was, how long you'd worked here, if you were married, that kind of thing."

Danielle went very still. She worked hard to keep her face clear of all emotion, but when Ruth pressed the cotton to her skin, the sharp sting made her wince. God, she'd been so careful, covered her tracks so cleanly. "Who?"

Ruth kept dabbing. "A man."

The dread circled closer, tighter. No wonder she'd been edgy all afternoon. He'd finally come looking for her, the brother she'd not spoken with in two long years. Her heart leaped at the prospect, then abruptly slowed.

Her brother wouldn't ask about her marital status—but there had been another man earlier in the week. He'd seemed charming enough, but Danielle had seen through the aristocratic manners to a muddy aura that warned her to keep her distance. "What did he look like?"

The assistant manager looked up from her handiwork. "I'm surprised you didn't notice him. He's been sitting in the big leather wing chair most of the afternoon. Dark hair. Tall." Ruth let out a dreamy sigh. "Very, very tall."

With eyes like pools of midnight on a cloudless night.

"The guy in the gray button-down?" Danielle asked, and her heart beat a little faster. A lot harder.

"That's him," Ruth said. "Real good-looking guy."

Intense, Danielle silently corrected. Striking.

Gone.

"All better," Ruth pronounced, but the words barely registered. Danielle stared across the lobby, toward the elegant wing chair that now sat empty, the newspaper abandoned on the floor.

The quick slice of unease made no sense. "Where did he go?"

"He's right—" Ruth's words broke off. "That's strange. He was there just a second ago."

Frowning, Danielle glanced around the lobby, toward the elevator, the sweeping staircase, the elegant front doors. Found nothing. Not the man, anyway. There were other patrons, the businessmen, the elderly couple from Wichita, the honeymooners from Madison, but the tall man with the flat eyes was just…gone.

Except she still felt him. Deeply. Disturbingly.

"You going to get that?" Ruth asked.

Danielle blinked and brought herself back, heard the low melody of her mobile phone. Through a haze of distraction she reached for the small black device to which only four people had the number—her manager, her sister and her son's school and day-care center. "Hello, this is Danielle."

"Turn around."

She stiffened. "Come again?"

"Paste a smile on that pretty face of yours and turn around, away from the old woman."

Everything flashed. The motion of the lobby dimmed, slowed, seemed to drag. "I don't understand—"

"Just do it."

Her heart started to pound. Hard. Instinct warned her to obey, even as an age-old rebellious streak dared her to lift her chin and defy. She'd done that before, many times. And the cost had been high.

Slowly she turned from the comforting din of the hotel lobby and took a few steps away from Ruth. "Okay."

"Good girl." The voice was distorted, genderless.

"Who is this? What do you—"

"I have your son."

The world stopped. Fast. Violently. She no longer faced the hotel guests, but knew if she turned around, she would see nothing. No movement. No life.

But then the words penetrated even deeper, beyond the fog of shock and the blanket of horror to the logical part of her, the part Jeremy had honed and fine-tuned, sharpened to a gleaming point, and another truth registered.

She was being watched. Someone, someone close, knew her every move.

The man. The man who'd been watching her, asking questions. The one who had vanished but whose presence lingered.

"You what?" she asked, slowly indulging the need to look. To see.

"Don't move," the voice intoned, and abruptly she froze. "If you want to see him again, you'll do exactly what I say."

The world started moving again, from dead cold to fast forward in one horrible dizzying heartbeat. Everything swirled, blurred. Blindly she reached for the counter. Her son. God, her precious little boy. Her life.

"No cops," the man continued. It had to be him, she thought. The man from the lobby. The one who'd been watching her, asking about her. The one who'd vanished mere seconds ago. "Call them and negotiations end."

She wasn't sure how she stayed standing, not when every cell in her body cried out, louder and harder than the distorted cry she'd picked up an hour earlier. And she knew. God help her, she knew why she'd been on edge. Why she'd been disturbed. Her son. Someone had gotten to her son, and on some intuitive level, she'd known danger pushed close.

But just as with his father, she hadn't been able to protect.

"What do you want?" she asked with a calm that did not come easy to her Gypsy blood. She'd been in situations like this before, dangerous, confusing, never with her own son, but she'd gone where law enforcement could not go.

"Call the day-care center. Tell them Alex walked home on his own."

She swallowed hard. That was feasible. The center was only a few blocks from her small Rogers Park home. Alex knew the way. He was an adventurous kid, clever, daring, always in constant motion. It would be just like him to wander off when no one was looking.

"Then what?"

"Wait for instructions."

Deep inside she started to shake. It was only a sick joke, she wanted to think. A prank. Payback for the sins of her past. But she'd met relatively few people since moving to Chicago and could think of none who would be so cruel.

It was a mistake, she thought next, but even as hope tried to bloom, reality sucked the oxygen from her lungs. She wanted to spin around and run, to shout at the top of her lungs as she searched for the tall man with the dark eyes. But with great effort, she kept herself very still.

"I'm calling them now," she said with the same forced calm.

"Good girl." A garbled sound then, something between laughter and scorn. "Do not betray us, my sweet. One word about this call to anyone, and your son will pay the price."

The line went dead. And for a long, drowning moment Danielle just stood there, breathing hard, praying she wouldn't throw up.

Then she ran.

"Thank God, Ms. Caldwell. We've been looking for him for the past ten minutes. We were about to call the police."

"Don't do that." The words burst out of Danielle like a wild animal released from captivity. Her whole body shook. If the day-care director called the cops, Danielle would have to produce her son. And if she couldn't, there would be an investigation. An Amber Alert. A full-scale search. In all likelihood, she would become the number-one suspect. She'd be hauled down to the station, detained, questioned.

And the man—the man with the dead-sea gaze, the one from the hotel, who'd sat and watched her for over an hour, who'd coldly issued his threats—would know.

And Alex would be punished.

"Everything's fine," she said, clenching the steering wheel with one hand as she raced north along Lakeshore Drive. "We're headed out of town for a few days and Alex was just excited." She had to get home. Fast. She needed to be in the small frame house she and her son had picked out, the one littered with his toys. Maybe he was already there. Maybe he'd gotten away, had run and run and run. He could run fast, she knew. He had the same uncanny knack for skirting trouble that she'd had.

Once.

A long time ago.

Before she made the wrong choice, and the wrong person paid the price.

"We're so sorry," the director was saying. Fear drenched her voice. The poor woman's livelihood wobbled at stake. A day-care center that lost children in its care would not stay in business long. "I don't know how he wandered off. We were watching him the whole time—"

"It's not your fault, Elaine." Danielle put on her blinker and zipped around a slow-moving minivan.

"But it is," Elaine insisted. "This is inexcusable."

Fear crawled through Danielle, as dark and slimy as an army of the earwigs she'd always hated, but she managed to keep her voice steady as she explained it would be several days before Alex returned to the day-care center. By the time she pulled into the cracked driveway of her little white house, she'd convinced Elaine Myers she wasn't going to press charges.

"Alex!" She called his name the second she pushed open the car door. "Alex!"

Nothing.

The house looked so still, still and dark and quiet. Too quiet for the house of a six-year-old boy who didn't even hold still when he slept.

She unlocked the front door, shoved it open and ran into the darkened foyer. "Alex!"

Nothing.

Her whole body started to shake, and this time she didn't have to pretend. Didn't have to hold back. She let the tide crash over and around her, let it push her to her knees.

The sobs came next, big, gulping sobs. "Oh, God," she whispered. "Oh, God, oh, God, oh, God."

Breathe, she told herself. Breathe. Think. But she couldn't. She'd never felt so helpless in her life, not even the horrible rainy night she'd watched a car spin out of control and crash, then burst into flames. She'd run toward the wreckage, screaming, her brother Anthony trying to hold her back. But there was no one here now. No one to hold her back. No one to hold her, period. No one to help. Her son was missing. Gone.

Images assaulted her then, darker than the fear, the horror, the rage snaking through her. Her little boy. His dark hair and laughing blue eyes. His impish smile. He'd never spent the night away from home. Away from her.

He could be anywhere. His abductors could be doing anything to him. Bile backed up in her throat, and this time she couldn't stop the churning of her stomach. She gagged, lost what little lunch she'd consumed.

She wasn't stupid or naive. She watched the news. She knew about child predators. Knew too much.

Anthony.

Her brother's name came to her on a shattering rush of memory, and with it came more tears. Dear, dear Anthony. So tough and brave, wounded on a level few would ever suspect. He'd taken on a man's responsibility long before he was able to wear a man's clothing. And for a long while, he'd succeeded. He'd protected her and her sister, Elizabeth. He'd sheltered them, saved them from the bad man.

But she'd turned her back on Anthony, on them all.

Blindly she staggered to her feet and ran to the kitchen, grabbed the phone. She had to call Anthony. He would know what to do. He wouldn't turn his back on her. Not now. He would be on the next plane to Chicago and—

One word about this call to anyone, and your son will pay the price.

Danielle sagged against the small white tiles of the counter and let the receiver drop from her hands. She couldn't make the call, couldn't take the risk.

The contact came thirty-three minutes later. She was staring at the phone, waiting for it to ring, but the noise resonated from the foyer. A knock. At the door.

She stood there a minute, stunned, before her training kicked in and she calmly dragged a chair to the cabinet and removed a lock box from the top shelf. Inside, the trusty Derringer awaited her. By rote, blindly, she retrieved the clip from a second box and slid it into place, all the while the knocking continued. Louder. Harder.

Sliding the gun into the waistband at the small of her back, she walked to the front door and pulled it open.

Nothing prepared her. Nothing could have. He stood against a wash of late-afternoon sun, the play of shadows and light stealing the details of his face, but not the force of his presence.

Danielle saw what the shadows stole. She saw the aura of

danger, the hard, dark eyes, the sharp lines of his cheekbones, the square jaw. And she knew. Instinct urged her to draw the gun, cram it against his jugular and curl her finger around the trigger, while demanding he lead her to her son. But something else, sanity—caution—prompted her to stand very still, with the air-conditioning slapping her back and the hot summer sun blasting her face, not moving other than a slight tilt to her chin.

"You're awfully bold, aren't you?" she asked.

The big, tall man who wore confidence like body armor blinked. "Excuse me?"

Her fingers itched for the cool steel of the Derringer she'd received in honor of her sixteenth birthday. "It's daylight," she pointed out, glancing beyond his wide shoulders to the quiet suburban street, where Jonah Johnson raced by on his dirt bike. "Someone might see you."

His lips, ridiculously full and soft for such a grim, hard man, twitched. "And would that be such a bad thing?"

"Not for me," she said with a cold smile. "You're the one taking the risk."

"I see." Slowly, very slowly, never taking his eyes from hers, he slid a hand into his pocket.

Danielle's breath slowed to the slide of his fingers. Adrenaline ebbed, flowed, guided her own hand behind her back, to the waistband of her tailored black skirt. She'd stood face-to-face with monsters before. Talked with them. Pretended. Played their game.

"It's a good thing I like risks, then, isn't it?" His question was casual, as unexpected as the dimple that flashed with his smile. He stepped closer, lowered his voice. "I have to say, though, this is hardly the greeting I expected."

"No?" Her fingers curled around the cool metal. "Did you expect to find me quivering in the dark? On my knees? In a puddle waiting to be mopped up and pushed aside?" If so, the man was sadly mistaken. Danielle had learned at an obscenely early age that the best defense was a strong offense.

If she let this man see the stark fear slicing her to thin painful ribbons, gave him one clue how hard it was to stand there and face him, to keep her voice calm, then his power over her would grow.

"Look," he said, "I'm afraid—"

"You should be." Slowly, calmly, she pulled the gun and pointed it at his chest. "Very, very afraid."

The man went still. She saw his eyes flare in surprise, then narrow in confusion. His mouth thinned to a flat line. His body, straining against the dark-gray of his wrinkled button-down and black jeans, froze.

"Doesn't feel very good, does it?" she asked, enjoying the brief upper hand. Pray God she wasn't making the biggest mistake of her life. "Now get inside and tell me what the hell is going on."

In another lifetime Liam might have laughed. In another lifetime he might have quickly and efficiently knocked the gun from her shaking hands, jammed her arm up behind her back and shoved her against the faded siding of her little house. In another lifetime he might have felt a flicker of fear or compassion or…or something.

But he felt nothing now, only the cold certainty that, once again, his informant had been right.

She was the one.

He saw it in the stark fear in her eyes, a fear she tried hard not to show behind the defiance and bravado, but which glimmered bright like the fire of highly polished opals. He saw it in the red rim around her eyes, the tracks of the tears down her pale face, a face that had been lively and vibrant only hours before, when he'd watched her at the hotel. He saw it in the mouth he was quite sure she didn't realize trembled.

A trickle of admiration leaked through, but he quickly stanched the flow. He was not here to admire this woman, no matter how appealing she'd looked earlier in the day, all snug and tidy in her chic little crimson jacket and tight-fitting black skirt. He'd watched her for the better part of an hour, observing her mannerisms, her movements, watching the way she artfully arranged the roses and lilies, learning all that he could before making his move.

A man in his line of work could never be too prepared, and this woman did not fit the profile. She worked an average job and lived in an average house. She had no visible ties to anyone in the spotlight. According to the assistant manager, she didn't even date.

But she didn't hesitate to pull again, when she felt threatened.

Slowly, he lifted his hands. "Whoa," he said in a low, soothing voice, one that was rusty and scraped his throat on the way out. How long since he'd last soothed someone? How long since he'd last cared?

Not cared, he amended. He didn't care about her, only about the hunt.

"Do you have a permit for that?" Liam asked.

"You really think a permit matters?"

"Yeah," he said slowly, confidently. "I do."

She angled her chin, jabbed the gun closer. "You don't need a permit where you're going."

No, he didn't. That much was true. But he didn't need a bullet hole through his heart, either. He looked at her standing there and wondered if she had any idea how provocative she looked, a tall, beautiful woman with streaks of dark hair slipping from her barrette and falling against her tear-streaked face, her pale lips trembling, a damn fine gun in her shaking hands. Her body screamed fear, but her eyes glittered with a fierce determination he recognized too well.

Deep in his gut, the truth sunk like a deadweight. "Jesus, I'm too late."

She blinked. It was the first chink in her armor. But then she rallied, narrowed her eyes. "That depends upon what you have in mind."

The words were tough, gutsy, but they hid a pain he didn't

want to hear. Didn't want to know about. He *was* too late. Again.

Frustration lashed at him. He'd left New York the second he'd received the scribbled note, used all his resources to find her. But just as he'd been for the past three years, he was one step behind.

The senator lying cold and dead in a New York morgue bore silent testimony to that.

"Look, Danielle." It was *his* voice that wanted to shake now, *his* hands that wanted to tremble, *his* past that wanted to leak through. "You don't need to be afraid," he said, and for a change, he didn't strip away the emotion. He changed it. Glossed over the hard edges, sanded down the splinters. "I'm here to help."

Her eyes narrowed. "I suppose that's why you were asking questions about me this afternoon at work? Watching me? Because you want to help?"

"That's right." Slowly, he released the edge of the black wallet he'd been holding in his hand, allowing one side to fall open and reveal the tarnished badge. "Special Agent Liam Brooks," he said very slowly, very deliberately. "FBI." He paused, watched the shock, the disbelief, the horror, wash over her face. "Now lower the damn gun before I do it myself."

Chapter 2

Danielle was a smart woman. Not the learned, book smart that came from school and study, but street smart, the kind that came from hard knocks and foster homes. She'd learned how to read between the lines. She knew how to recognize trouble, how to know when to stay and when to go, how to take care of herself. Her sister had insisted Danielle could make a nice living setting up at carnivals, charging a fee for the intuition that came to her naturally.

There wasn't much that got by her, wasn't much she didn't understand.

But standing there with a gun pointed at this grim-faced stranger, with her heart racing and her knees trying not to knock, she watched his mouth move, heard the deep tenor of his voice, but didn't understand. She didn't understand what he was saying. She didn't understand why his badge looked so real. Didn't understand how her life could shatter in the space of only an hour, not after all the measures she'd taken to protect her son. He was just a little boy. Only six. Innocent.

But worst of all, most damning of all, she didn't understand the dizzying desire to believe this man, to trust him, to think that the badge was real, that somehow he could help.

One word about this to anyone, and your son will pay the price.

"You're lying." That had to be it. He was fabricating a story to gain her trust, her cooperation. Or maybe he was testing her, trying to trick her into disobeying his instructions.

His eyes locked onto hers, dark, commanding. "Why would I lie?"

The gun grew heavier, like a weight on her heart, but she kept her hands steady. "You tell me."

He answered not as she'd expected, as she'd hoped, but with a low stream of curse words. "I'm too late," he said again, and this time his voice cracked on a hard edge of frustration and disgust and remorse.

Danielle wanted to step back from him, from the crazy way he made her feel, the confusion, the hope. But she forced herself to stand very still, even as he took a step closer, so close that the barrel of the gun jammed against his chest.

"What has he done to you, Danielle?" The question was soft, laced with a vehemence that chilled her blood. "Tell me what that bastard has done to hurt you."

The walls, the certainty, started to crumble. "No one has hurt me."

His face hardened. "Don't lie to me, damn it." The words were hard, not at all preparing her for the way he lifted a hand to skim a finger beneath her lashes. "I see it in your eyes."

Naked. She suddenly felt completely exposed, as though she stood before this man without a stitch of clothing on. The way he looked at her, with that dark, penetrating gaze, made her feel as though he could see beyond the fabric of her uniform, deeper than the flesh, to the fear snaking through her like cold slime.

"You don't need to be afraid," he said in a voice that no

longer resonated with anger but soothed like a warm summer breeze. "Not anymore. Not of me."

Her throat tightened. For almost two hours she'd been holding all the jagged pieces together, the fear, the uncertainty, the desperation, willing herself to be strong, to stay in control. For Alex. But now, in the face of this man with the hard eyes but soft words, who offered her a gift she couldn't accept, the gift of help, everything started to slip, and it sliced to the bone.

"What do you want?" she asked with a valiance she no longer felt.

His dark eyes narrowed. "Right now," he said very slowly, very softly, "I want you to put that gun down." The hand at her face, the fingers that feathered along her cheekbone, lowered, dropping to the Derringer.

No! someplace deep inside screamed. Fight him. Don't let him have his way with you. But she could no more move, no more look away from him, than she could push time backward and bring Alex home.

"I'm going to help you," he murmured, uncurling her fingers and taking the weight of the gun from her hand.

She watched him, saw his square palm, his long fingers, the bronze of his tan against her pale wrist, but just like earlier at the hotel, when she'd stared at the patrons milling about the lobby, she couldn't bring the moment into focus.

"See?" His voice was low, soothing. "We're putting the gun down." In a svelte move he removed the clip and shoved the barrel into the waistband of his jeans. "Good."

A trap, she told herself. A trick.

No, came the voice deep inside, the voice she'd once staked her life on but could no longer trust.

"Now we're going to go inside," the man was saying, and before she could pull away, he had a hand at her waist and was guiding her into the cool confines of her small foyer. She knew she should fight him, stop him, but lethargy stole through her, numbing like a sweet, forgotten drug.

The man, Liam he said his name was, an FBI agent, led her into the cluttered family room, where the puzzle of the United States she and her son had been working lay unfinished on the old pine coffee table. He guided her to the denim sofa, the one Alex had picked out, and encouraged her to sit.

She did.

He sat beside her, didn't release her hand. She hadn't realized how cold she was, hadn't known she could be so cold while the sun still blazed outside and blood still pumped through her body.

Ty.

Ty had been this cold. But then, her son's father had been dead. She'd stared at him in his casket, a tall, lanky man in dark gray trousers and a black dress shirt, sandy-blond hair combed obscenely neatly for such a perpetually unkempt man, the soft lines of his face, the whiskers she'd begged them not to shave. Ty wouldn't be Ty without his scruffy jaw.

Anthony had been by her side, strong and protective as always. He'd stood to her left with a steadying arm around her waist, Elizabeth to her right, also lending an arm in support. They'd held her up, tried to stop her when she stepped forward with a picture of her son in her hand. She'd meant only to lay it on Ty's chest, but she'd lifted her hand higher, skimmed it over his mouth, his cheek.

Cold. So horribly cold.

But there was no cold now, not from the man seated next to her. The heat of his body blanketed her, soaked through her palm and into her blood, fighting with memory and reality.

The desire—the need—to lean into him stunned her. It would be so easy. There wasn't that much space between them. She had only to let go, lean against his chest.

She pulled back abruptly, putting as much space between them as she could while he still held her hand.

"Talk to me," he said in that darkly magical voice of his,

the one that both threatened and coerced. "Tell me what's going on. Tell me what he's done to you."

She wanted to. God, against every scrap of sanity and caution, she wanted to. The forgotten force of need burst through her like a punch. "I don't know what you're talking about."

"Yes," Liam said, never releasing her hand, her eyes, "you do."

She watched him, much as he'd watched her earlier, noting the lines at the corners of his eyes, laugh lines on some men, but not this man. These lines carved deeper, screamed of life and lessons that had nothing to do with humor. His face was tanned, not quite leathery, but not smooth like Alex's. At his jaw she saw the gathering of whiskers and wondered when was the last time he'd shaved.

He wasn't her friend. He wasn't her ally. No matter how strong the temptation to lean on him, trust him, the possible consequences screamed through her. She didn't know who he really was or what he really wanted. Badges could be faked. Compassion forced. He could be involved.

Or he really could be FBI. Which would almost be worse. The caller had made it clear what would happen if the authorities got involved.

"It's just been a long day," she hedged.

"And that's why you pulled a gun on me?"

The question landed with unerring accuracy. Pulling a gun on a stranger was not the mark of a calm, content, rational woman. "I...I thought you were someone else."

"Who?"

She shook her head. "It doesn't matter."

He let out a rough breath and looked away from her, staring at the half-finished puzzle on the coffee table. Just beyond, a pair of dirty sneakers lay near the back door. "You have a kid?"

Her heart jumped. "A son," she admitted, because she knew the safest lies grew from the truth.

"Where is he?"

"At day care," she lied automatically.

"Are you sure?"

"I talked to them less than an hour ago." The truth.

"Why didn't you pick him up on the way home?"

The questions just kept coming, one after another. "I was hoping to rest for a few minutes, get rid of my headache." Hoping the phone would ring and she would receive her next set of instructions.

Before Liam could fire off another query, she launched one of her own. "Maybe you should tell me what's going on," she suggested. "You say you're with the FBI. What could you possibly want with me?"

From the time she'd pulled the gun on him, something had changed. His stony expression had softened, the hard edges to his voice had vanished. He'd been almost human. But that all changed now. The man from the lobby returned, and with his arrival, the oxygen fled the small family room.

"I—" He hesitated, swore softly, rolled to his feet. He paced to the window overlooking her shady backyard and just stood there, with his hand braced against the frame. The sinking sun cut in around him, casting him in silhouette, forcing Danielle to wonder what he saw. She didn't need her intuitive Gypsy blood to realize it wasn't her son's deserted jungle gym.

"Look," she said, standing. Part of her wanted to take his wrist and drag him to the front door, just as he'd led her to the sofa. Another part of her wanted to step closer, put a hand to the wrinkled cotton shirt stretched across his wide shoulders.

She did neither. "I really need to start dinner—"

He swung toward her. "Three days ago Senator Gregory of New York was found dead in his hotel room."

Danielle went very still. She wasn't a news junkie, but she'd have to be a hermit to have missed the story that had dominated the media for the past several days. Gregory was a young man, a political golden boy lauded as the next great hope for the country. And he'd been in prime health.

Until he turned up dead.

The hotel room had been locked from the inside, Danielle recalled. They'd had to break down the door to get to him, after he failed to answer the phone. The coroner estimated he'd been dead for several hours before they found him. There were no marks on his body, no signs of trauma or physical distress. The autopsy had revealed nothing.

The man's heart, strong and healthy, with valves not the least bit blocked, had simply stopped beating.

Her own heart kicked up a notch. "What does that have to do with me?"

Liam scrubbed a hand over his face. "I— Christ, I don't know."

It wasn't the answer she was expecting. Somehow, she hadn't figured Liam Brooks, allegedly special agent of the FBI, was a man to admit he didn't know everything. "Then why are you here?"

He closed the distance between them, making the room shrink with each step he took. She stood fascinated, wondering how he could cover in three steps the same territory that took her at least six.

"A note," he said roughly. "I received a handwritten note with your name on it."

Her breath caught. "*My* name?"

"Your name, and the mention of Chicago."

And now her son was gone. "I don't understand." She'd never met the senator from New York, had no idea how her son's disappearance could be connected to his alleged murder.

Liam's expression hardened. "Neither do I," he admitted. "Neither do I."

The dark clouds she'd sensed all afternoon rolled closer. She swallowed against a horrible sense of inevitability and reminded herself nothing had changed. This man's story didn't change the instructions she'd received, instructions she intended to follow.

"You can see everything is fine," she said, overriding the voice inside, the one that scraped against her throat, screaming for her to tell him what she knew. Let him help. She'd never been one to play by the rules, after all. She'd always preferred following her own path. Finding a loophole or a workaround.

But with her son's life on the line, this time she had no choice. "If anything happens, I'll—"

"Damn it." He moved so fast she never had a chance to back away. He took her shoulders in his hands, his big, strong, surprisingly gentle hands, and held on tight. "If anything happens, it will already be too late, don't you understand that?"

She swallowed hard. "I'm sure it's all just some misunderstanding," she forced herself to say. She needed him to leave, damn it. "Maybe there are two Danielle Caldwells in Chicago."

His mouth flattened into a hard line. "You can hope." He put her Derringer onto the table, then flipped open the wallet with his badge and handed her a small embossed card. "I'm staying at the Manor. Call me if something changes."

She ran the tip of her index finger along the raised, blue letters of his name. "I will." The words hurt, because she knew they were not true. She would not call him, would not ask for his help. "Thanks for checking on me," she said with a casualness at complete odds with the tension arcing between them. Forcing a smile, she led him to the front of the house and opened the door.

He stepped into the hazy shades of early evening. A warm breeze blew in from the lake several miles away. "You'd better go get your son."

They were simple words. Easy. Casual. And yet they destroyed the tenuous hold on her emotions. "Yes."

He held her gaze a moment longer than was comfortable,

his dark, penetrating eyes lingering on her face, much the way he'd held her hand longer than necessary. "Just be careful," he said at last, then turned and walked away.

Come back! The words vaulted from deep inside her, but Danielle refused to give them voice. She stood there in the open door of her small home, watching Alex's neighborhood buddies across the street shoot hoops, as FBI Special Agent Liam Brooks, and any help he might be able to offer, drove away.

She was hiding something. That much Liam knew. She put up a good front, played a good game, but Liam was too well trained to miss the clues. He'd spent years watching people, studying them, analyzing them. He knew how to read between the lines, the lies. And even though Danielle Caldwell pretended valiantly that her life was in perfect order, he'd seen the truth in the way those startling green eyes had glittered, the way her fine-boned hands had trembled.

Liam pushed away from the window of his fourteenth-floor suite at the Stirling Manor and stalked toward the bottle of scotch he'd ordered from room service. He poured the single malt into a tumbler and lifted it to his mouth but didn't throw the warm liquid back. He wasn't ready to numb himself. Wasn't ready to take a short cut and stop thinking.

Wasn't ready to turn his back on Danielle.

She didn't trust him, didn't want his help. She'd made that abundantly clear; he just didn't understand why. He was one of the good guys, but she'd looked at him with abject horror, as though she'd expected him to suddenly grow horns and do horrible, lewd things to her.

Or her son.

The thought stopped him cold. Her son.

A child changed everything, introduced vulnerabilities sick and sinister and powerful enough to turn even his stomach. When someone became a parent, their personal welfare fell to the background, replaced by that of the child. There was no better way to hurt a parent than to hurt his or her child.

That, Liam knew too well.

Frowning, he picked up the tumbler and tossed back the liquid, savoring the burn clear down to his gut. He was still savoring when his mobile phone rang five minutes later.

He grabbed it from the bed. "Brooks."

"Tell me you're not in Chicago."

The voice was soft but strong, friendly yet concerned, and Liam couldn't help but smile. Mariah Ingram, fellow FBI agent and longtime friend, didn't pull any punches. "I'm afraid I can't do that."

"Liam," she said in that way of hers, a soft voice that registered like a quick smack to the side of his head.

"Don't start with me, okay?" He sank down to the bed and leaned against the headboard. It was the first time he'd allowed himself to sit since charging out of the cab from the airport that morning.

Mariah sighed. "Bankston said you took a few days' leave. But that's not what you're doing, is it? You're not on vacation. You're chasing shadows again, aren't you? You're on another wild-goose chase."

He stared at the blank television screen, wishing the woman didn't know him so damn well. They'd worked together off and on over the years, more closely after he'd lost his partner, Paul Lennox, during the investigation into the theft of hundreds of billions of dollars from the World Bank.

The case had gripped the nation in panic, forcing the Bureau to allocate every available resource to hunting the perpetrator. Other casework, unless there was a clear and present danger, fell to the background. They'd worked tirelessly, sifting through bizarre allegations of conspiracy and treason, corruption that reached into all echelons of the government and, ultimately, allegations of genetic engineering—which had turned out to be true. Gutsy Mariah had plowed in headfirst and proven instrumental in wrapping up the case. In the process, she'd fallen in love and married one of the men at the center of the circus, renowned financier Jake Ingram.

Frowning, Liam reached across the bed to the antique nightstand and pulled open the drawer, retrieved a small plastic bag. Inside, a stack of three postcards taunted him. The first had been in his possession for three long years, since the week before the World Bank case stole headlines and resources. The second had been found stashed in Senator Gregory's day planner. The third had shown up in Liam's New York hotel room only the day before, waiting like a pal beneath a little piece of gold-foil-wrapped dark chocolate.

"I received a tip," he said. The handwriting on the first two was identical, but someone else had penned the third. Someone desperate.

"A tip," Mariah repeated skeptically.

He fingered the back of the postcard, stared at the image of the obscenely quaint pastoral farmhouse. "He's back, Mariah." He didn't give a damn if no one believed him, if they all thought he was crazy. The truth hummed through him like a chill to the bone. "That bastard is back." And this time, if it was the last thing Liam did, he was going to stop the man and the syndicate he headed, before more lives were destroyed. "Titan."

Just saying the name of the reputed but elusive European crime lord turned his stomach.

"You think he's connected to the senator's death?"

Liam ran his fingers over the three neatly printed words that had eaten away at him for what seemed like a lifetime.

My deepest sympathy.

He'd never known three little years could drag so slowly.

"Without a doubt." The fact that the senator's death mirrored a string of deaths across Europe was indication enough, but the presence of the postcard sealed the deal.

"But why?" Mariah hesitated. "What possible motive could there be?"

Liam shoved the baggie back into the drawer, pushed it closed and stood. "That's what I'm going to find out."

"Then what in the world are you doing in Chicago?"

The bottle of scotch called to him, with its sleek lines and smooth edges, smoky amber liquid, but Liam refused to let himself move. Refused to let himself take the easy way out. To be like his father. "There's a woman—"

"A woman." Weariness and concern thickened Mariah's voice. "Do you hear yourself, Lee? Your job is to bring down Titan," she reminded softly. "Not play protector to every damsel in distress."

Images of Danielle fired through him, standing in the doorway of her small frame house with her thick hair falling from the barrette behind her head, slumberous eyes drenched with courage and fear and determination, shadows and secrets and pain he understood all too easily, the gun in her shaking hands.

"That's not what I'm doing," he gritted out. He didn't do rescues. His skill set ran toward the other extreme.

Across the phone line, from her beautiful home in Dallas, Mariah sighed. It was a weary sound, that of a friend's concern. "You can't bring her back." The words were soft but they landed hard. "You have to let it go." She hesitated before adding, "Let *her* go."

This time Liam did cross the room and grab the bottle. He poured, not a full glass like his old man had done, over and over and over, but just enough to take away the sting of the truth.

"I have," he muttered, throwing back the liquid. He waited for the sweet burn, but the liquid streaked through him like acid.

The urge to run, to pound his feet against the pavement and suck in deep gulps of acrid air, like he'd done that long-ago night, burned through him. He had moved on. He'd had no choice. Time never stood still.

But he would never let go, not so long as the loose ends

lingered like smoke after a fire, thick and pungent, oppressive. Damning.

He barely even remembered those first few days and weeks and months. He'd existed on autopilot, behaving like a good little agent, when all the while the memories he tried to scrub away followed him like a starving, rabid animal from case to case, town to town. He learned how to answer his supervisors' questions, how to feed the division shrink exactly what she wanted to hear, but the truth was never far away. It festered like polluted ground water just beneath the surface, making its presence known during the long dark hours of the night when he would go to extreme measures to find sleep, only to see her as she'd been in the predawn darkness of that last morning. His wife, standing in the doorway of the bathroom, with a sleek ivory negligee draping her newly rounded curves and with devastation in her eyes.

Twenty hours later she'd been dead.

Liam slammed the tumbler down on the elegant cherry sidebar and turned his back on escape. Tomorrow morning would not be one of countless sunrises he'd once greeted with bleary eyes and an empty bottle cradled against his chest. He'd waited too long for Titan to return to lose his edge now.

"What about you?" he asked, shoving the conversation in a different direction as he headed toward the window. Subtlety had never been his calling card. "You're feeling okay?"

Mariah hesitated before letting him off the hook. She knew what he saw in the darkness. She knew the images that invaded his dreams. "Wonderful," she finally said. "Hungry as a horse and bone tired, but absolutely, gloriously wonderful."

Liam stared out over the city, the twinkling lights down below, the glimmer of the moon over Lake Michigan, the high, thin clouds whispering across the darkness. "That's so great," he said, and meant it. Once he, too, had wanted a family. Not immediately, but someday.

Titan had made sure that would never happen.

"And Jake?" he asked of her husband. Ingram was a good man, loyal and honorable, surprisingly normal considering the strange circumstances of his birth. Genetic engineering. When the first news stories had broken about the birth of superbabies in the 1960s, Liam had laughed them off, much like Elvis sightings. But then facts replaced rumors and reality overrode science fiction. The government really had experimented with altering genetic makeup—and in a handful of cases they had succeeded. Jake Ingram and his siblings were living, breathing proof of that. "You letting him take care of you?"

Mariah laughed. "He's doing great," she said. "Busy, as always. He's out for a run now, trying to clear his head."

Liam breathed easier, welcoming the benign, normal conversation. "Something up?"

"Just his imagination," Mariah said wryly. "I think the prospect of becoming a father is starting to spook him. He came home today convinced he'd heard me crying out in pain."

"You? Cry out?" Not in this lifetime. Not Mariah.

She snorted her agreement. "Exactly." Then she sobered. "It really rattled him, though. He's been acting weird all evening. Worried. He even called his brothers and sisters to make sure they were okay, convinced that if it wasn't me, it must have been one of them."

"Sounds like that man needs a vacation," Liam said, then wished he hadn't. The last time he'd planned a vacation—

He broke the thought off. His last planned vacation no longer mattered. He'd never taken it, never wanted another since, never taken time off from the Bureau.

Until now.

Frowning, he let his thoughts return to the woman with the wild hair and slumberous green eyes, the one who'd angled her chin and insisted everything was fine, even after pulling a gun.

She was so lying.

* * *

The wind whipped off the lake and sent sand dancing in a frenzy of motion. High, thin clouds played hide-and-seek with the stars and the nearly full moon. A strawberry moon, she knew. In just a few days the June full moon would ride high in the sky, its rosy hue pulling tides and disturbing sleep, filling emergency rooms and keeping the cops on their toes.

Danielle shivered. She'd been born under a full moon, the cold moon of December. The winter equinox. Full-moon babies are special, she remembered someone telling her once, a voice from a distant past, a life she remembered only in shadowy fragments and horrifying splinters. The life before she and her sister had crouched in a closet, hidden among their mother's clothes, breathing in her scent of fresh gardenia, while in another room, Deanna Payne screamed and begged, cried, then went horribly silent.

Danielle swallowed hard, forced back the memory. She didn't want to think of her mother's murder tonight, didn't want to think of any death. Not while Alex's life hung in the balance.

The chill needled deeper, despite the warm, muggy air blowing off Lake Michigan. She wrapped her arms around her middle and glanced at her car, parked in a deserted lot a hundred yards away. Uncertainty stabbed her throat. She'd feel better there, secure in the small front seat, with locked doors on either side of her, much as she'd felt that night in her mother's closet.

But the caller had been clear.

"Midnight," the mechanical voice had intoned shortly after sundown. "Come alone, walk to the water's edge and wait."

So she stood, and she waited. Beyond, waves swished and crashed against the rocky shore, sending an occasional spray of cool water against the back of her arms and legs. All the while she scanned the beach, watching, waiting, fighting memories that grew stronger with every gust of the wind. A storm was pushing close.

Just like the memory.

"Sailboats!" The moment Danielle released a four-year-old Alex from his child seat, he bolted from the car and ran across the dirty sand. His little legs moved with an uncanny grace, much like his father, carrying him closer to the edge of the lake—and the small drop-off.

"Alex!" Danielle raced after him, her heart pounding so hard it hurt. He was so like his father, in so many ways. Bold, daring, fun-loving. Except Alex was alive, whereas Ty was dead. "Alex, stop!"

Her son kept running, right up until the last minute, when laughing, he skidded to a halt and spun toward her. "Can I have a sailboat, too?"

Breathless, she caught up with him and pulled him to her, hugged his little body to her legs and fought a stinging wave of emotion. "Someday," she promised thickly, because she knew if it was something Alex wanted, he, like his father, would find a way to make it happen. Even if it proved to be the death of him. "When you're older."

He pulled back and gazed up at her through his father's crystal-blue eyes, uncannily wise for a boy so young. "Mommy, why are you crying?"

The question, pure and innocent and impossible to answer, pierced her heart. "It's just the sand," she said, blinking against the moisture, the truth. "I got some in my eyes."

Alex nodded sagely. "Here," he said, shoving his little hand into the pockets of his baggy denim shorts and pulling out the pair of Spider-Man sunglasses she'd bought him the week before. "Maybe these will help."

They had. Much to a laughing Alex's delight, she'd slipped his small sunglasses onto her face, and the two had settled down for a picnic.

Swallowing hard, Danielle refused to indulge the surge of emotion. Now was not the time for memories. Now was not the time to fall apart. She had to be strong now, for Alex, even if that meant going against every instinct she had and standing alone on the beach in the middle of the night. The clouds had grown thicker, blotting out much of the moon's gauzy light. If she turned, she knew she would no longer see it playing on the surface of the lake.

But she didn't turn, wasn't about to look away, not for one fraction of one second. Her brother thrived on wide-open spaces, couldn't stand being confined. But Dani—

She heard it then, just a soft sound, a slight disturbance to the cadence of the warm breeze. Footsteps.

Finally.

Her heart slammed hard against her ribs. Once, she'd hidden from her nightmares. Once, she'd run from her fears. But now she didn't hesitate. She slid a hand to the gun at the small of her back and pivoted to her left.

Nothing. Just shadows shimmying across the sand and rock that locals called a beach.

"Who's there?" She stripped every ounce of emotion, every ounce of fear, from her voice, but not her body. Jeremy had taught her how to use both.

The wind whipped up, sending sand and whispery raindrops against her face. She blinked against the sting but didn't look away. "I did what you asked, damn it." She squinted, seeing nothing but sensing the presence. Shaking, she stepped toward it. "What do you want with me?"

She realized her mistake too late.

"Well, well, well," came a low voice from behind her.

She spun, but he was too close, too fast. He caught her before she could lift the gun, knocked it from her hands. She lunged after it, but his foot came down on the Derringer before she could make contact. Panic backed up in her throat. She tried to dance out of his way, but before she could move, before her heart could so much as beat, he snagged her wrist and dragged her toward him.

For a cruel moment time stood still. The gently falling rain, the gusty wind, the fury of the waves against the shore all faded into a void of nothingness. She struggled to breathe, to think, to formulate a plan, but intuitively she knew this was not a man she could outrun.

"Where is he?" she bit out with a bravado she didn't come close to feeling. Refusing to cower, she forced herself to look up and felt the breath leave her lungs on a painful rush.

A grim smile curved FBI Special Agent Liam Brooks's mouth. "Is this how you greet everyone, Danielle, or is it just me?"

Chapter 3

No. Denial screamed through her. Her throat knotted. Her stomach clenched. Danielle stared up at him, his big body blotting out the lingering light of the moon, reducing the world, the night, the beach, to just the two of them. One man. One woman.

She'd forgotten how tall he was. Or maybe, safe and secure inside the four walls of her house, she hadn't realized the threat. But here on the beach, with the dark lake gaping on one side and the deserted strip of Lakeshore Drive stretching along the other, over a hundred yards away, awareness hit like a swift blow to the gut. Liam Brooks, or whoever he was, had taken her son.

Her mistake burned.

This man had been in her house. She'd had him in her grasp, but instead of leveraging her advantage, she'd let him disarm her. She hadn't even put up a fight when he'd put his hands to her body. She'd let him touch her, hold her hand. Worse, far worse, she'd let the warmth of his body seep into hers, let it dull her senses, her defenses, as she'd wondered for a few crazy minutes what it would feel like to lean closer, to accept his lies as truth and—

"I'm here," she said, lifting her chin. The wind whipped harder, blowing long strands of tangled dark hair into her face. She made no move to push them back. "I'm here just like you instructed. Now where the hell is he?"

The man from the hotel, the one who'd come to her house, who'd touched her and lied to her, who claimed to be with the FBI but who knew things there was no way he could know, lifted a hand and eased the hair behind her ear. "It's your little boy, isn't it? He's in trouble. Someone's taken him."

It was the gentleness that got her. It was the gentleness that pushed her over the edge. "Is this how you get your kicks?" she asked hoarsely. "By playing twisted mind games?"

Through the darkness, she would have sworn the hard lines of his face gathered into a wince. "I'm not playing, Danielle."

The words, so soft and grave and ominous, chilled. "Then what do you want?" The question ripped out of her, followed by a sobering truth. She would do anything—*anything*—to bring her son home safe and sound. There was no price she wouldn't pay. No sacrifice too great. Nothing she could lose that mattered more than Alex.

But Liam—if that was really his name—said nothing. He just looked down at her through those dark, somber eyes of his.

"Is it me?" she asked, ripping at the buttons of her shirt. "Do you want me? Because you can have me, right here and right now."

He caught her hand before she bared her breasts. "Danielle, stop it."

She stared up at him, into those dark, dark eyes, not at all understanding what she saw. The shadows and secrets were there, yes, but something else glistened like the little pings of rain against his cheeks. "Then what?" she asked, and God help her, this time her voice broke. "What do you want?"

"To help," he said quietly, transferring both her wrists into one of his hands. Then he shrugged out of his black jacket and draped it around her shoulders. "Why didn't you call me? Why did you come here alone?"

The breath sawed in and out of her. She fought his voice, the concern softening the rough edges, the same concern she lavished on Alex when she sat on the side of his bed, easing him from a nightmare.

"Come on," he said softly, then slid his hand to clasp one of hers. "We need to get you in your car before the storm hits. Then we can talk."

The rain fell harder, cool and wet, but she didn't move.

"He's not coming," he said even more quietly. And his eyes, hard and penetrating before, gentled. "Whoever it is you thought you were meeting tonight, he's not coming." He tugged her toward the parking area. "Now, come on. Let's get you out of the rain."

Deep inside she started to shake. There was no lightning with the storm, no thunder, but the truth flashed as garishly as though shards of light split the sky.

She'd always been a woman to trust her instinct. Luck, her brother and sister had called it, a byproduct of the Gypsy blood that flowed through them all. Creepy, Ty had always said.

Regardless of the label, Danielle had learned to listen to, to trust, the voice inside of her, the intuition that served as sentinel for them all. Over the years the whispering had warned of trivial things, like thunderstorms and blizzards, of impending accidents like the time she'd slammed on the brakes at a green light seconds before a drunk driver had careened through the intersection and mowed down the car next to her.

Later, her knowledge of events before they happened had helped them know when to stay and when to go, which door to open and which to leave closed, who to trust, where danger lay hidden. Her Gypsy intuition had never let her down, not until that hot summer night when she'd watched in horror as Ty's car wrapped around a tree, and exploded.

In the days and months and years since then, she'd quit listening to the voice. She no longer trusted the gentle prodding she'd once considered a gift, not when it had failed her in the most fundamental way imaginable. Eventually the whisperings had gone quiet. Or maybe she'd just trained herself not to hear them.

But now from that place she'd tried valiantly to wall off, the Gypsy instinct on which she'd once relied screamed, much as it had been doing since the moment she'd looked up to find the impossibly tall man with the dark eyes in the hotel lobby. At first she'd interpreted the uneasy hum as paranoia, maybe even a primal attraction she had no interest in exploring. Then, when Alex turned up missing, it had been so easy to blame him.

But now as she stared up at him, at his hard face and shadow-drenched eyes, at the lingering shards of a pain she recognized all too well, a sobering truth drilled through her.

He wasn't the one who had taken Alex.

He wasn't the one who wanted to hurt her.

He wasn't the one she'd come here to meet.

Which could only mean one thing. He really was FBI.

"No," she whispered, fighting the truth, the implication. The warning had been explicit. Tell no one. Come alone. But here she stood, on an open expanse of beach where anyone could see her with a federal agent.

Horror convulsed through her. She hadn't meant to, she'd been willing to play the nasty little game, but in the end she'd disobeyed the cardinal rule, and now her son was the one who'd suffer the consequences.

"No," she said again, this time louder, and before Liam could react, she twisted from him and ran.

* * *

Liam had seen a lot of ugliness in his life. He'd prowled crime scenes, studied photographs of grisly murders, listened while a child molester recounted how a five-year-old boy from Kansas City had ended up dead in a Mississippi canal. He'd walked among the wreckage of downed airliners and bombed buildings. He'd seen the shell-shocked faces of the survivors, listened to desperate descriptions of relatives searching for their loved ones. He'd seen the grim determination of rescue workers. He'd seen and touched, smelled and tasted. And through it all he'd learned.

He knew the masks people wore to hide their pain. He knew the bravado that concealed sheer desperation. He knew how to recognize the tattered fabric of someone just barely holding on.

He knew, and he hated, but he never felt. He never felt the pain, the desperation. He never felt the fear. He'd walked like an automaton from crime scene to crime scene, investigation to investigation, wearing the same masks as those he encountered, because, God help him, he was one of them.

Until tonight.

For three years he'd suppressed everything, biding his time, waiting for a day he knew would come. Now the day he'd craved, the one he'd lived for, planned for, was here. But he'd never counted on Danielle.

She didn't fit. She didn't belong. Titan's trail of destruction was littered with wealthy, influential, often political figures. He dabbled with the worst of them, piped drugs into elite circles all over the world. His name had even turned up during the World Bank investigation, linked to the reputed General DeBruzkya of Rebelia, who'd had deep ties to the Coalition.

Anonymous women in the heartland of America did not match his profile. Hurting kids wasn't his style. He always aimed higher.

But now here was Danielle, this woman who teetered on

the edge of a dark abyss Liam recognized too well but who refused his help. Hell, maybe Mariah was right. Maybe he really was chasing shadows. Maybe there was no connection between the woman with the wild green eyes and thick dark hair, the woman who now ran down the rain-soaked beach.

But somehow that possibility didn't seem to matter. Whoever the hell she was, she was in trouble, and she needed help, and there was no way Liam could stand in the shadows and watch her fall apart.

So he ran.

"Danielle!" His strides were long, powerful, determined. The tight fit of his dark jeans didn't slow him. Nor did the damp, clinging sand. "Wait!"

She didn't. She ran with the grace of a wild gazelle with a predator hot on her heels, down the beach, away from him and her car. The rain whipped harder, merging with the wind to slap her in thick horizontal sheets. And still she ran.

"Danielle, please," he called to her, gaining ground.

She glanced over her shoulder, saw him, staggered forward.

"This isn't the answer," he said, surprised by how hard he was breathing. He ran ten miles every day. A short sprint down the beach should have been little more than a warm-up.

He caught her from behind and realized he had two choices. He could tackle her and ensure she didn't get away from him or he could snag her by the arm.

The image of Danielle sprawled in the sand, beneath his body, with her chest heaving and her eyes flashing, dark hair spilled around her face as she glared up at him, appealed in ways that almost made him lose his step.

"It's over," he said, reaching out to close his hand around her arm.

She had no choice but to stop, but she didn't turn around, just stood with her back to him, gulping in deep breaths of air and rain.

"Hey, now," he said, trying not to spook her. "I'm not letting you go, not until you tell me what's going on."

Nothing prepared him. Nothing could have. Slowly she turned and looked up at him with those big horror-filled green eyes. "Why?" she asked, and God help him there were tears in her eyes. "Why won't you just leave me alone?"

There was water all around him, the lake to his right, the rain pouring from the sky, but it was in her eyes that he almost drowned.

"Because I can't," he ground out. He tried to grab hold of the rough edges cutting through all those walls he'd tacked up after Kelly's death, but they were too sharp, and he was too tired. "Because I know," he added, pulling her closer.

He knew he shouldn't do it. He knew better than to put his arms around her, anchoring her to his body, but he could no more stop himself than he could stop the intensifying storm.

"I know," he said again, as time turned backward and accelerated. Everything blurred: the days, the weeks, the months, the investigations, the people whose lives he'd walked through, carrying him back to the cold night he'd run down the quiet suburban street, clogged and congested with fire engines and police cars.

"I know what it's like to be afraid," he told her, his voice pitched low. "I know what terror tastes like and smells like." The primal instinct it unleashed. "I know what it's like to be willing to trade anything." It sickened him that this proud, brave woman had been willing to strip for him, to give herself to him, in exchange for her son.

It sickened even more the way his body had reacted, the jolt of lust that had fired through him at the sight of the soft, creamy swell of her breasts.

He stared down at her now, at the way she gazed up at him, the wet, tangled hair in her face and clinging to her slightly parted mouth, the noncomprehension in her eyes.

"I know what it's like to beg and plead." He forced himself to go on, ignoring the ridiculous desire to ease the hair from her face, not with his hand as he'd done before but with his mouth. "To be willing to do anything, only to realize in the end there's no option but to run."

As she had done.

As he had done.

But there'd been no one there to catch him. No one there to stop him. He'd run and run, during the day, the night, toward the house, then away from the charred ruins, but no matter where he went, no matter the time of day, the truth was always there waiting.

He'd killed his wife.

"Let me help," he said quietly, lifting a hand to wipe the rain from her face. "I can."

Her eyes, wide and dark and utterly exhausted, locked on to his. "Don't."

The urge to pull her closer blindsided him. "Don't what?" he asked, skimming his fingers along her cheek. "Don't help you?" He'd forgotten how soft female flesh could be, forgotten the way a simple touch could make him want so much more. Forgotten what it was like to want something that had nothing to do with bringing down Titan. "Or don't touch you?"

She twisted from him, but this time she didn't run. She just sucked in another deep breath and angled her chin in an endearingly defiant gesture.

"I don't know who you really are or what you want, but you shouldn't be here right now. You shouldn't have followed me."

Like he'd had a choice. After hanging up with Mariah, he'd returned to his rental car and retraced his path to her little house north of the city, where he'd sat waiting in the quiet suburban street. He'd watched the single light glowing from a window in her house, wondering, like some deranged pervert, if it was her bedroom and what she was doing inside. A hundred times he'd told himself to go home, to quit playing

Peeping Tom. But instinct had hummed too loudly. There was no way he could have slipped beneath the cool, soft cotton sheets of his hotel bed when he knew this woman was in trouble.

"I wouldn't have needed to," he said very slowly, very quietly, "if you hadn't lied."

Her eyes flashed. She glanced desperately around the beach, toward the parking area, the road beyond, then back at him. "My God, do you have any idea what you've just done?"

He was starting to. "Tell me."

"If anything happens to him…"

Her words trailed off, but he heard what she didn't say. "I'm not the enemy," he told her, willing her to believe him, yet knowing she wouldn't. "I'm here to help."

She shoved the hair back from her face. "You can't, don't you get it?"

"Yes, I can, honey." Because the endearment flowed from him with alarming ease, he cleared his throat and let the roughness return. "I know things you don't know." About Titan. His handiwork. The trail of devastation in his wake. "I have resources you can't even begin to fathom."

"I don't want your resources," she shot back. "Why is that so hard for you to understand?"

A fresh surge of fury shot through him. What had Titan done to her? Taken her son, to be sure. But it didn't take years of investigative training to realize that he himself had done more. Worse. That he'd threatened her, as well, pinned her against a wall without so much as laying a finger on her.

God help him, Liam wanted to lay far more than a finger on her.

"Because you're scared," he told her, even though he didn't understand. Bringing down Titan was the only thing he'd thought about, dreamed about, wanted, for the past three years.

"Because I stood in the shadows watching you for over

an hour." Because he'd seen her shaking, shivering. Because he'd stood there with his hands shoved deep in his pockets, fighting the urge to go to her, pull her into his arms and promise her he would find her son.

"Because I'm your best chance," he added, even though the reality, the hypocrisy, of that statement terrified him. "You need me, Danielle." Just as he needed her. To lead him to Titan, he amended. That was all. "And whether you want to admit it or not, we both know it."

Slowly, her eyes met his, but in them he no longer saw the stark fear or punishing desperation, only the soft glow of a resolve he saw every morning when he looked into the foggy bathroom mirror and lifted a razor to his face.

"I don't need you."

Her words shouldn't have stung. She was right, after all. There were those at the Bureau who swore playing chicken with an oncoming freight train was smarter than putting your faith and your future—your son's life—in Liam Brooks's scarred hands.

He looked at her standing there, sleek and drenched and vulnerable in ways he knew she hated, and once again shoved his hands in his pockets. It was harder this time, because the thick denim was drenched and sticking to his body. Not because the urge was stronger. It was only human compassion, he assured himself, even if he hadn't felt any in years. Hadn't felt a woman, either. Hadn't touched, hadn't tasted.

Hadn't wanted.

Until tonight.

"Yes, you do," he said, and the words scraped on the way out. "You do." He stepped toward her, again lifted a hand to her face. "You need me in ways you can't even begin to imagine." And he needed her even more. "That's why I can't leave you alone."

Stopping the rain falling from the darkened sky or the wind lashing waves against the shore would have been easier.

Then, because he wanted to step closer, because he knew he'd pushed hard enough for one night, he turned and walked away.

He didn't belong here.

That was her first thought. It was too dark, too quiet and spooky. Too far from home.

He was awfully brave. That was her second thought. The little boy with the sandy hair and skinned knees lay curled on a narrow white bed, staring into the darkness. He wasn't crying, like she wanted to, wasn't calling for his mommy, like she tried to do but couldn't.

The small room was cold, not like the winter in Boston when big fat fluffy snowflakes fell for hours and hours and she wanted to go play but Daddy wanted her to stay inside by the warmth of the fireplace, but like the dark corner of the basement. And it was so still and quiet. Too quiet.

"Who are you?" she wanted to ask, but her voice didn't work here.

The boy looked up anyway, looked directly at her, startled her with wide, red-rimmed eyes.

"I'm Alex."

His name echoed through the quiet, strangely smelling room, even though she never saw his mouth move. "Are— are you okay?"

He didn't look hurt, just scared.

She didn't really expect him to answer, because her voice still wasn't working. But his little mouth puckered, and he nodded. "I wanna go home."

So did she. She wanted to be back in her safe little pink and white room, in her cozy house with her mommy and daddy just a few doors down the hall. She wanted to open her eyes and see her favorite pink teddy bear, to hug it close to her body, to breathe deeply and smell the soft scent of powder and lotion, not this nasty smell that reminded her of mud puddles several days after it rained. She couldn't remember the word her mommy used to describe that icky smell, but she knew it was a bad word.

Just like this was a bad place.

"What are you doing here?" the little boy asked. "How did you get here?"

She looked around, started to shiver. She didn't know where she was. Didn't know how she'd gotten there. It had all happened so fast. The last thing she remembered was crawling into her bed, her daddy reading a story, saying their prayers together, then him kissing her on the cheek and turning off the pink poodle lamp Santa had brought her for Christmas.

Swallowing a sob, trying to match his bravery, she studied him more closely. She couldn't understand why she felt as if she already knew him.

He chewed his lips, glancing across the small room to where light leaked in from under the door. "We gotta get out of here."

She knew that. She may have been only two, but she knew she had to help the little boy get out of there. He was scared, and he was in trouble, and even though she was scared, too, and just a girl, she was the only one who could help him.

But she didn't know how.

The only thing she knew how to do was draw. Her mommy said she was the best. Her daddy called her a prodigy, whatever that was.

"I'll try," she promised bravely, then spotted the table and the crayons scattered on top. She didn't want to move, didn't want to walk across the room, but knew she had to. Biting her lip, she forced her legs to carry her, even though they felt all heavy. It didn't matter how hard it was. It didn't matter how scared she was.

All that mattered was the little boy named Alex and finding some way to get him back to his mommy and daddy.

So she could go back to her mommy and daddy. And her pink teddy bear.

"What are you doing?" Alex asked, peering queerly at her.

She wasn't sure, just knew she had to draw. "Just wait," she said, picking up a crayon and pushing it against a blank sheet of paper. "Maybe this will help."

Chapter 4

The first pinkish rays of dawn stretched lazily against the horizon. The sky lightened, from a smeared, drab gray to streaks and swirls in a soft palette of pastels. The storm had moved on, unleashing its fury for a short time, then hurrying southeast, leaving an eerie calm in its place.

Through it all, Danielle had stood by the lake and waited.

But no one had ever come.

She looked at her watch now, saw the hour nearing seven, felt the scratch of inevitability against her throat.

Just a little longer, she told herself. She'd stand here, and she'd wait, by herself, and she'd prove to them that she had not intended to disobey. She'd done just as instructed, even though it grated at her. She'd never been one to follow instructions, no matter who issued them. Except her mother. She remembered so little of the exotic woman with wild dark hair and laughing green eyes, just bits and pieces. The smell of gardenia. And her voice. It had been a soft voice, gentle, filled with love. Even when she'd lost her patience with the triplets, she'd disciplined them lovingly.

And Danielle had always, always responded.

It had been a different story with her father. She remembered less about him, just his big, booming presence. He'd looked neat and tidy, and he'd smiled whenever they had company, but when no one else was around, he'd turned into a different person, a person none of them liked very much. He'd order them around, his face turning red, his eyes bulging. That was her first memory of being defiant. She'd known she should obey him, that the consequences of disobedience were bad, but even at a young age, her Gypsy blood had been strong, and she'd been unable to follow his rigid rules.

Sometimes she and Elizabeth had hidden from him to avoid the belt. Usually they wedged themselves under the bed, sometimes in a closet—like they'd done the night their mother died. She'd lost them both that night, her mother to violence, her father to a question mark. Benedict Payne had simply vanished.

That night marked a transition in her life, but patterns instilled by her parents remained. A wild child, one foster family had called her. A bad seed. A hellion. But if the names were supposed to wound, they never had. If anything, they'd encouraged her. She'd seen what happened to her mother when she bent to her father's will like nothing more than a flimsy sapling in a gale-force wind. She remembered the arguments, the tears, and she'd resolved to never, never let anyone dominate her. To never blindly follow someone else's rules. To follow her own path, her own calling.

And she had.

Until yesterday.

The breeze whipped off the lake, cooler now, no longer warmed by the lingering heat of the day. She turned toward the endless expanse of blue, stared at the lone red-and-yellow sail already visible in the distance. Her clothes were still wet from the rain, her hair sticky, but she wasn't ready to leave yet. Wasn't ready to give up.

The irony burned. For the first time in thirty-one years,

she'd been willing to play by someone else's rules. She'd been willing to go along with the request, do whatever was required to get her son back. With a stab to her throat she remembered the way she'd torn at her clothes, offering herself to Liam in exchange for Alex. She would have done whatever he wanted, gone down with him in the sand, let him have her, use her.

But he'd stopped her.

Frowning, she tried to focus on a lone gull dipping over the blue, blue waters of the lake. Instead she saw Liam, the way his eyes had darkened, not grimly, but like smoke. She remembered the feel of his hands grabbing hers, not cruelly or harshly, but tenderly. She felt the brush of his fingers along her breasts, the startling tingle of awareness. That was only physiological, she knew. A purely female response to the first male touch in more than two years.

"Danielle."

The sound of her name on his voice, so low and hoarse, whispered through her like a caress. She closed her eyes to the feeling she didn't want, didn't trust, but her heart kicked up a notch, anyway.

His hands, big, strong, deceptively gentle, settled against her shoulders. "It's time to go home, honey."

She opened her eyes to the bright blue of early morning, the truth she didn't want to see. "Not yet."

"No one's coming," he said quietly. "You can wait all day, but I'm the only one who's going to be here."

She spun toward him, ready to lash out at him for ruining everything, for watching her at the hotel and showing up at her house, for following her to the beach and ruining her chances of getting Alex back. But when she saw him, the shadows beneath his eyes, the stubble at his jaw, the same damp clothes he'd worn the night before, words failed her. So did her breath.

"They'll make contact again," he promised in that low,

raspy voice of his. "But you need to be home to get the call."

She swallowed hard. "You didn't leave."

"Not with you here by yourself, no."

She wanted to be angry at him. She wanted to blame him. But standing there in the hazy light of a storm-washed morning, she could find no anger, no blame. There was only the memory of the torrent of words he'd unleashed on her last night, the admissions that lingered in his gaze.

I know what terror tastes like and smells like.

Last night she'd been too lost in her private hell for the words to fully register, but they swirled through her now, dark, dangerous, unearthing the crazy desire to lift a hand to this man's face and wipe away the shadows.

I know what it's like to be willing to trade anything.

Even his soul. Because he had, she knew instinctively. It was there in his eyes, the aura of black that surrounded him like his own personal storm cloud.

The voice deep inside, the one that had finally started speaking to her after weeks and months of dormancy, whispered a little louder. *What happened to this man? What had hurt him so? What had he lost?*

But the voice of logic and reason, the one she'd forced herself to live by, refused to let the questions past her throat. Whatever had happened to this man didn't matter. He didn't matter. Only Alex did.

Behind him a snarl of traffic already inched its way down Lakeshore Drive, streaming south into the city, just like countless other days. Odd that life could march on in a cloud of normalcy, when with one simple phone call, her entire world had turned upside down.

"Come on," he said, reaching for her hand. His fingers curled around hers, bringing with them a staggering infusion of warmth. "We need to get you out of these clothes—"

She couldn't help it. Her eyes flared all by themselves.

"—and into some dry ones."

Danielle the wild child, the hellion, the rebel, would have fought this man, his command. She would have dug in her heels and refused to go anywhere with him.

But the Danielle who'd stood on the deserted beach all night long, in the rain and the wind and the soul-shattering dark, waiting for a rendezvous that had never come, the woman who'd ripped at her blouse and offered herself to this man, who'd seen the pain hollow out his eyes, heard it drench his voice, the one who was so tired she could barely walk, that Danielle wanted nothing more than to be home again, in the small house she and Alex had picked out, where his picture sat square and center on the mantel, where the phone could ring, and she could find some way to convince his abductors that last night had been a mistake. That she really was willing to play by their rules.

Pay their price.

Whatever it was.

With one last look over the light chop of the lake, where a second sailboat had joined the first but the gull remained solitary, she let Liam lead her across the expanse of sand and rock, allowing herself to think only of Alex. She refused to think of the way the warmth of Liam's hand seeped into her, beyond flesh and bone, to the core, where for the first time the chill didn't pierce quite so deeply.

The little house, with its faded siding but bright window boxes brimming with petunias and impatiens, sat still and quiet, much too still and quiet. Liam eased his rental to a stop at the curb while Danielle pulled into the driveway. He didn't know how much longer she could function without collapsing.

He'd walked away last night, even climbed into his car and driven away, but within minutes he'd been back. No way was he leaving her there alone during the long, dark hours of the night, waiting for Titan or one of his goons to arrive. Especially not after the way she'd thrown herself at Liam, willing to trade her body in exchange for her son.

The memory sickened him, even as it sent a blast of heat licking through him. A lesser man—

He shoved the thought aside, the punishingly erotic image of her on her back in the sand, not wanting to think about what a lesser man would have done to her.

What he himself had wanted to do.

He'd come to Chicago in search of Titan, not to get laid. It wasn't really Danielle Caldwell that fired his blood, wasn't she who made him feel alive, made him want, for the first time in years. That was just the case, the prospect, the sweet anticipation of finally getting something long denied.

Liam shoved open the car door and stood, readjusted jeans that had suddenly become too tight. He'd never thought of his quest for Titan as sexual, but now that the thought had seeded itself, the analogy needled deeper. There was nothing like that achingly sweet moment of culmination, the moment of triumph that could come only after long bouts of denial, of wanting and hungering, burning and craving.

He watched Danielle now, the way her lithe body moved with catlike grace despite her disheveled appearance. The lake breeze had dried her hair, leaving it wild and wavy and falling loosely around her face. No makeup remained, but with her dark coloring and expressive eyes, she didn't need makeup to make an impression. Her dark shirt and jeans were still damp, clinging to her body in a way that could make a monk's mouth water.

Frowning, Liam followed her, reminding himself he'd slipped into this woman's life because she represented the first active, tangible, *living* link to Titan he'd unearthed in years—not so that he could tangle his hands in her hair, taste her exotic mouth and chase away the fear she so staunchly denied.

"How do you take your coffee?" he asked, joining her at the front door.

With the key slid into the lock, she tossed him a look over her shoulder. "Alone."

He refused to indulge the smile that wanted to form. "Not an option." He put his hand to hers and turned the knob, pushed open the door. "Stay here while I check things out."

He heard her sharp intake of breath only moments before she lifted stricken eyes to his. "You don't think—"

"I don't know." But he knew Titan, knew the man with a disgusting intimacy, even though he'd never laid eyes on the bastard. It galled him to know he could walk by him on the street and never even know it. The man was shadowy and elusive. There were those who claimed there was no Titan. It was all a myth. A twisted urban legend. A phantom evil created to blame for a trail of otherwise unsolvable crimes. The authorities' way of saving face.

But Liam knew otherwise.

He knew, even if he had no proof.

Through Danielle, he stood to gather the evidence so many in the Bureau said didn't exist. But he didn't want to gather it at the expense of her son.

"Everything's probably fine," he told her, hating the lie, the horror darkening her eyes. "Just a precaution."

He expected her to fight him, the way she'd done from the moment he'd walked into her life. But she didn't. At least not fully. "I'll go with you," she said, stepping closer to him. "He's my son. I can't just stand here on the porch and wait, if there's something inside to find."

Liam wanted to argue with her, tell her it was best for her to wait outside. But he couldn't. Not when he knew the frustration and helplessness of being held back. Sometimes, when he couldn't stay awake any longer, couldn't resist the draw of sleep, his eyes would slide shut and his heart would start racing, and he'd be on the street again, the quiet, tree-lined boulevard in a sleepy Kansas City suburb. Running. God, he'd run so fast. The flames and smoke had drawn him.

It had taken four police officers to hold him back. He didn't want to go in there, they'd said with a grim stoicism that still chilled Liam's blood. Whatever there was to find, he needed to let the authorities find it, do their job.

He'd tried to shove past them, the need to see and find for himself burning hotter and brighter than the fire that claimed the house he and Kelly had never quite turned into a home. But he'd been just one man, and there'd been so many cops. They'd held him back, refused to listen to his demands. Even when Lennox had shown up, with his quiet skills of persuasion, the police had held their ground.

It was hours later, when the flames had cooled but the acrid smell of smoke lingered, when the dark of night was giving way to the first streaks of dawn, that he saw the body bag.

"Liam?"

He blinked and dragged himself out of the past to see Danielle staring up at him. Her eyes still looked alarmingly dark against the unnaturally pale skin of her face, but in them he didn't see the stark horror of moments before, only a concern that reached inside of him and touched a place that hadn't been broached in too many days and weeks and months to count.

"You're right," he barked, then took her hand and led her into the quiet house. Like the exterior, the interior was dark and still, cooled by the whisper of air-conditioning. It was a comfortable house, a surprising throwback to the seventies. Brown carpet covered the floor, dark paneling the walls. On the mantel sat a red lava lamp. He couldn't see much of the kitchen from this small room, but the mushroom wallpaper and avocado-green refrigerator were impossible to miss.

The decor charmed him, even as he wondered why a woman like Danielle hadn't taken advantage of the numerous design magazines and television shows to update her little house.

Only the television, sleek and large, hinted at the twenty-first century.

Sunlight streamed through the uncovered window overlooking the backyard. He looked from the denim sofa to the puzzle on the coffee table, the dirty sneakers and soccer ball abandoned by the door.

The scatter of pictures on the mantel stopped him cold.

There was Danielle, younger but just as striking, beaming from a wheelchair with a swaddled baby in her arms. A laughing Danielle flanked by a young man and woman whose dark hair and flashing eyes left no doubt that they were related. Another young man, this one with thick wavy hair the color of California sand, holding a little boy in his arms—a little boy who shared his eyes, his chin and his smile.

"We need to call your son's father, let him know what happened."

A stricken look moved into Danielle's eyes. "He can't help us."

"Alex could be with him—"

The color drained from her face. "He's not."

"We have to be sure."

"I am," she said with a hard note of finality. "It's not even possible."

Questions snaked through Liam, but he slipped his Glock from the shoulder holster and forced them back. His interest in Danielle pertained to her link to Titan. Not her family. Not the fact that no ring glittered from her left hand, or that she claimed it wasn't possible for a son to be with his father.

"What is it?" Danielle asked, moving closer. The soft swell of her breast brushed his arm.

"Nothing." The word came out gruffer than he'd intended. He glanced at her, saw her staring at the gun. "Just a precaution."

She responded by pulling the Derringer from her purse.

The sight of this gutsy, exhausted woman standing by his side in a wash of morning sunlight, holding a gun and ready to face whatever unknown evil may be lurking in her house, pulled at Liam in a way he didn't like. "You don't need that."

She checked the clip, then looked up at him and angled her chin. "He's my son, Liam. Don't tell me what I need."

Frustration tangled with admiration. He wanted to grab the gun from her hands and shove it in his holster, to sit her down on the sofa and demand that she wait until he could make sure the house was safe and she was safe, that no nasty surprises awaited in one of the bedrooms. But he couldn't do that to her. Not when he saw the fierce glow of a survivor in her eyes. He didn't know what this woman had been through, what she'd endured, but on a gut-deep level he knew asking her to take a back seat was like asking her to cut off her hands.

"Point taken," he said on a low growl. Then he thought about the bedrooms, what could be awaiting them. A message from her son's kidnapper, a warning, or worse. "Just don't do anything stupid."

A grim smile curved her lips. "Like trust a strange man with a gun?"

Liam just stared. He didn't know how she did it, made him want to laugh when only moments before a dark dread had pulsed through him. Made him want to draw her against his body and put his mouth to hers, taste the smile that wasn't supposed to affect him but did.

"Something like that," he grumbled, then led her from the bright light of the family room and down a small hall. Three doors greeted him, all open. The first led to a bathroom, a narrow strip of linoleum with a basic white sink and toilet and shower curtain drawn open. Poppies, he noted. Bright splashes of red and blue and yellow tumbled over the crinkled plastic.

He knew what the next room would contain before he ever looked through the open door. Danielle's body tensed as they drew close. Her breath caught. Apprehension bled through the bravado she had erected around her like body armor.

Chaos. That was his first impression. Utter, sheer, jubilant little-boy chaos. There were clothes strewn everywhere, another soccer ball, more tennis shoes and a race track cluttered with a mismatch of miniature stock cars. Books overflowed a set of shelves, and the bed, covered by wrinkled Spider-Man sheets and a matching spread, looked like a disaster area.

"How old is he?"

"Six."

Earlier, Liam had wondered what it would be like to hear a soft cry tear from Danielle's throat, but the broken sound that echoed through the quiet room was not what he'd wanted. He looked from the mess to the woman, saw her biting down on her lip as she stared into her son's room.

"Danielle," he started to say, but she spoke before he could finish.

"He was going to clean it last night," she whispered. "There's a carnival down by the lake. I promised if he cleaned his room, we could go this weekend."

The words, soft, drenched with love and fear, had Liam drawing her closer. "You'll take him to the carnival," he promised lamely, fighting the urge to pull her into his arms. The senselessness of the situation ripped at him. Titan moved in circles as far removed from this woman as her small house was from the streets of Europe where he thrived. That he would target her and her son, now, here, like this, just didn't fit.

"You'll see," he said, anyway. Because she would. He would figure it out. He would get this woman's son back, and Titan would be punished for a rap sheet of crimes that extended from one side of the Atlantic to the other. Drugs, at least in the conventional sense, were just the beginning.

Before she could protest or deny or torture herself further, Liam led her from her son's room to the final door. "Yours?"

"I didn't make my bed, either," she said as he stepped into the utterly feminine sanctuary that smelled of roses and baby powder.

In Alex's room the messy sheets had screamed little boy. But in Danielle's room the tangle of soft blue covers and the abandoned black chemise tossed carelessly at the foot of the bed evoked an entirely different image. He didn't see a little boy tossing and turning, but a woman with untamed dark hair and equally untamed eyes, soft and naked, arching and accepting, demanding more.

"No harm in that," he muttered, then almost choked on the words. There was a hell of a lot of harm in the images clouding his mind. "Let me just look around—"

"The answering machine." She pushed past him and ran to the table beside her bed, where from the phone a small red light blinked.

Adrenaline surged past the wall of calm. "Let me—"

But she was already pushing a series of numbers, standing woodenly with the receiver at her ear. He wanted to take it from her, but he saw the bloodless grip of her fingers and compromised by putting his hand to hers and leaning close, so they could both hear.

"You were warned."

That was all there was. A distorted, mechanical voice, impossible to discern male from female. Then a dial tone.

You were warned.

And suddenly it all made a horrible kind of sense. Danielle's suspicion of him, the way she'd violently rejected him even after he'd convinced her he really was FBI, the stark fear lurking in her eyes. The way she'd lashed out at him, demanded that he leave her alone, when clearly she needed help.

Needed him.

Why she'd never called the authorities to report her son missing and activate the sophisticated Amber Alert system designed to saturate the media with pertinent information.

"Danielle." He said her name softly, took the receiver from her icy hands and dropped it to the floor, then turned her to look at him. He tried like hell to breathe. "Tell me."

Her eyes were huge, dark. "You shouldn't be here."

The words, barely more than a cracked whisper, confirmed Liam's darkest suspicions.

"Damn it," he growled, biting back an inventive stream of curse words that wouldn't do either of them any good. But Christ, he hated seeing her like this, as robotic and mechanical as the voice on the phone. That wasn't Danielle Caldwell. She was a woman of courage and bravado, of fire. Not one of defeat.

"They threatened you, didn't they?" The thought sickened him. So did the piercing realization that he'd prevented her from carrying out their demands. "They told you not to involve the authorities or something horrible would happen to your son."

"I told you to leave me alone," she whispered, but her voice broke anyway. "I *begged.*"

The word, the way she spit it at him, landed hard and low in his gut. He didn't want to hear Danielle Caldwell beg, not ever, ever again. Except—

He shoved aside the inappropriate thought, appalled by the image that automatically formed.

"If anything happens to him…" She squeezed her eyes shut, opened them a heartbeat later, but the horror remained. "If anything happens to him, his blood will be on your hands. Is that really what you want?"

Liam was a strong man. Physically. Emotionally. From the time he'd been a small boy, absorbing his father's alcohol-smothered, hate-filled words, the lash of his two-holed belt, he'd taught himself not to react. In Quantico he'd been trained to withstand stress, trauma, torture. He'd stood with a gun pointed at his head without so much as blinking. He'd crawled into the dirty underbelly of organized crime and pretended to be someone he wasn't, day after day after dirty slimy day. He'd buried his wife—and come as close to breaking as he would ever allow.

But standing there in Danielle's erotically cluttered feminine bedroom, with the soft light of morning pouring around them and those huge, lost, emerald eyes staring at him in accusation, it took all of his will not to stagger back from her, run into the bathroom, lean over the toilet and throw up.

His blood will be on your hands.

Liam didn't need more blood on his hands. Especially that belonging to a little boy.

"That's not going to happen," he said as levelly as he could. He still held her shoulders in his hands, and he wanted to shake her gently, make her believe him, but he'd never used force with a woman, not even a playful shove against his obnoxious cousin who, as a nine-year-old, had thrived on trying to discover what it took to make her cousin lose control.

"They're not going to hurt him," he told her, ignoring the annoying drone of the phone, left too long off the hook. "He was taken for a reason. You have to remember that. Hurting him won't get them what they want."

Please, God.

Emotion, as unexpected as it was jarring, boiled through him. "You have to trust me," he went on, because she said nothing, just stared up at him as if he'd ripped her heart out. "I'm not going to let anything happen to your son."

Finally she moved. Finally life registered in her eyes, her face. She shook her head, sending hair falling around her face. "Why?" Her voice was stronger now. "Why won't you just go away? Why won't you leave me alone?"

"Because I can't." The truth spilled from him like the acid burning his stomach. "Because I know who has your son. I know how he thinks, how he operates." How he destroyed, how he killed. "And so help me God, I'm not going to rest until I make sure that bastard never hurts another."

Danielle's eyes widened. "Who is it?"

"Who doesn't matter—"

She shoved against him with surprising force considering she looked on the verge of dropping. "The hell it doesn't," she snarled, twisting against his grip. "He's my son, damn

A Cry in the Dark

it. *My* son. Not yours.'' She broke from him and staggered back, stood with her hands balled into tight fists as she glared up at him. ''I have every right to know who's responsible.''

Time stood still. He looked at her standing there in the pale morning light, the dark circles ringing her eyes, the mutinous line to her mouth, and wished like hell he could turn back time. That he'd gotten to her sooner. That he'd warned her. That they'd never stood on that beach last night, waiting for a rendezvous that had never come.

That they weren't standing here now, in this rose-scented feminine sanctuary, next to a bed whose tangled sheets made him remember a side of life he'd trained himself to forget— hot nights and long rainy mornings.

He wanted to argue with her. He wanted to deny her claim. He wanted to tell her to just let him do his job. But he couldn't. Not when she was right.

Nor could he stand seeing her like this, all patched together on the outside, but empty and broken on the inside.

''Okay,'' he said, and the word tasted bitter on the way out. ''You're right. You deserve answers.''

A flicker of surprise flitted through her gaze like a black butterfly against a creamy flower, there one moment, gone the next. Never giving an inch, she lifted her chin and wrapped her arms around her middle and waited. ''I'm listening.''

Her clothes were still damp, her shirt molded to her breasts. ''And I'll talk,'' he said, stepping toward her. He expected her to pull back, but she didn't, not even when he reached for her. ''But only after you shower and get into some dry clothes.''

That would give him a few minutes to regroup.

''I don't want a shower.''

''But you need one,'' he said, steering her toward the small bathroom attached to the bedroom. Clutter greeted him there, as well, a scatter of feminine toiletries across the counter, hair brushes and barrettes, jars and bottles of lotion and powder and other concoctions.

He'd forgotten how enticing a woman's bathroom could be.

"You're exhausted," he said, leaning over to turn on the hot water, "and still damp from the rain." He tested the water, added the right amount of cold. A bright yellow scrunchie thing dangled above the faucet. On the side of the tub, another collection of bottles decorated the rim.

"You'll feel better after you're warm and dry." He looked at her then, reminded himself this was where he had to stop. He could lead a woman to water… "Do I have to take off your clothes, too?" he asked gruffly.

Her eyes flared, but she didn't step back from him. "Is that part of your job description?"

He had no job description. At least not one to which he adhered one hundred percent of the time. "Whatever it takes, honey. Whatever it takes."

Chapter 5

A soft little sound broke from her throat, dangerously close to the one he'd let himself imagine earlier. "How dedicated," she said, stepping back from him. "But I think I can take it from here."

He knew she could. He just wished—

He wished a lot of things. None of them mattered. "When you're done, I'll tell you everything you want to know."

Or at least everything he could.

Her hair fell in a tangle around her face, drawing his attention to her mouth, a pair of full lips made for laughing and kissing, not frowning and crying. "You're not going to leave me alone, are you?"

Very little emotion stained the question. Not accusation, sure as hell not gratitude. "Nope," he said, with one last glance at the running water. "We can work together or against each other. That choice is yours." He hesitated, met her eyes. "But no, I'm not walking away."

He couldn't. Not yet. Not anymore.

Confusion clouded her gaze. "I don't understand."

And for once Liam saw no point in evading, pretending.

"Neither do I," he muttered, then before he could do something stupid, something he hadn't wanted to do in more than three long years, he turned and did exactly what he'd promised he wouldn't do.

He walked away.

The smell of coffee seduced her long before she stepped from the shower. She'd tried to give up caffeine, once, about four years before, after reading an article about its adverse effects. She'd managed nine days without coffee. She'd even gotten through the withdrawal headaches. But then she'd walked into the kitchen one morning, seen her brother and sister and Ty and Jeremy all seated around the table with the newspaper spread before them and coffee steaming between them, and she'd caved.

That first sip, after nine days without, had been like a jolt of pure heaven.

One vice, she'd decided. She could allow herself one vice.

The rich smell of a Kona blend mingled with the steam swirling through the shower, enticing her to breathe deeply. It galled her to admit it, but the FBI man was right. And that was how she wanted to think of him. As the FBI man. His name, Liam, made him too real. More of a man than an authority.

She didn't want to think of him as a man.

Danielle squeezed liquid soap onto the scrubbie and ran it along her body, trying not to remember the way he'd looked standing in her room, by her bed, so big and tall and disheveled from a night spent in his car. If she let herself, she could still see him standing in the rain—

She refused to let herself.

But the ripple of vulnerability still ran through her, an uncertainty she hadn't felt in a long, long time. Because of the circumstances that brought them together, she reasoned. But then, he'd shattered the line between impersonal and personal by leading her into her bathroom. She realized the truth: she wasn't used to having a man in her house.

Once, men had been an everyday part of her life. First Anthony, the brother with whom she'd shared every day until two years ago. Then there'd been Jeremy, the kind-hearted man who'd taken in three street orphans and given them a home. Then Ty. For a while they'd all lived together under one roof.

Then Ty died, and everything had changed.

Since then there had been no one. Not romantically, not even a salesman or the father of one of Alex's friends. There'd been no man in her home. Until now. Until Liam.

Frowning, she scrubbed harder. The FBI man, she corrected. The grim-faced federal agent who'd barged in uninvited and unwanted, violating the instructions she'd been determined to follow.

Hurting him won't get them what they want.

The water was hot, but a chill snaked through her. Alex. Her son. Her precious little boy.

"I promise, Ty," she'd said, kneeling in the rain and leaning over his broken body while Anthony had tried to drag her away, scared the remains of the car would explode. Water had streamed down her face, clouded her vision.

Or maybe those had been tears.

"I promise I'll take good care of him. I won't let anything happen to our son."

He'd gazed up at her through vacant eyes, given her a weak squeeze of his hand. "I...I...love you."

And then he'd left her. His eyes had slid shut and his body had gone limp, and she'd been left hovering over him in the rain, holding his still-warm hand and begging him to come back to her, just like that hot summer night a lifetime before when she and Liz had hovered over their mother's lifeless body, begging her to come back.

Now Alex, too, was gone.

Fighting tears she'd grown to despise, Danielle slammed

off the water and yanked open the curtain, stepped from the shower and reached for a towel. This time would be different. This time she would do more than beg. She would do whatever she had to do to get her son back.

Even if that meant calling a truce with a federal agent.

Resolve hammered through her. She glanced at the lotion and powder on the counter, wasn't about to waste one second on pampering. She allowed herself only a comb through her hair, hacking through the tangles then combing the thick mass back. No makeup. No time.

Her robe, the soft gold chenille Jeremy had given her one Christmas so long ago, the one she always, always slipped into after showering, threadbare now at the elbows, hung on the back of the door, but she knew better than to face Liam—the federal agent, she corrected—with bare breasts and bare legs.

Do I have to take off your clothes, too?

The darkly erotic words followed her to the small closet in her bedroom, where she pulled on a pair of gray yoga pants and a soft shirt.

No way would he have carried out the threat she'd seen glowing in the darkness of his eyes.

Danielle left her bedroom and hurried down the hall, allowing only a brief glimpse into Alex's room.

The aroma of coffee grew stronger as she neared the kitchen, joined by a mix of other scents and sounds. She turned the corner ready to demand that Mr. FBI lay it all on the line, but all the words she'd arranged so carefully in her mind jumbled into a nonsensical mess on the floor.

Liam stood at the old, icky avocado stove she'd never found the money to replace, with his shirtsleeves rolled up, a dish towel over his arm and a spatula in his hand. Sunlight splashed in through the striped curtains she'd made last spring, landing on his hair and revealing reddish gold highlights she hadn't noticed before. Natural, she knew in an instant. A man—no, an FBI agent—like the brooding, no-

nonsense Liam Brooks would never consent to having his hair professionally highlighted.

In the old iron skillet eggs crackled and sizzled. Bacon waited on a folded paper towel beside the stove. In the toaster, two slices of bread stood ready.

The sight was jarring.

A man in her kitchen. It was another of those peculiarly comforting intimacies she'd walked away from all those years before.

"Hungry?" He turned toward her even though she'd not made a sound, moved a muscle. That kind of incredible timing had always been *her* game, walking into a room just as Jeremy hollered her name. Picking up a phone and greeting a friend by name, long before the invention of caller ID.

"No," she said, shaking her head and reaching for one of two mugs sitting by the coffeepot. They were all that remained from a set of six she and Alex had made in a pottery class last fall. Her son was skilled with a soccer ball, but his little fingers were clumsy. "Coffee is all I need."

"Wrong." He slid the spatula under one of the fried eggs and eased it onto a plate. "When was the last time you ate?"

She reached for the coffeepot and poured the steaming liquid into her mug. "Yesterday," she hedged, not about to admit it had been yesterday at lunch, close to twenty-four hours before.

"You need your strength," he said casually, comfortably, as though they shared a kitchen and breakfast every morning.

Danielle ignored the unwanted niggle of familiarity and brought the mug to her mouth, sipped deeply of the strong coffee. "What I need are answers."

He strolled past her and set a plate on the table. "It's a package deal," he said. "If you want answers, you have to eat."

A protest rose to her throat, but she bit it back. Now was not the time to engage in a battle of wills.

Shooting him a sharp, sideways glance, she took her place

at the table and stabbed her fork into the egg, brought the bite to her mouth. "Why me?" she asked, chewing, refusing to acknowledge the growl low in her stomach. "Why Alex?"

For such a tall, shadow-shrouded man, he looked jarringly comfortable in her kitchen. He made up his own plate then strolled toward her. "I got a tip."

She brought a piece of bacon to her mouth. "A tip?" The thought chilled. "About Alex?"

"About you." He sat across from her and picked up a quart of orange juice he must have put on the table before she'd joined him. "In my hotel room in New York."

Danielle watched him pour, watched him bring the glass to his mouth. His hands were big and strong, his fingers wide, making her wonder how he could hold such a dainty glass without shattering it to bits. "I don't understand."

He set down the glass, now empty, and met her eyes with his own. "Neither do I."

The admission surprised her. She was used to those in authority clinging tightly to the reins of control, never admitting when they were wrong, when they didn't know something. "What did the tip say?"

He gestured toward her plate. "Eat."

She glared at him, but when he just kept watching her through those penetrating eyes, she picked up her fork and brought another bite to her mouth.

His gaze never left her face. "Do you do drugs?"

Her fork clattered to the table. "Excuse me?"

"Drugs," he said again. "Marijuana, cocaine, ecstasy, the basic street stuff." He rattled off the list as if they were discussing a shopping list of fruits and vegetables. "Do you dabble?"

Everything inside of her went tight. Memories flashed of a subculture that consumed everyone who stepped too close.

She'd never stepped too close.

Because of Jeremy. He'd intervened before she and Elizabeth and Anthony had been absorbed by the anonymous streets on which they'd once lived. But later, when they were older, there'd been those times when Jeremy had sent them back onto those streets, and she'd realized, starkly and horribly, how close she and her siblings had come to never making it out.

"I'm a mother," she said, working hard to keep the grinding emotion from her voice. "I have a child who depends on me."

Liam poured more orange juice. "What about before Alex was born?"

"What kind of woman do you think I am?"

Slowly Liam lifted his eyes to hers. "I have no idea what kind of woman you are." His gaze flitted down her face to her mouth, lower still, along her neck, to her chest, covered by the ratty Philadelphia Eagles shirt, making her grateful she'd not slipped into her robe.

Abruptly he looked back up. "That's what I'm trying to find out."

Heat rushed through her, as unexpected as it was unwanted. "I don't do drugs," she said coldly. "Not now, not ever."

The lines of his face, hard and unreadable moments before, softened. "I didn't think so," he said, and even his voice was softer. "But I had to be sure."

She sat there, breathing deeply, wondering how this man could jerk her emotions around so easily. The Gypsy blood she'd inherited from her mother didn't require much provocation to flame, but this man seemed especially skilled.

"What about Europe?" he asked. "Know anyone there?"

She blinked. From drugs to over the pond in under three seconds. "No."

He took another sip of orange juice. "Ever been?"

She watched him swallow, saw his throat work. "No, but—" Another memory washed over her, this one sweet but fractured, hazy, not quite in focus. The music, lively and joyful. The colors, bright and vivid.

"But what?"

Emotion surged through her, despite the passing of twenty-eight years. It had never made sense to her that she could mourn something she'd never really known, didn't fully remember. "When I was a little girl, I used to dream of going to Romania."

"Romania?"

She indulged a small smile of memory. "Not quite what you were expecting?"

He brought a piece of toast to his mouth. "Hardly." She hadn't thought it possible, but the corner of his mouth tilted up in something oddly close to a smile. Rusty, but a smile all the same. "Got some kind of latent vampire fantasy?"

Her breath caught. "Not vampire," she said, fighting the ridiculous urge to lift a hand to her neck and ward off an invisible attack. Across the table, he wasn't close enough to touch, much less bite. "Gypsy."

Just saying the word filled her with warmth and regret.

"Ah." It was more sound than word. "Now it makes sense. The hair, the coloring…" His eyes glimmered like black diamonds. "The temper."

She couldn't help it. She laughed. It was a quick lapse, a burst of emotion and memory. She had a temper, that was true. Like fire, Jeremy had always teased, quick and volatile and prone to flare out of control.

But it was nothing compared to her brother's.

A quick stab of guilt killed the moment, because her son was missing, and this man, this FBI agent, had coaxed a laugh from her.

"My mother's from there." The heaviness to her heart returned, thicker and more constricting, like a wet wool coat ten sizes too small and shrinking. "She immigrated to the States a few years before I was born."

The sun glinted in from the window, playing with the highlights in Liam's hair and drawing her attention to the whiskers along his jaw. But the shadows she sensed about him, the dark aura that consumed him, deepened. He was quiet a moment, but she could see his mind working, see him chewing on what she'd said as thoroughly as he'd chewed his breakfast.

"It's a possibility," he muttered after a few tense moments. Then he met her gaze. "I'd like to talk to her."

"So would I." The words slipped free before she could stop them, followed by a quick slice of emotion. It had been twenty-eight years, but sometimes the wound gaped as raw and fresh as though the murder had just happened. "But she's dead."

Liam winced. "I'm sorry."

"It's okay," she lied. It took effort, but she kept her voice level. "I was young." Three years old. "I barely remember her." She felt her, more, alone in her bed at night, in the whisper of the breeze. "Just vague impressions of stories from the old country, the old ways." The bright flashing eyes and thick raven hair, the loud vibrant music, bright colors and festive clothes. The laughter. The love.

"That's why you wanted to go to Romania."

It was a statement, not a question. "Sentimental journey," she acknowledged. But then Alex had been born, and Ty had died, and things like sentiment and dreams had quit meaning anything.

Because it hurt to remember, she shoved everything back under the heavy carpet of her mind. "Drugs, Europe, what does all this have to do with Alex?"

Frowning, Liam looked at the scraps of fried egg still on his plate, but didn't lift his fork. "Does the name Titan Syndicate mean anything to you?"

A chill whispered down the back of her neck, along her spine. "Should it?"

He sat close enough to reach out and touch, just across the old farmhouse table she'd found at a garage sale, but the few feet separating them elongated, gouging out a distance of time and space. He never moved, but as she watched him, his expression, the tight lines of his big body, she saw him travel far, far away.

"It's a European-based organization," he said in a low, tense voice, and she was suddenly glad he no longer held a glass of orange juice. He would have shattered it, and the shards would have cut to the bone.

But even without the cuts, this man bled. "Vague, elusive, linked to black-market drug deals."

"And that's why you asked if I did drugs?"

"Titan deals in the big-time. He moves in elite circles. Politicians, old money, fallen royalty... There was even talk of an alliance with the Rebelian dictator DeBruzkya."

Her blood ran cold. She'd heard about DeBruzkya, his thirst for blood, his hunger for power. He'd been linked to the World Bank heist several years back that had nearly destroyed the American economic system.

"What would someone like that want with my son?"

Liam's eyes met hers. "I don't think he wants your son," he said calmly. "I think he wants you."

She tried not to wince. She tried to be just as impassive and matter-of-fact as he was. But her heart leaped and her breath caught, and there was no way she could just sit there calmly while he speculated that a European criminal mastermind had designs on her.

"That's ridiculous." The legs of her chair scraped against the linoleum as she surged to her feet. "I'm nobody."

Now it was Liam's turn to wince. He stood and stepped toward her. "Not true," he said, and before she realized his intent, he was around the table and lifting a hand to her face. "Everyone is somebody."

She tried to breathe but couldn't. Tried to step back but couldn't. The counter blocked her. "That's not what I meant," she said, but his eyes, so deep and dark and all-knowing, weren't so quick to let her off the hook. "All I meant was there's no reason a man like that would want me."

His gaze heated. "I wouldn't be so sure of that," he muttered. "Maybe he saw you somewhere. At the hotel. The Stirling does a strong international business, doesn't it? Maybe he liked what he saw."

Denial vaulted through her. Disgust chased close behind. "You think my son has been kidnapped because some sicko saw me—" The words jammed in her throat. Her heart jammed in her chest. The room started to spin. "Oh my God."

Liam took her by the shoulders, held her, those big strong hands of his bracing her against the memory, but the room, the world, wouldn't slow down. Wouldn't focus.

Crazy. It was so crazy.

"Danielle." His voice, low and strong and sure, was an anchor.

She grabbed for it, held on tight. "There *was* a man," she whispered, and the memory almost sent her to her knees. But Liam was holding her, and instinctively she knew he would not let her fall. "At the hotel."

A hard sound broke from his throat. "Tell me."

She closed her eyes and focused on the evening barely a week before. The tall, salt-and pepper-haired man with the graying goatee. The vague, cutting sense of familiarity. She'd felt him before she'd seen him, the old awareness she'd quit listening to surging with renewed force. There'd been a tingle within her, a rip. Something not quite right. "He was… watching me."

"Christ." Liam's grip on her tightened. "At the hotel?"

Numbly, she nodded. "Last…Wednesday, I think."

"Did you talk to him?"

She could still see him, dressed in a European-cut black suit, a swagger to his walk. "He had an accent," she murmured, unable to break the trancelike state of her voice. Her mind. "He…"She gulped in a deep breath, drew in the forgotten scent of man. "He had an accent."

A vicious curse echoed through the kitchen.

"He asked me out," she said, looking into Liam's eyes,

not understanding what she saw. Interest, yes. Concern. But there was a hunger there, as well. A complex hunger she didn't understand, which stirred her blood. "He was very persuasive."

"Did you go?"

She met his gaze. "After I got off, he was waiting in the lobby. He—" Horror kicked in with the memory. "He offered me a drink." She'd stood there, acutely aware of her co-worker's amused interest, staring at the benign-looking drink in his hand. Tonic and lime, he'd said. Her favorite.

And it was.

"I didn't take it," she whispered. *Lucky, lucky, lucky.* The long-ago childhood chorus, the one Liz and Anthony had always harassed her with, ran through her mind like a warped record. "I don't know why."

But that was a lie, and she knew it. She hadn't taken the drink because of the hum deep inside, low, insistent, persuasive.

"Thank God," Liam muttered, then stunned her by lifting a hand to her face. "It was probably drugged."

She absorbed the words, the implication. "You think it was him."

"I'd bet my life on it." His eyes, so dark and unreadable moments before, suddenly glowed with life. "If it was, you can identify him."

She stepped back from him. "No."

"Yes, you can," he went on, faster now, more intense. "Don't you understand, Danielle? I've been hunting this man for years, but no one knows what he looks like. There's a very real chance you could provide the first big break."

She swallowed hard. "I can't do that," she said, backing away from him. "Not if he's the one who has Alex."

"When did he check out?" he asked, as though she'd never denied him.

"I don't know. The next day he was just…gone." Ruth had teased her incessantly about her mystery man with the charming, continental manners. "It was as though he'd never been there to begin with."

Liam scrubbed a hand over his face. "Danielle," he said, and suddenly the brisk tone of the FBI agent was gone, replaced by a gentleness she didn't want to hear. "I know you're scared. You have every right to be. But playing Titan's game isn't going to bring Alex home." He stepped toward her. "Only I can do that."

She didn't want to believe him. She didn't want to admit he was right. But standing there in her small kitchen, with the sun spilling so cheerfully around them, the buzz started again, the hum deep inside, and she realized her choices were limited. She didn't have Jeremy and Anthony anymore. They weren't standing by, ready to fight, to defend—

The memory hit her hard and fast, almost sending her to her knees.

"Are you out of your mind?"

Danielle stared at her brother, so tall and strong and wounded, the green of his eyes flashing with a contempt that scorched deep, and felt her heart crack wide open.

"Maybe," she whispered. "But it's a chance I have to take."

"I won't let you," he barked, as he always did when one of his sisters went against his wishes. "It's too dangerous."

"I'm a big girl," she returned. She knew he loved her, but he didn't understand. She couldn't stay, not one second longer, not without being suffocated beyond repair. "I can take care of myself—and my son."

"You think so?" His voice was acrid now, nasty. "You think you can just walk away from what we've been doing? What if someone finds you?" He stepped close and lifted his arms to her as though he meant to grab her, but at the last minute he exhaled roughly and let them fall to his sides. "What if someone discovers you broke away? What if someone finds out where you are? What if someone decides to use you to punish us all?"

"Danielle?" Liam's voice broke the memory, but the sick feeling lingered. "What is it? Did you remember something else?"

She looked up at him, saw the ferocity of his gaze and wanted to tell him. Wanted him to know. To help. But this was her battle. What she and her siblings had done, the potential consequences, had nothing to do with the FBI or Liam Brooks or some power-starved lunatic in Europe.

"Just thinking," she said, not lying. Not really. The possibilities kept roiling through her. She and Anthony and Liz had made their share of enemies over the years. Some of them were bound to be out of jail by now. Many of them had sworn revenge.

He touched her again, a hand to her face, a quick slide of damp hair behind her ears. "You look ready to drop."

She looked up at him and felt her throat go tight. "You don't look so good yourself," she said with a strained smile, but that was a lie. He looked exhausted, but on him the signs of strain and exhaustion only heightened his masculinity. His eyes gleamed darker. The lines of his face were sharper. The whiskers at his jaw made his mouth look softer. The wrinkles in his shirt destroyed that aura of imperviousness about him and made him seem totally, dangerously approachable.

She wanted to touch him, too.

"You should go," she said, ripping away from him. "Sleep would help us both."

He didn't move at first, just stood there and watched her, his gaze lingering on her face and making her heart thrum a darkly erotic rhythm. The longing blasted in from nowhere and streamed thickly through her blood. The desire to ask him to stay, to let him help. Because he could, she knew on some instinctive level. This man was like a big, strong, gorgeous dog with a bone. A Great Dane, maybe.

Once he staked a claim, made a promise, he didn't back down.

So long, she thought with a stab to her heart. It had been

so long since she'd let anyone close. Let anyone help. What would it feel like to have those arms of his close around her and hold on tight, to feel the vibration in his chest as he promised her everything would be okay? That he would make it okay, through sheer force of will alone?

"I'll…I'll call you if I remember anything else."

His eyes darkened, gleamed like black diamonds in the rough. "You're not alone anymore, Danielle," he said, his voice suddenly hoarse and raw, tired. "I'm here now." As though to prove his point, he spread his hand along her jaw, slid his fingers up against the side of her face. "You've got to trust me, work with me. Lean on me."

The words did cruel, cruel things to her resolve. Outside the kitchen window, the old air conditioner rattled noisily, but rather than fill the sunny kitchen with cool air, the oxygen was being sucked out, molecule by painful molecule.

Why, she wanted to ask, but refused to let the question slip past. Yes, Liam had said he wanted to bring her son home, and she believed him, but she also knew she and Alex were just a means to an end. Something else drove this man, chased him. He wanted something, needed something, that extended far beyond bringing home a little boy he'd never even met.

What would it take, she wondered fleetingly. What would it take to chase the shadows from this man's eyes?

The truth scraped hard. It would take something she didn't have, and he didn't want.

Because she wanted to step closer, anyway, she turned from him and headed for the front door.

"I mean it, Danielle," he said, his heavy footsteps closing the distance she'd put between them. "I don't want you taking any more chances." She pulled open the door—and stopped dead in her tracks. She must have made some kind of noise, because Liam was by her side in a heartbeat, swearing softly and putting his big body between her and the package sitting on her welcome mat. "Get back in the house."

But she couldn't move, couldn't breathe, could only stare at the four words printed neatly in big black letters across the brown wrapping.

DON'T DEFY US AGAIN.

Chapter 6

"They were here." Danielle's words were barely more than a choked whisper. "At the house. While we were inside."

Adrenaline crashed through Liam. He kept his body between Danielle and the package, scanning the front yard, the driveway, the street beyond, for anything out of the ordinary. A young mother pushed her baby along the cracked sidewalk. Two houses down three boys practiced hockey shots. Across the way an elderly man pruned his roses.

But other than that, there was nothing, just the package sitting on the doormat of faded yellow sunflowers.

The sun blasted from high in the sky, but the darkness pushed closer, and everything inside him went cold. While he'd been sitting inside, playing house and trying not to lose himself in Danielle's big wounded eyes, Titan, or one of his men, had made a move. Ventured close. Close enough to grab, if only Liam had been paying attention.

"Alex," she whispered, reaching for the package.

He acted without thinking. He acted without finesse or caution. He acted on pure blind instinct, and black boiling horror.

"Don't!" He lunged after her, caught her before she touched the perfectly square box.

She twisted toward him, lashed at him first with her eyes, then with words. "I have to know what's inside."

"Me first," he bit out, wrestling the ugliness he didn't want her to see. The possibilities he didn't want to consider. The box was large enough to contain any number of things, some benign, some horrific, some deadly.

Images clouded his mind, of nasty surprises other agents had found.

Nasty surprises he himself had found.

"Please," he said, holding her upper arms. "Trust me on this one. Just go inside and wait."

Horror darkened her eyes. "You don't think—" She brought a shaking hand to her mouth. "No."

"I don't know," he said honestly. "It's probably nothing," he added, fighting the crazy urge to pull her into his arms and hold her, just hold her, to take the chill from her body and give her the heat of his, to find some way to make the ugliness go away.

"Just give me a few minutes," he said. "Alone." Because she just kept staring over his shoulder, down at the package, he brought a hand to her chin and lifted her face up toward his. "Trust me."

Slowly her gaze met his and damn near sent him to his knees.

"Come on." He turned her toward the spill of cool air from the open front door and walked her to the family room, where pictures of Alex smiled at them from the mantel. "I'll be right back."

She nodded, and he turned and walked away from her, each step feeling as if he dragged heavy slabs of lead behind him.

Training took over. He stepped onto the small front porch

and closed the door, knelt in front of the package. Carefully he lifted it, brought it to his ear, listened. Nothing. No ticking, no whirring.

Relief flashed hard and fast, not just because the package didn't make noise, but because it was dry. No liquid—clear, brown, red or otherwise—oozed or leaked from within. And it was light. Beautifully, gloriously light. Whatever was inside—if anything—didn't weight much at all.

The sickness he'd been fighting, that dark ball of dread that had lodged in his throat lightened, and the dry grit in his eyes dissipated. He sat there a moment on his knees on her porch, with the sun beating down on him and a lightweight brown package in his hands, not at all understanding why the world had gone watery.

Very carefully he eased back the brown paper and found the box within, then lifted the top.

The shoe was small, not clean, but dirty in only an innocent sense—stains made from mud and grass. Not blood.

Then he saw the videotape.

Swallowing hard, Liam looked up at the deceptively blue sky, the cumulous clouds building to the east, and said a silent prayer of thanks. He hadn't wanted to think something gruesome lurked inside the box, but years ago he hadn't wanted to believe the phone call from his neighbor, either. He hadn't wanted to believe the flames licking against the night sky were coming from his house.

And, God, he hadn't wanted to believe that the impersonal black body bag, like so many he'd seen over the course of his tenure with the FBI, contained the body of his wife.

"Liam?"

He looked up to find the door open, Danielle standing there with uncertainty hovering in her eyes.

"It's okay," he said, pushing to his feet. "It's—"

"His shoe." She had the small white sneaker in her hands before he could warn her about tampering with evidence, but just as quickly he realized it didn't matter. Neither one of them was about to involve the authorities. Danielle wasn't going to risk angering Titan, and Liam, well, he had his own reasons for avoiding exposure.

"Come on," he said, sliding an arm around her. Her bravado made her appear tough, almost untouchable, but when his hand settled around her waist, when his fingers skimmed her rib cage and he realized he could count each bone, a sobering truth pierced deep. All that strength she projected, all that bravery, protected a vulnerability she skillfully hid from the world.

Deep inside something tightened, squeezed. A heavy, forgotten rhythm pounded through his blood. Frowning, he fought the sensation, the fledgling urge to protect, to defend—urges that had been brutally murdered one night long ago.

Urges he never wanted to feel again.

With grim determination, he steered her inside and kicked the door shut behind him. In the family room he ejected a video cassette from her VCR and inserted the plain black one from the box, turned on the television and hit the play button.

On the screen the room was small, dark, almost clinical in appearance. A cot occupied one corner, and on the cot lay a little boy.

"Alex…" Danielle sighed.

Liam swore softly, stepped closer to her.

"Oh, God," she choked out, and this time Liam didn't try to stop himself. He pulled her into his arms and held her. He held her while she trembled, held her while she turned her head from his chest and stared at the dark, fuzzy image on her television, where sometime in the not too distant past, somebody had watched a video called *Lilo and Stitch.*

"He's not moving."

"Just sleeping." The words practically tore out of him. There was nothing gentle inside of him, but somehow he managed to keep the movement of his hands along her body tender, reassuring. He skimmed one hand low, stroked the other along the damp hair at the back of her neck. His fingers itched to thread deeper, to tilt her head back and let him see her face, but the intensity hacking through him was not what she needed.

Not what he needed.

"Just sleeping," he murmured again. He wasn't quite sure what he said after that, how long they stood there in her small cluttered family room, with the sun whispering in to them, holding each other, him running his hands along her body, both of them staring at the image of her son, who lay as still as death on a cot in a small dingy room.

But it was well after noon when he left.

He'd wanted Spider-Man shoes. Not the kind with Velcro straps for little kids, but the gray ones with the red and blue Spider-Man crawling up from the bottom, with big-kid laces. Little Jimmy Leonard had a pair, and from the second Alex had seen them, he'd been in love.

Swallowing against a tight throat, Danielle stared down at the plain white tennis shoe that she'd purchased at the discount store, stained now with mud and grass. Alex had been so excited when she'd come home from the store. He'd taken the bag from her hands and retrieved the box, eagerly pulled off the lid.

Then he'd just stood there, for what had seemed like forever but had only been a minute or so, staring at the plain, boring, generic white tennis shoes.

"What about Spidey?" he asked at last, looking up at her through his father's big soulful eyes.

She'd wanted to cry. "I'm sorry, ace," she'd said, feeling like the worst mother in the world. The next day she'd gone to the mall and hunted down the shoes he'd described to her, purchased them and put them away for his birthday. As far as she knew, Alex had no idea.

Now he might never know.

Swiping at tears she'd trained herself not to let fall, tears that signified defeat, Danielle forced her hand to release its death grip on the dirty white shoe. Gently, lovingly she placed it on her dresser.

Breathing deeply, she turned toward her bed and pushed aside the memory of the FBI agent standing there, all big and strong and rumpled. "Get some rest," he'd ordered before leaving, and for a crazy moment, she'd thought he was about to kiss her. Not on the mouth, not romantically or passionately, but a gentle brush of his lips across her forehead. He'd had a hand on her face, a big square palm resting softly against her cheek, and he'd leaned close, but then he'd abruptly released her, as though the physical contact had hurt him somehow.

Then he'd walked away.

It was what she'd wanted, what she needed, but for a long time after he'd left, she'd just stood there at the front door, watching, aching, not at all understanding the hollow feeling of loss.

On impulse she crossed to the small stand by her bed and picked up the phone, punched out ten digits she knew as well as her own phone number. Of course, they'd once been her number. Her heart kicked up a notch when she heard the first ring. The second.

It flat-out stopped when the gruff male voice came across the line. "This is Anthony. Make it good."

His voice, so deep and strong and…harsh, rushed over her and through her, and despite the rough edges that could easily cut to the quick, a happy little song sang through her.

"Who is this?" her brother barked.

Longing jammed into her throat, preventing words, breath. Two years. Two years since she'd heard his voice, seen his face. Two years since the bitter argument that had severed the once-strong ties of family. She could still see him, though, her brother, her triplet, so big and tall and imposing, with a mane of thick black hair that would make almost any woman envious, the wicked little gold hoop in his ear. The fierce glower on his face.

And despite the sun slicing through the window, she started to shake. One word. That was all it would take. One word and he'd come charging in on his big black stallion, ready to save the world. Save the nephew he'd once cradled in his big arms and rocked to sleep while humming the haunting melodies their mother had once sung to them, melodies from the Old World, of the old ways, their words long since faded with time.

It's me, some place deep inside of her wanted to shout. *It's Lucky.* There was a hum to her blood, low, fierce, an energy that came only from Elizabeth and Anthony. *Don't you feel it, too?* she wanted to cry.

But then she remembered the note on the package, the warning that chilled her blood.

"Don't defy us again."

"Look, I don't know how you got this number," he growled, "but I don't have time for games."

And then the line went dead. "Anthony," she whispered, and his name scraped her throat on the way out. The truth hurt even more. It was too late for him to hear, too late to undo the past. Too late for so many things. Her brother hadn't understood her need to put distance between herself and her old way of life. He'd taken her decision personally, yet another abandonment in a lifetime of unexpected goodbyes.

She stood there for a long time after that, in her bedroom with the droning receiver in her hand and memories flooding her heart, her son's dirty little tennis shoe sitting on her dresser, the FBI agent's words echoing louder with every beat of her heart.

You need me, Danielle.

You're not alone anymore. I'm here now.

She needed, that was true. There were so many things

she'd tried so hard to deny. But she didn't know how to lean. Not anymore.

If she leaned, she might fall. And if she fell, this time she might never get back up.

The moon, almost full, hung high and bright over Lake Michigan. The dark waters shimmied in the mercurial light, shifting, restless, unsettled.

Liam could relate.

From his hotel window he stared into the night, looking for a pattern that refused to materialize. A French industrialist. A United States senator. And now a gap-toothed six-year-old boy in Chicago. The first two dead, linked only by a postcard and a hunch. The third, missing, linked by a tip.

It didn't make sense.

Frustration ground through him, but he refused to indulge the dark desires, the ones that had him wanting to spin away from the window and pick up the phone, call her. Again. Go to her and run his fingers along the smooth curves of woman, or worse, reach out to the bottle that sat on the antique sidebar. He ordered the scotch wherever he went, but allowed himself one glass and one glass only.

The remainder of the bottle served as a test every bit as demanding as the ones he'd aced at Quantico, one he had not failed in two years, seven months, three days, and—

Liam glanced at his watch. Fourteen hours.

Too well he remembered the face staring back at him from the mirror the last time he'd failed. The dark, vacant eyes. The white rim around the mouth. Too well he remembered the woman he'd found sprawled in his bed, the one whose name he'd never even asked. And too well he remembered the vow he'd made in that dismal little hotel room in a town he'd never been to before or since.

He would not slip, would not fall, would not fail again.

But now here he was, alone in an antiques-packed hotel

room in Chicago, and God, how he wanted to indulge. Just one call. One touch. One more sip.

No one could see him, catch him, hear him, but he muttered a stream of vile curse words out loud, anyway, then dropped to the floor and stretched out on his stomach, balled his hands into fists and pushed himself up, then down. Up, then down.

She was hiding something. He'd seen the flicker in her pale-green eyes that morning in her house, over breakfast, just after she'd told him about the man who'd approached her in the hotel lobby, a drink in hand.

That fit the pattern. Several of Titan's victims had been found with narcotics in their system. Nothing strong enough to kill, just to maim. To render unconscious.

But why?

Turning it over in his mind, he pulled his right arm behind his back and continued his regimen with only his left. Up, down. Up, down.

She'd been aloof when he'd called earlier in the evening, robotically formal, talking to him as though he'd not held her in his arms a few hours before, as though she'd not held him back, not rested her head against his chest. She'd said there'd been no further contact, that she was fine. That no, he did not need to come over.

And while he believed her on the former, the latter, uttered in that defiant way of hers, had reeked of lies.

Breathing harder now, his heart beating a little faster, he pushed up high with his left arm, released himself and slammed his balled fists against each other, then continued the routine with only his right arm.

He wanted to go to her, but didn't trust himself to be near her. Not tonight. Not with all these sharp, jagged edges cutting to the bone. He'd already stepped on the line. He would not let himself cross it.

Except, five hours later he did. He'd learned how to test himself, how to deny himself while he was awake. But when exhaustion consumed him and his eyes slid closed, when the world went dark and he began to drift, it was during those shadowy, tenuous moments that the demons came out to play.

There was Danielle on the deserted strip of beach, standing stoic and alone, her thick hair blowing in the breeze. Then she was in his arms. Her body was soft and warm, accepting and demanding. Then it was shaking, rejecting. There was a gun in her hands, then it was gone and she was pulling him close. Her mouth was trembling, then it was on his. Chaste, then desperate.

The images blurred, merging with the shadows. Dazed, dizzy, fighting what he recognized as wrong even for dreams, he shoved back from her, staggered back.

Her hair was no longer thick and dark, but long and straight and blond. Her eyes no longer flashed vitality, but froze him with an icy blue. Her mouth no longer trembled, but slid into a hard, condemning line.

"You think this is all it takes?" she asked, gesturing toward the sleek little black chemise he'd ordered for her from Paris. "You think this makes up for the past nine months?"

No, he didn't think that, not at all. He just thought—

"Just admit it, Liam, okay? Just put us both out of our misery and admit the truth."

He reached for her, Kelly, his wife, but she twisted away. "I almost wish there was another woman. That, I could fight. That, I could understand. But your job—"

He hit back a sound low in his throat. They'd had this conversation a hundred times. "Sweetheart, I know, and I'm sorry. It's just this case. Give me a few more weeks—"

"A few more weeks won't change anything." Her voice, normally so confident, broke. "Don't you get it, Lee? I could die, but it wouldn't matter. Your life wouldn't change, because you'd still have your passion. Your job."

The accusation sliced in with unerring precision. He reached for her to explain, but his hands swished through empty space, and his heart staggered hard. "Kelly!" He tore through the darkness, pivoted and found her standing behind him. But her hair was dark now, her eyes untamed, her mouth full and lush and curled with challenge. And in her hands, she again held the gun.

"No!" Jarred awake, Liam sat bolt upright, the sound of a single gunshot echoing insidiously through his mind. Breathing hard, his naked body hot and clammy, he stared across the room, lit by the gauzy light of the moon. The bottle sat where it had all evening, on the sidebar, sleek and tempting, but he refused to move.

Refused to indulge.

Kelly had been wrong. Dead wrong. Her death *had* changed his life, brutally and irrevocably. And he couldn't let it happen again. Titan would not win. No matter the cost, Liam would not let Titan destroy another woman, another family.

"Where's your shoe?"

The little boy with the messy hair and brave eyes glanced down at his feet. A dirty tennis shoe covered one, but on the other there was only a sock. "They took it."

"Took it?" Frowning, she looked at her pink fuzzy slippers and curled her toes against them. "Why?"

"Dunno," he said. "They just did."

She shivered. The room was the same as the night before, still and dark and cold, icky smelling. But the boy no longer lay on the cot. He was sitting on the edge, swinging his legs. He didn't look scared anymore. Now he just looked mad.

"How did I get here?"

He shrugged. "Dunno."

She didn't, either. She remembered the night before, when they'd first started speaking in their minds, but she had no memory of the day. And surely there had to have been a day. There was always a day.

But she only remembered the night, the darkness. The boy.

"Does anyone know we're here?" she asked, trying to

keep her bottom lip from trembling. If her daddy knew, he'd come get her. Maybe she should scream, she thought, cry out. Her daddy always came running when she had a bad dream, always slipped in bed beside her and held her until she fell back asleep.

But when she opened her mouth, no sound came forth.

"They won't hear you," the boy said. Alex, she remembered. His name was Alex. "I've already tried."

"What about your daddy?" she asked, shuffling closer to the bed. "Daddys always hear."

Alex's eyes, so calm minutes before, filled with sudden moisture. "I don't have a daddy."

She stared at him. "Everybody has a daddy."

His bottom lip trembled. "Mine went to heaven."

That stopped her. Heaven. She knew about heaven. Heaven was where her goldfish went. It was also where her grandma Violet went a long time ago. She'd cried over her goldfish, even though her mom had bought her a new one. She'd never met her grandma, but she'd heard her mommy cry, sometimes when she was alone in her bedroom.

"Then we'll just have to count on my daddy," she said. "He'll help us."

Alex's mouth twisted. He balled his hands in his Spider-Man T-shirt, looked at her real weird. "Your daddy can't help me."

"Yes, he can," she said, her little heart pounding. "He's a pwivate inwestigator." If only she knew how to reach him. How to tell him. Chewing on her lip, she turned around, saw the table, the one that looked exactly like the one in her bedroom. And she remembered. The crayons were still there. So was the paper.

"Just watch," she said, scampering to the small chair. She picked up a black crayon and started to draw. "You'll see."

Chapter 7

Art Dealer on Parole.

Dragging her third cup of coffee to her mouth, Danielle stared at the small news story she'd found on the Internet. Adrenaline pumped dizzily. Her heart raced. Finally, after hours of bleary-eyed searching, she'd hit pay dirt.

Sal D'Ambroni. He'd been one of Chicago's most prominent art dealers, traveling in exclusive circles, living high above Michigan Avenue in a gleaming penthouse, never giving a second thought to all those he'd cheated. Antiquities, he'd called his merchandise. From the holy land. Rare, priceless relics.

Oh, but he'd charged for them, all right. Extraordinary, mind-boggling, fraudulent prices. Because that was what his merchandise had been. Fraudulent. Cheap replicas made in Taiwan.

But no one had known. No one had suspected. He'd played a good game, until one of his clients had grown suspicious. The authorities, even the insurance company, had turned up nothing, but one client, Margaret Wentworth, had been relentless—and furious. She'd contacted Jeremy, desperate for help. And help Jeremy had.

Six weeks later, Sal had been arrested.

Six months later, on trial.

Seven months later, in the state penitentiary.

Except, now he was a free man and again living in Chicago.

Danielle closed her eyes and saw the man as he'd been that last day in court, after the jury had rendered the verdict and the bailiff was leading him away. He was a distinguished man, with a mane of long silvery hair that he wore in an elegant ponytail. He'd glared at Danielle, the woman who'd posed as his assistant, but who instead had been digging through his files and uncovering his dirty little secrets.

"You'll pay," he'd sneered. "You'll all pay."

She opened her eyes to the bright light of early morning and stared at the small set of wind chimes outside the breakfast window. They tinkled with the breeze, a soft melody that should have brought a smile to her face but didn't.

Within her, determination surged. Fury chased close behind. She pushed to her feet and ran to her bedroom, slipped out of her robe and reached for a pair of jeans.

Lost in anticipation, she just barely heard the ringing of the phone. Pulling on the jeans, she hobbled across the room. "Hello," she answered breathlessly.

"Danielle."

Just his voice, low and hoarse and uncomfortably intimate, that was all it took to stop her wriggling into the faded black jeans. It stopped her breath, her heartbeat. Ten hours had elapsed since his last call, ten long hours when she'd roamed the dark house, searched the Internet, tossed and turned in her bed, determined to prove he was wrong. Her son had not been kidnapped by a European criminal. There was no reason the FBI needed to be involved. No reason *he* needed to be involved. She did not need the tall man with the dark, haunted eyes.

"Nothing has changed," she said as matter-of-factly as she could. "There's been no further contact."

A rough breath scratched across the phone line and sent a shiver down her spine. "I'm on my way over—"

"No." The word shot out like a sharp gust of wind off the lake. "I—" Her mind raced for a suitable excuse. Work would have been nice, but he was staying at the hotel and could easily verify she'd secured some time off when she'd called yesterday. "I just need to be alone right now."

"I don't think that's a good idea."

"But I do," she said, even as some place deep inside protested. "I didn't sleep much last night."

"Neither did I."

The image formed by itself—Liam's big nude body twisting restlessly in the hotel's fine, Egyptian cotton sheets. She looked down at her own unmade bed and suddenly wished she'd pulled on a shirt before answering the phone.

Questions slinked in next, questions whose answers she was better off not knowing. Why hadn't he slept well? What demons chased him through the darkness? What pain had caused the aura of shadows to form around him?

What would it take to make him sleep through the night?

Her chest tightened with a compassion she didn't want to feel. "Then neither of us will do the other much good, will we?" The remark came out sharper than she'd intended, and despite the quick sting of remorse, she went with it. "There's no reason for you to be here," she said. "Not unless something changes."

"You really believe that?" he asked quietly.

Her pulse skittered. "Please," she said, and this time her voice softened. She moved away from the bed, away from images she didn't want to see. "Just give me a few hours." She reached for a black scoop-necked T-shirt. "I'll call you if anything changes."

"Sure you will," he muttered, and then the line went dead

and she was left standing in the dim recesses of her closet, in only her jeans and a bra, wondering why it felt as if she'd just failed a pivotal test.

The gallery was small and nondescript, nothing compared to the discreet establishment that had once dominated a corner of Michigan Avenue. A single brass sign hung out front, a simple plaque that paled in comparison to the exclusive sign that had once greeted customers from all over the world. Treasures, it said. That was all.

Anticipation quickened through Danielle. So did a vein of unease. She'd felt it from the moment she'd stepped from her car, the forgotten echo of awareness. The same low hum she'd felt a few days ago in the lobby of the Stirling, mere hours before she'd learned Alex was missing. The unnerving hazy insight into the future that had once ruled her life.

As kids, Liz and Anthony had called it her lucky sense, but Jeremy had insisted her ability to sense events before they happened was far more than luck. Skill, he'd said. A gift. Just like her knack for seeing, for reading the auras of color that surrounded all living creatures. Liz and Anthony had gifts, as well, uncanny, unusual abilities that had frightened their foster parents and helped the triplets survive on the streets. Abilities Jeremy had fine-tuned and honed, taught them to use, to trust.

Now she glanced around, taking in the run-down buildings lining the street. They were all crammed together, some of them occupied, all of them in disrepair. The one in front of which she stood looked as if it was ready to be condemned. The siding desperately needed paint. The windows were grimy, cloudy, letting little light squeeze out from inside. And the steps, three small stairs leading to the weathered front door, reeked of termites.

How far we fall...

She blocked the thought, the quick stab of unease, and hurried up the steps, turned the knob and pushed inside. It was broad daylight and she had her mobile phone and her gun. She wasn't afraid. She'd undertaken far more dangerous missions than this in the not-so-distant past, when Ty had been alive and her family had been whole. If her heart raced a little too fast, that was only the rush of adrenaline. And if one man's name kept echoing through her mind, louder and fiercer with each beat of her heart, that was only because—

She blocked that thought, as well.

A single bell dinged when she entered the dimly lit room, and she drew up short.

Old warped shelves lined the walls, as desperately in need of paint as the siding outside. A threadbare replica of a Persian rug sprawled across the dirty, scarred hardwood flooring. And the dust, it was everywhere.

So was the junk.

And that was what it was. No glistening replicas of fine artwork, no gleaming urns, no parchment-thin textiles. No display of intricately carved crosses. No arrangements of jeweled goblets. Just junk.

Slowly she moved toward the nearest shelf, ran her hand along an old, tarnished toaster. Next to it sat a tattered teddy bear, dirty mason jars and a stack of old yellowed paperbacks.

Junk.

"Can I help ya?" came a tired voice from behind her, and even as her heart thumped hard against her ribs, she spun around and saw him. Sal D'Ambroni. Or at least a man who'd once been Sal D'Ambroni.

Shuffling from behind a counter, the old man limped toward her. His face, once a study of elegant lines and refinement, was haggard and worn, tired. And his eyes, once sharp and gleaming, looked dull. "Do I know ya?" he asked.

Danielle took an instinctive step back. She'd known the trial had broken him. She'd known he'd lost everything—his fortune, his dignity. Even his family had abandoned him. But nothing had prepared her for the man she now faced.

"I—" she started, but then hesitated. She'd ignored the

niggle that insisted this was a dead end and charged south of town, clenching the forced hope that she'd found the man who'd taken her son. Now, staring at this broken old man, doubt became certainty. "I was just…looking for someone I used to know."

"No one here but me," he said with a tired smile, but then his face went hard, and she saw the gleam of recognition. And contempt. "You."

She swallowed hard. "Hello, Sal."

"You got a lot of nerve showing up here, girlie," he snarled, moving toward her.

She went to step back again, but her heels bumped against the wall of cluttered shelves.

"Does this make you happy?" he sneered, stepping so deep into her personal space that she could smell the day-old sweat on his body. "This what you came to see?"

"No," she said, holding up a hand. "It's not like that. I—"

"Then what?"

The quick slice of guilt made no sense. This man had made his own bed. He'd cheated countless people out of large sums of money. And yet, seeing him like this, she couldn't help but think he'd paid for his crimes.

She knew what it was like to lose everything.

"Git out," he said, and his hand clamped down around her wrist. His arms looked like little more than toothpicks, but they were surprisingly strong as he dragged her toward the door.

"Take your hands off her."

The voice, low and hard and deathly quiet, reverberated through the small shop. A sound broke from Danielle's throat as she swung around to see Liam, a tall, dark-eyed man all in black striding through the door he'd thrown open.

"I mean it," he snarled in a voice so deadly quiet it chilled her blood. "Take your filthy hands off the lady, and do it now." He slid a hand inside his sport coat, retrieved a sleek pewter handgun. "Don't make me say it again."

Danielle's heart staggered. The room, dirty and small to begin with, started to spin. She reached for balance, grabbed Liam's arm. "It's not what you think," she said.

But he wasn't paying attention to her. His eyes were dark, furious, focused only on Sal. "No?" There was a harsh clip to his voice. "I walk into this shop and find this man with his hands all over you, dragging you against your will, and you tell me this isn't what I think?"

"I wasn't gonna hurt her," Sal said, and when Danielle glanced back at him, she saw that his grizzled face had lost all color. "I just wanted her gone."

"It's true," she said, looking back at Liam. "The mistake was mine." And it had been. She should have listened to the voice she'd once trusted with the lives of those she loved, the one that had insisted Sal had nothing to do with Alex's disappearance.

Finally Liam looked at her, and when he did, when his eyes met hers, the breath abandoned her body on one sharp swoosh. In the short time she'd known this man, she'd seen more facets to his personality than a prism had colors. She'd seen him remain calm when she pulled a gun on him, seen him fiercely protective when he found her on the windswept beach at midnight, seen him in agent mode as he questioned her about drugs and Europe. She'd seen him alert and edgy when they'd found the box on her doorstep, oddly comforting when she'd fallen apart at the sight of Alex lying so still on that dirty little cot. She'd seen him cook breakfast and drink orange juice, she'd seen him by her bed, his eyes dark as he looked at the rumpled covers.

She'd seen him in her dreams.

But she'd never seen him like this, with the lines of his face all tight, the glint in his eyes like shrapnel. Cold fury radiated from him in a dark toxic cloud, and it sent her pulse into a low, deep thrum.

"Liam, please," she said, and only then did she realize Sal had released her and was shuffling back. She took Liam's hands in her own, indulging only briefly in their solid warmth, and stared into his eyes. "Let's just go."

"Not until you tell me what the hell was going on here."

"I already told you," she said, hating the edge of desperation to her voice. She was the one who should be furious with him. He'd followed her, after all. He'd followed her after she'd told him to leave her alone.

But now here he was, and no matter how hard she fought it, she couldn't silence the fierce song in her blood. "I made a mistake."

"Is this the man?" he asked in a voice stripped of all the warmth, all the tenderness and emotion he'd given her earlier. "The man from the hotel?"

She shook her head. "No."

"I ain't been to no hotel," Sal put in.

"Then what the hell are you doing here?"

She tugged Liam toward the door. "I'll explain later." And she would have to, she realized. She'd have to tell him about her past, about Jeremy, about the assignments he'd taken, shadowy assignments the police had turned their backs on.

Assignments Liz and Anthony still worked.

Assignments that had gotten Ty killed.

"I promise," she said, letting her voice go soft.

Debate darkened his eyes. Doubt. She'd already lied to him once, after all, and while she'd felt justified at the time, now regret nagged at her.

"Don't let her fool you," Sal snarled from behind her. "She'll tell you whatever she thinks you want to hear, if she thinks it will get her what she wants."

Her heart oddly heavy, Danielle swung around and saw the way he was looking at her, like a malnourished dog who'd just been kicked. "Sal…" She started but didn't know what to say.

"Come on." She wasn't quite sure how it happened. One minute she'd been holding on to Liam, her hands curled around his forearms, but then his hand was closed around hers, and he was dragging her toward the door.

She hurried to keep up with him, his angry footsteps thudding loudly against the old wood floor. And when the door opened and they stepped into the muggy air of midafternoon, when the sun cut down on them from a dizzyingly blue sky dotted by wispy clouds, she knew there'd be no retreating to the shadows. Not this time. Not with this man.

His hand curled tightly around hers, he led her down the rickety stairs to the sidewalk, where he didn't stop walking. He just kept right on going, leading her to where she'd parked her car several buildings away.

And finally she knew. She knew why the ancient sensation had crawled down her spine, why unease had whispered through her. She had been followed.

By Liam.

He released her, but she still couldn't get away from him. He had her wedged between his body and her sturdy car, his broad chest blocking the row of clapboard buildings, the rest of the world. He seemed even taller here, more imposing, the unsettling aura around him darker.

Her heart thrummed low and her hands went clammy, but when she looked up and met his eyes, she wasn't afraid. Not really. Not in a primal, life-or-death sense.

But on another level, a deeper one.

"Do you mind telling me," he said very slowly, very deliberately, "just what the hell you thought you were doing?"

Liam stared down at her, at her defiant eyes and the mutinous set to her mouth, at the wisps of dark hair that had escaped her ponytail and now curled around her flushed face, and didn't know whether to expose her to the ugliness rampaging through him, or pull her into his arms, kiss her senseless and discover once and for all whether she would taste as untamed as she looked.

"I was trying to find my son," she said in a voice that

betrayed not one sliver of unease. Caught in his, her hand was clammy and her pulse point fluttered wildly, but other than that, her composure showed no cracks.

"Here?" he demanded, forcing his gaze from hers and down the seedy street south of town. He'd been parked down the block from her house when he'd called earlier in the morning, unable to suppress the niggling thought that he should not leave her alone. So he'd watched, and he'd waited, and sure enough, shortly after noon he'd realized his gut had once again been right.

She'd lied to him.

The thought, the reality, shouldn't have tripped the fuse deep inside. Somehow it did.

During the long night before, thoughts of Danielle and Kelly had circled him like a merry-go-round out of control. They'd whirred and blurred, laughed and taunted.

Long before the sun broke over the lake he'd given up on sleep and had once again pored over his notes, the facts, the three postcards.

Danielle was the link, instinct insisted. She was the one. The one, the woman, who could lead him to his quarry. Titan.

That explained his need for her, he told himself, why thoughts of her clouded his mind. That explained why he wanted her to trust him, work with him.

That explained why he'd been so furious when he'd seen her back out of her driveway and head down Lakeshore Drive.

But God, it was all he could do to cage in the rawness creeping through him, a rawness he had not felt in a long, long time.

He wanted to be angry with her. He wanted to be furious. But the relief flooding his body was too strong.

"That man is a convicted felon," he said. He'd run a quick check before entering the shop, had learned the owner had spent time in the state pen and was out on parole. When he'd walked inside and found D'Ambroni with his hands all over her, touching her, dragging her—

"I know."

Her voice was quiet, resolved. Calm.

And it blasted one more link on the cage. "You know?" The information should not have surprised him. This was, after all, the woman who'd gone willingly to a deserted strip of beach in the middle of the night, armed only with a flimsy little handgun, ready to confront Titan's men on her own. The woman who'd been willing to do anything, risk anything, to get her son back.

The woman who'd ripped at her own clothes, ready to make a trade that had the power to make Liam's blood run cold.

He knew the answer before he voiced the question, but still, he asked. "What in the world made you come here alone?"

Her mouth twisted, into a frown or a smile he couldn't tell. "Because I'm the one who got him convicted."

There wasn't much space between them, barely enough for the sunlight to squeeze through, but he stepped closer. His hands itched to touch, but he kept them by his side. "You did what?"

She angled her chin. "I was the one who got him convicted," she said again. "I was the one who proved he was a fraud."

And because of that, she thought he'd taken her son. For revenge. "That's why you came here looking for Alex."

"Yes."

He swore softly. "Damn it, Danielle. I've already told you who's responsible for taking Alex."

"But you don't know that," she returned. "Not for sure one hundred percent."

"Yes," he said very slowly, very firmly, "I do."

She just stared at him, her face still tilted, her mouth still tight.

"And even if I didn't know that, even if there was a chance this Sal character was involved, you should not have come here alone."

Her eyes flashed. "I can take care of myself."

The words were sharp, confident, but behind them he heard the quaver of vulnerability she tried to hide from the world. Or maybe just from him. She wanted to take care of herself and her son, that was true. She was determined to prove that she didn't need anyone, that she could walk alone.

And while Liam understood the sentiment with a precision that never quit cutting, he also recognized the danger. The danger for her. His circumstances were different. He was a trained agent. He'd survived tests and trials designed to break the ordinary man. He'd been through Quantico.

He'd been through hell.

So had she, some voice deep inside insisted. She'd been through hell, and like him she'd survived. She'd come out hardened, determined, but she'd survived.

"But you don't have to," he said, letting his voice go quiet. All that anger inside of him, the anger that boiled and festered, shifted suddenly, softened, like pellets of ice transitioning into flakes of snow. "That's what I'm here for."

The warm breeze blowing off the lake picked up, playing dangerously with the tendrils of hair curling against her face. "Liam—" she started but didn't finish, just looked at him with a futility and longing that squeezed his heart.

Because he wanted to lift a hand to her face, to touch her cheek and ease the hair behind her ear, he curled his fingers into a fist.

"I didn't realize you'd been in law enforcement," he said.

She blinked. "Law enforcement?"

"You said you were the one who got D'Ambroni convicted."

Her expression, open and seeking a moment before, instantly closed. "I wasn't in law enforcement."

Earlier he'd stepped closer, so close his hips brushed her stomach. Now he stepped back. "Explain."

He hadn't known Danielle long, but he'd already learned she wore composure like most women wore heavy wool coats on a bitterly cold day. It draped over her curves, protected her from the elements. He'd only seen it slip once, and that was when she'd stared at the image of her son lying as still as death on the narrow cot in the dank little room.

But now it faltered again, as though the wind had blown open the edges of her coat. He saw it in her eyes, the way her lower lip trembled. She held his gaze for a long moment, then looked away.

He wasn't sure if it was a gesture of surrender or defiance, but either way it left a sour taste in his mouth.

"I'm waiting," he said.

Frowning, she returned her gaze to his. "I don't suppose you're going to accept 'it's none of your business' as an answer, are you?"

He stared at her mouth, the way it had quirked when she'd spoken the words. And something deep inside him lightened. "No."

She sighed. "You're not going to like this."

He wanted to laugh. God help him, the rumble started low and made it all the way to his throat before he stopped it. "There isn't much I like about what's happening right now."

Her eyes, normally an obscure shade of green so light and pale they were almost translucent, darkened. She lifted a hand to her face and swiped the hair back, exposing him to the sharpness of her cheekbones. Exotic, he realized, then remembered what she'd told him about her Romanian heritage, and couldn't help but wonder if the wildness he sensed came from Gypsy blood.

"It seems like another lifetime," she said, and her voice was soft, faraway, "but before I moved to Chicago, I used to…" She hesitated. "How do I say it?" she said, more to herself than to him. "We used to take on odd jobs. Jobs nobody else wanted or would touch."

He absorbed the information, all she'd left unsaid. *"We?"*

She nodded. "My brother and sister and I. And Ty."

"Ty?"

She looked down and away, let out a breath that could only come from memory. "Alex's father."

Something sharp and volatile flared through him. He'd known the child had a father. That was a given. But the assistant manager at the hotel had let it slip that Danielle was single, and she herself had told him Alex's father was of no help to them. Now images formed he didn't want to see, of Danielle and this faceless man, the life, the child, they'd shared.

"Odd jobs?" He ignored the dark streak within him. "What kind of jobs?"

Again her mouth twisted. "You are *so* not going to like this."

But this time no laughter surged within him. "I don't like a lot of things." He paused, stripped the growing unease from his voice. "Tell me, anyway."

She fiddled with her hair again, lifting a hand to slide it from her face, even though the wind had yet to blow it back. "Jeremy always called them making things right."

"Who's Jeremy? Your boss?"

The softness returned to her eyes. "I suppose it looked that way to the world at large, but he was more of a father than anything else."

Interesting. Her mother was dead, but she'd not mentioned anything about a father. He filed the information away, knowing now was not the time to pursue why this Jeremy was more like a father than the man who'd given her life. One nugget at a time. "What kind of things did you make right?"

She glanced toward D'Ambroni's shop. "Take Sal, for example," she said, then explained about the antiquities business he'd been running. The scam. "The police saw no evidence of crime. It's highly likely he had someone in their ranks on his payroll. So one of his customers, Margaret, who'd been taken for a bundle, came to Jeremy, asking for help.''

"For help," Liam repeated, awareness growing within him.

"To prove Sal was a fraud," Danielle said, looking up to meet Liam's gaze. "That's where I came in. I posed as an ancient-art enthusiast and quickly got a job as an assistant in his gallery.''

"But you were really snooping." He didn't mean for the words to come out so condemning, but they did.

"Investigating," Danielle clarified.

"Without any kind of legal sanction or protection.''

Her chin came up. "I wasn't the one breaking the law. He was.''

God, Liam thought. What had this woman been involved with? And worse, if this was the kind of covert world she'd lived in, was it possible one of her assignments had brought her in contact with Titan? That she'd crossed him somehow? Hurt him? That now he was back, seeking revenge, just as Sal D'Ambroni had promised to do?

"You're the one who brought Sal down," he said, and incredulity blasted him. What kind of man was this Ty, that he let his lover, the mother of his child, operate in such a dangerous, seedy line of work?

For the first time since he'd found her in the dirty little shop, she smiled. "Yes.''

And she was proud of that fact. A little vein of pride ran through him, as well, at her courage, her tenacity, but he quickly clamped it off. "You did other jobs like this.''

She nodded. "We all did. Elizabeth and Anthony and I. We each had our own—" she hesitated "—talent.''

It was the way she said the word, more than the word itself, that grated like nails down a chalkboard. "Talent?" The bad feeling he'd been fighting grew worse. He had no doubt that this woman had talent, all kinds of talent. Talents he knew better than to let himself explore. "And what was yours?"

"Luck," she said, and her voice twisted. "Pure blind luck."

But she didn't think so, he could tell. Not anymore. "The kind of luck that prevented you from taking the drink from the stranger in the hotel lobby?"

A hard sound broke from her throat. "The kind that runs out," she said in a flat voice. "The kind that died cold and fast the night a job went bad and Alex's father bled to death in my arms."

Whoa. He looked at her standing there, at the shadows that had suddenly consumed her eyes, and realized he'd just stepped into a mine field. The urge to touch her, to lift a hand to her face and comfort somehow, stunned him, so he did the only thing he could.

He took another step back. "Danielle—"

"Satisfied?" she asked, and he could literally see her wrapping the thick wool coat of composure around her curvy body. "Did your little interrogation get you what you wanted?"

"This wasn't an interrogation." But the truth curled around his throat like a rough, braided rope. He had been interrogating, pressing for information, trying to understand. And now he did. Too well.

"Then what would you call it?" she asked.

The question landed hard, dangerously close to an area he didn't care to explore. "Trying to help," he said very carefully, denying the rest. Caring. Protecting. "Trying to understand how deep the waters are that we've waded into."

An old El Camino rattled down the street, but she didn't spare it a passing glance. "We?"

"We." He glanced toward the sky, no longer a deep blue but whitewashed now. The sun was in its descent, signaling late afternoon. "Let's get out of here," he said. "Go home, cool off."

"And if I say no?"

"Wouldn't matter."

"Because you're going to keep following me, aren't you? No matter what I say, what I do? You're not going to leave me alone."

He gestured toward his rental, parked along the street two buildings away. "I already told you," he said, retrieving the keys from his pocket. "We can work together or against each other, but working without me is not an option."

The house was quiet. Too quiet. Memories crouched in every room, every corner. She could see her son camped in front of the computer or the TV. She could see his gap-toothed smile, hear his laughter, feel the tears he hated to shed, tears that came less often now as memories of his father faded.

That was why she'd agreed to dinner, she told herself, seated in the passenger side of Liam's rental. The only reason. Because she didn't want to spend one more minute alone in the house. She had her mobile phone, a lifeline she carried with her everywhere, even into the shower. She'd forwarded her home number. There was no reason to sit around and torture herself, let her imagination run down cruel and horrifying paths.

Alex.

She bit down on her lip, choked back tears she would not let fall. Jeremy had taught her how to narrow the world to finite tasks, not allowing the bigger picture to paralyze. It was a lesson she'd learned well. They all had.

Later, when Alex was home, safe and sound and tucked in his bed, and she stood in the doorway watching him, listening to his every breath, then and only then could she fall apart.

"What are you hungry for?"

Liam's voice was low, hoarse, and as always it sent an electric charge through her pulse. She glanced at his profile, the way his big body dominated the seat next to her. There was an alertness to him, a readiness that defied the casual manner with which he had one hand draped over the wheel, the other resting on one of his jean-covered knees. The pose suited him. If ever there was a man born to be in the driver's seat, it was this man.

Agent, she corrected. FBI special agent. Not man.

"I'm not sure." She looked away from him, away from the aura that drew her no matter how hard she tried to resist, and out the passenger window. And that was when she saw it. Her heart kicked hard, then slowed to a crawl. The pain was instant, blinding.

"Oh my God," she said on a low breath. Then she turned and grabbed the steering wheel, pulled right. "Stop the car."

Chapter 8

Tires screeched and brakes groaned. Behind them a horn blared. Liam swore softly. "What the hell—"

"Here." Danielle's voice was little more than a raw whisper. "Turn here."

It was the alarm that got him. Alarm she normally hid from him. Feeling a nasty rush of adrenaline, Liam plied away the fine-boned feminine hand that had curled in a death grip around the wheel. With his other hand, he maneuvered them from the stream of slow-moving traffic and onto the dirt drive.

"What is it?" he asked, looking first at the uneven rows of cars parked along the makeshift lot, then at the stricken expression on Danielle's face. Her eyes were wide, almost sightless. Her skin was too pale. And he knew if he touched, he would find it cool again, clammy.

"Talk to me, honey," he said with a calm that defied the rush of his pulse. "Tell me what you see."

"Alex…"

And his world just about stopped. "Where?" He slammed on the brakes, reached for his door handle.

Danielle beat him to it. She threw open the passenger door and ran from the car, kicking up dust behind her.

He grabbed his gun, crammed it into the waistband of his jeans and took off after her. "Danielle, wait!"

There were people everywhere, men, women and children. Young, old, everywhere in between. Some were laughing, others crying. Mothers pushed strollers while fathers held toddlers high on their shoulders. Teenagers walked with their arms draped around each other's waists, their hands tucked in each other's back pockets. They all stopped and stared, pointed at Liam as he tore through the crowd like a crazy man. "Danielle!"

He found her at the edge of the clearing, standing as still as a statue, except for the dark hair blowing wildly in the warm breeze. She had her back to him, but he could tell she had one arm lifted, a hand to her throat.

The pose horrified him. Recognition flowed hard and fast and brutal. He knew that pose, he'd lived that pose. For one fraction of one second, as he'd skidded to a halt at the police line half a block from his burning house. He'd stopped, and he'd stared, and in that one chilling instant, his whole life had flashed and crashed.

Then he'd run.

But Danielle was just standing there. Staring.

He approached her from behind, cautiously, much like a negotiator might approach a jumper perched on a ledge hundreds of feet in the air. The urge—the need—to touch almost blinded him. He wanted to lift a hand to her back, lay his palm against her shoulder and pull her against him.

But even more, he wanted to see what she saw, what had galvanized her so. All he saw was life and vitality and happiness, and—

A carnival.

"Danielle, honey?" Unwanted compassion choked him, but he kept his voice low and calm. "Tell me what you see."

At first she said nothing, just kept staring in the direction of the carnival, where a giant Ferris wheel revolved slowly against the soft crimson streaks of the early-evening sky. Families surged around them, moved as though drawn by magnets to the entrance, where lively music blasted.

He moved in front of her, turned to face her, felt the quick slice somewhere deep.

"Danielle?" he asked again, and this time he couldn't stop himself. It was her pain, but it swirled around him, sucking him closer, deeper. He lifted a hand to her face, eased back her hair. "I can't help if I don't know what's going on."

Slowly her eyes, those deep, distinctive pools of green, met his, and in them he saw a hell he'd hoped to never see again. He'd never had the chance to meet his child, to know if the baby Kelly carried was a girl or a boy, if the baby looked like him or his wife or some incredible combination of them both. But those four tenuous weeks between learning of her pregnancy and her death had been enough to trigger a ferocity in him unlike anything he'd ever known. He'd loved that child, the one he'd never seen, never touched, never held.

He could only imagine how deep that love must grow with each passing day, as the years rolled by. As a parent held a child, soothed them when they cried, read bedtime stories and sang silly nonsensical songs, taught them to walk and talk and love and laugh.

"I promised," she whispered, and the ragged edge to her voice assaulted him somewhere deep inside. "I promised him we could go to the carnival this weekend."

But now he was gone, and Danielle stood here alone, on the periphery of the carnival, staring at evidence that life marched on, even when hers stood still.

"Don't do this to yourself," he said, and just like that, his determination to stand back from the line between them shattered. Only a dead man could look at her and feel nothing, and even though Liam hadn't felt anything in three long years, he was not a dead man. Not even close. He couldn't just stand there and watch her hurt, not when she'd found a way to tap into the trickle of humanity still left within him. He didn't know whether it was the edge to her voice or the desolation in her eyes, or something else, something he wasn't ready to explore. He only knew he had to step over the line.

"Come here," he murmured, drawing her into his arms. He expected her to fight, but what she did was almost worse. She just stood there, woodenly, neither rejecting nor accepting.

"Honey, you have to quit torturing yourself like this," he said quietly.

Slowly she looked up at him. "Do you have children?"

The question lanced his heart. "No."

Her eyes glistened. "Then don't tell me what I should or shouldn't do."

The ancient pain flashed, but he pushed it aside. Now was not the time for his personal demons. "Just because I don't have children doesn't mean I don't know what it's like to lose," he said with a rough tenderness. "It doesn't mean I don't know what it's like to hurt."

"He's my son," she said. "My little boy. I'm supposed to protect him, to fight for him—"

"And you are." He wanted to brush back the hair that blew into her face, but he liked the way it looked, streaking against her cheeks and her mouth. "But being here isn't the answer."

Slowly she shook her head. "You don't understand." She stepped back from him. "I feel closer to him here. I feel…" She pulled in a deep breath, let it out slowly. "I need to be here."

He wished she was right. He wished he didn't understand. But he did. He'd gone back to his house the evening after the fire, and the next night, and the next, until he'd lost count of how many times he'd found himself poking around the burned-out lot that used to be his home. Once, he'd seen the lady next door, a close friend of Kelly's, seen the pity in her eyes, the concern, but even that had not been enough to keep him away.

"Then I'm going with you," he said. No way in hell was he leaving her to face this alone. Not when he knew the dark urges that drove a person to walk unblinkingly into the fire.

Without giving her a chance to protest, he took her hand and walked with her among the crowd, toward the bright lights and whirring specter of the carnival.

Alex loved carnivals. He loved the exciting confusion of the midway, the Viking boat that rocked back and forth and always made Danielle queasy, the Fun House, but most especially, he loved the games and the Ferris wheel and the funnel cakes.

"We brought Alex to his first carnival when he was only six months old."

"You and Ty?" Liam asked.

They walked side by side, hand in hand, down the crowded midway. Hawkers called to them, begging, teasing, but she barely heard. "And Elizabeth and Anthony," she said, and the old warmth filled her heart. Memories tittered like the rings tossed onto the tops of row after row of cola bottles. "You could say he was a group project," she explained. "Ty and I were his parents, but his aunt and uncle doted on him."

"You and your brother and sister are close, then?"

Danielle glanced to the right, where children and adults lined up to shoot streams of water into the open mouths of clowns. "You could say that," she said with a sharp twist to her heart. They'd been inseparable then. "We're triplets."

Liam stopped walking. "Triplets?"

She nodded, used to the surprise. "Anthony is the oldest. Liz was born twenty minutes later. I came along last."

His lips twitched. "The baby of the family."

It was a simple statement, and it was true, but a faraway echo dimmed her smile. "So they tell me."

"I'd think that would be a matter of record."

The carnival whirred around them, but above the chatter and clatter, the vendors calling out and the children laughing, Danielle heard only one sound—the sound that had haunted her during the early years after her mother died. "For the longest time Liz and I thought we had a younger brother or sister who somehow got lost in the confusion."

Liam sidestepped a herd of running adolescent boys, all wearing dirtied baseball uniforms. "Got lost?"

She shook her head, but the sound grew louder, more insistent, worming its way into her consciousness like a splinter under the skin. "Got left behind," she clarified. Vanished with their father—or worse, met the same fate as their mother.

The planes of his lean face hardened. "You don't remember?"

It was a simple question, a logical one. It shouldn't have sliced through her with the precision of a surgeon's scalpel. But it did.

"We thought we did." They'd insisted, but no one had believed them. Not even Anthony. "We thought we remembered the sound of a baby crying, of mother singing softly, trying to restore quiet." The dull ache, one she'd trained herself not to feel, stung anew. "But the social worker explained that we were only imagining things." Danielle could still see the woman's sympathetic face as she'd looked at the two girls with what could only be called pity. The same woman had been responsible for changing the triplets' last name from Payne to Caldwell. For their protection, she said, in case whoever had killed their mother ever went looking for the children who may have witnessed everything. "She said it was perfectly normal, given what we'd been through, that we'd want to fabricate more family, to make up for what we'd lost."

Liam frowned. "I've heard of that happening."

"So have I," she admitted. As a teenager she'd even researched the phenomenon. "It just seemed so...real."

"And now?"

She drew a deep breath, laden with the sweet scent of funnel cakes. "More like a dream," she said. A dream that had infected the long hours of the night for most of her childhood. "Hazy, fuzzy."

His eyes, gleaming like black diamonds only minutes before, went dark. "Sometimes it's hard to distinguish between what happens in our minds and what happens in real life."

The statement was matter-of-fact and soberingly true, but Danielle sensed more to Liam's words than met the eye. His secrets, she knew. The ones he kept deeply buried. The ones that had hurt him. "Liam—"

"Three of you," he muttered as though she'd never opened her mouth. "I can hardly imagine." With a tug they were walking again, still hand in hand. So seemingly normal.

And the dark waters, the ones she'd wanted to test, were left behind.

"Triple the trouble," Danielle said flatly. She tried for a smile, for levity, but there'd been nothing funny about the conversation she'd overheard standing outside the study door.

With effort, she lifted a corner of her mouth. "At least, that's what our last foster family said."

The kids were wild, untamed. Got each other in trouble. They needed to be separated.

Of course, what that had really meant was Wayne Toliver didn't want Anthony around. Didn't want Anthony to know. Didn't want Anthony to kill him when he found out what he really wanted from the boy's thirteen-year-old sisters.

Because he knew Anthony would. He almost had.

Danielle blinked against the memory of her brother breaking through the door and charging into his sisters' small bedroom, an old baseball bat in his hands and murder in his eyes.

Elizabeth, in shock and clutching a torn shirt, had silently cried. Danielle had screamed. And Anthony had roared.

Wayne had cowered.

To this day, she still remembered the sound of wood slamming against flesh and shattering bone.

"Danielle?"

She blinked, stared up at Liam. "What?"

"I asked about your foster home. You had more than one?"

Different scents now, those of deep-dish pizza and popcorn and turkey legs. But above them all the smell of sweat and beer lingered. "Countless." Some of them had been nice. One, Danielle remembered, had given her a fairy princess room, complete with a white four-poster bed and a fluffy pink comforter with matching curtains. "The agency tried to keep us together, but no one wanted that responsibility. Then they tried separating us."

Liam steered them around a group of teenage girls gathered at a henna tattoo booth. "Something tells me that didn't work, either."

The memory wasn't funny, yet she smiled. "No."

"How many?" he asked.

But she didn't answer; she was done with this line of questioning. "Look," she said, dragging him out of the throng of men, women and children, toward a bald hawker with a red bandanna secured around his head. "This is Alex's favorite."

Liam took the lead, inserting himself between her and the big bald man.

"I can't tell you how much money I've wasted," she mused, "trying to knock over those infernal milk bottles."

Liam looked down at her. His eyes were gleaming again, thoughtful. "I thought you said your talent was luck."

She shrugged. "Like I said, it ran out."

The sun had gone down, casting the night into a darkness lit only by the artificial lighting of the carnival. Shadows played against Liam's face, but they weren't the dark, secretive kind. They were tempting, unusual shades of a puzzle she couldn't figure out.

"Now, that's where you're wrong," he said in a drawl she'd never heard from him, then before she could stop him, he was forking over a stack of bills in exchange for big fat softballs.

"Liam—"

He handed her two balls, tossed the third in the air. "Let me show you how it's done."

Behind the kiosk, the bald man's dark eyes glowed, reminding her of a spider sitting eagerly in the middle of its web.

"I mean it," Danielle said. "I don't want you throwing away your money on my behalf."

He didn't even spare her a glance. He wound his arm up and slung the softball toward the small pyramid of white milk jugs with a wicked side-arm delivery she'd only seen from the occasional professional ballplayer.

"Ah, just missed," the hawker said, smirking.

Danielle took his arm. "Liam—"

"I'm just warming up," he said. "Now toss me another ball."

Behind them, a little boy of no more than three tugged at his mother's sleeve. "I want Nemo! I want Nemo!"

Danielle's heart twisted. Last year was the first time she'd brought Alex to the carnival, just the two of them. No Ty. No Elizabeth or Anthony. He'd tried so hard to be grown up and hide his disappointment, but when the hours mounted and she failed to win him anything, not even a plastic key chain, his smile had wobbled and his eyes had dulled. "It's okay, Mom," he'd said on the way out, reminding her so much of her brother that she'd barely been able to breathe. "One day I'll be able to win stuff, like Daddy and Uncle Tony did."

Except "one day" was now, and Alex, the only one besides her mother who could get away with shortening Anthony's name to Tony, was gone.

"You might want to aim for the bottom," the hawker suggested.

"I might," Liam agreed, again winding up. He fired another side-arm throw at the dead center of the triangle—and sent all three bottles crashing to the ground.

"If I wanted to lose, that is," he clarified. He didn't smile, though, just kept his gaze on the booth operator, steady, penetrating, much as Danielle imagined Liam might stare at a suspect during an interrogation. "But when I play, it's to win."

Danielle's breath caught. Before she realized his intent, Liam had taken the third and final ball from her hands and slung it toward a second stack of milk bottles, hitting it exactly in the same spot. And once again, the pyramid toppled.

"He did it!" the little boy squealed. "He did it, Mommy! Now it's your turn."

"I believe that's two Nemos," Liam said in a voice so low and quiet it somehow drowned out the cacophony of the carnival.

"Two?" the hawker asked.

Liam nodded. "One for me, and one for my little friend."

The man's bald head turned a fascinating shade of red. Danielle thought he meant to argue, but he didn't. He ducked under a counter and came up with two giant, fuzzy, stuffed clown fish.

Liam took his prizes and turned, went down on one knee and offered one to the little boy. "For you, young man."

The little boy's eyes went wide. "Really?" he asked with a squeal. "Mine for keeps?"

His mother stepped in. "Oh, but we can't—"

"Of course you can," Liam smoothly interjected, placing Nemo in the boy's hands. "My friend here only needs the one."

Danielle's chest tightened. From the afternoon he'd walked

into her life, she'd schooled herself to think of Liam as an FBI agent. A highly trained operative who'd barged his way into her affairs and who wouldn't leave her alone, no matter how hard she tried to push him out the door. A government man who'd ruined her first chance to get Alex home.

His blood will be on your hands, she'd scolded him, but she stared at those hands now, square palms and strong sturdy fingers, a collection of scars and calluses, holding a giant stuffed fish. Man's hands, she thought with a twist. Attached to a man's body.

Given life by a man's heart.

A heart he worked hard to hide. A heart hidden behind the dark aura of shadows and secrets. A heart that had been badly hurt, as deeply scarred as his hands.

"You're so very kind," the young mother was saying, but Liam would have none of it. He insisted his gesture was nothing, then before she could protest, he'd again turned his attention to Danielle.

"For Alex."

They stood in the middle of the midway of a lively carnival, with music blaring and bright lights flashing, vendors jockeying for attention and money, mothers and fathers and children laughing, but for one narrow second, there was only Liam, this impossibly tall man with the shrewd eyes and brusque manners, holding a giant orange fish in his hands. And for that wobbly moment, she didn't see the dark aura. There was only strength and willpower, a driving, relentless passion that should have sent her running.

But didn't.

"Thank you," she said, fighting a ridiculous flood of emotion. Because she heard what he didn't say. The stuffed animal was for Alex, when he came home. Because Liam Brooks, FBI special agent by trade, man by heart, was determined that he would.

When I play, it's to win.

She took the animal and hugged it to her body but said nothing else. Words weren't needed.

His expression unreadable, Liam slid an arm around her waist and steered her from the booth.

Move away, some voice deep inside insisted. Step away from his touch. But another voice, this one louder, urged her to ease closer, to drift into him, lean on him.

Doing neither, she walked among the whirl of the carnival, but the sights and sounds barely registered. Only the stark realization that for the first time in two years, since the night Ty had died and her world had gone dark, since she'd said goodbye to her sister and ignored her brother's wrath, someone had communicated with her without words.

The realization dulled all those sharp edges inside, the ones that had been slicing her heart for so long she'd forgotten there was another way.

"You really don't think they'll hurt him?"

Liam's expression remained as closed and distant as it had been from the moment he'd given her the stuffed animal. It was as though the gesture had depleted him, left him operating on fumes. They'd walked for what seemed like hours but was probably only minutes, the silence between them thickening and pulsing with every beat of her heart.

Until he'd steered her toward the Ferris wheel. Then she'd pulled away from him, stopped in her tracks. Reality granted them no reprieves. They weren't lovers so lost in each other that the world around them didn't matter. They weren't out for an evening of fun. In her purse, her cell phone sat ready, waiting for a call that might never come.

"Trust me," Liam had said. "This is the best way to play the game."

Game.

The word stuck in her throat like a giant wad of Play-Doh.

"This isn't a game," she'd protested.

He'd taken her arm and led her into one of the small cars,

and now the giant, brightly lit wheel began its ascent. Liam
sat next to her, quiet, intense, staring toward the south. To
the right, city lights twinkled and sprawled; to the left, the
darkness of the lake gaped as far as the eye could see.

"Answer me," she said. "Do you think they'll hurt
Alex?"

A hard sound broke from low in his throat. "They have
nothing to gain from hurting him."

Instinctively she slid a hand into her purse and retrieved
her small phone, glanced at the display to make sure it was
still on. "Then why won't they call?"

Finally he looked at her, and when he did, when those dark
eyes of his skittered over her face like clouds across the
moon, her heart changed rhythms. "It's all part of the game."

Game. There was that word again, and this time it punc-
tured the thin veil of patience and control she'd been trying
so hard to hold on to.

"This isn't a game," she said again, and her voice broke.
Swallowing hard, she hugged Nemo to her body. "It's my
son's life."

For a moment he said nothing, he just looked at her. Then
he stunned her by reaching for her hand, chilled now, and
cradling it against the warmth of his. "I know," he said, his
thumb tracing small circles against her palm. "I know." His
eyes met hers. "But to Titan it's just a game."

She wanted to pull back from him, his world, but they were
alone in a small car suspended high above the ground with
the cool lake breeze rocking them. "But why?"

"They're playing you," he said with a matter-of-factness
that sent a nasty chill through her. "Priming you. Pushing
you to the edge, trying to drive you out of your mind with
worry. They want to unravel you," he added. "So the next
time they make contact, you'll be so desperate, you'll jump
at the chance to get your son back."

Her breath caught in her throat, and up so high above the
ground, she no longer smelled the sickly sweet scents of the

carnival. She wanted to deny his explanation, but couldn't deny its logic. With each second that crawled by, the longer the silence, the more leeway her imagination had to run wild. And the more her imagination worked against her—

In her mind flashed the memory of the night on the beach, the way she'd torn at her own shirt, willing to do anything, *anything,* to get her son back.

"You have to trust me," Liam said again.

This time it was Danielle's turn to look away, to focus on the string of airplanes streaking across the dark sky, a blur of slow-moving lights, one after the other, snaking across the city and out over the lake, making a U-turn to head back in for a landing.

Trust. "I wish it was that easy," she murmured.

"Danielle." It was just her name, a name she'd heard all her life, but when he said it, the way he said it, it was as though he spoke in some secret, ancient language. He lifted a finger to her chin and tilted her face toward his. "There's nothing easy about this."

The quiet statement wound around her heart and pulled. She felt herself lean toward him, reach for him. On some distant level she was aware of the way she tilted her face, lifted her mouth. The way he leaned toward her. The way her heart thrummed and drummed. The groundswell of want and need, twined so tightly it was impossible to separate one from the other.

The shock was instantaneous, a wild current rushing through her. His mouth brushed hers and his lips moved, but rather than a kiss, they formed a near-silent hiss, and then he was once again turning from her and staring into the night as the small car swung its way down the giant wheel.

And Danielle was left sitting there, hugging her son's stuffed animal and trying to breathe. This was a mistake, she knew. Coming to the carnival, spending time with Liam, letting herself see the man behind the FBI badge. She should have stayed home alone. She should have sent him on his way.

But now they sat side by side in the small cage of a Ferris wheel, rocking to the breeze blowing steadily off the lake. A smart woman would move away from him, stare off into the distance like he was doing. A smart woman would pretend that she'd not wanted, for one tenuous second, to feel the heat and warmth of his kiss.

She'd been alone for so long, she figured it was only natural. Maybe it was the memories stirred by being at the carnival, maybe the crushing disappointment of looking into the faces of so many children and not seeing her son, but for the first time in years she actually wanted to lean on someone else.

Except, he'd pulled away.

She watched him now, the acute stillness of his body, the uncompromising lines of his face, the shadows that had once again hidden his eyes, and even though she knew better, she lifted a hand to his face. He'd touched her so many times. He'd taken the gun from her hands. He'd caught her arm to prevent her from running from him. He'd brushed the hair from her face.

But this was the first time she'd touched him.

The first time she'd initiated contact with a man since the night Ty died.

He flinched.

The small gesture shouldn't have wounded her, but somehow it did. Still, it didn't deter her. Warning shrieked through her, but very slowly she let her fingers skim the rough planes of his face, felt the prickles clear down to her bone. "Who was she?"

From the car behind them, the sound of a child's giddy laughter filled the air, but Liam said nothing. Not with words. Only the tightening of his jaw confirmed her suspicions.

"She hurt you," Danielle said quietly, and even though it shouldn't matter, nothing about this man should matter, she couldn't just let him sit there and quietly suffer. Poison had to be drawn out. Bit by painful bit.

"She hurt you bad."

Slowly Liam turned to face her, exposing her to the saddest eyes she'd ever seen. "It wasn't her fault."

Danielle's heart kicked hard. Instinct warned her to retreat, but suspended high above the ground, there was nowhere to go. "You blame yourself."

For a moment he said nothing, just looked at her as if she'd stripped off a bandage and jammed a hot poker into a wound that had never healed. Then he swore softly. "Let it go."

The wind whispered harder, sending stray tendrils of hair into her face. "Hurting isn't a weakness," she told him, because intuitively she knew he thought it was. "Feeling makes you human."

He hissed out a low breath. "You really want to know what I'm feeling right now?"

The serrated edge to his voice should have warned her, frightened her. But it didn't. "Yes, I do."

His hands were on her face then, both of them, big, strong, holding her so that she couldn't move. And his eyes flashed. He leaned closer, rubbing a thumb along her lower lip.

"So do I," he said in that alarmingly quiet way of his, with a voice that had no business coming from a man of his size. "So do I."

Then he was gone, and just as quickly the ride ended and the attendant opened the car and Liam strode into the night, leaving Danielle sitting there hugging the stuffed animal to her heart.

And trying desperately to breathe.

Liam cut through the milling crowd, but could do nothing about the frustration winding him up inside like a top about to spin out of control. He'd done it again, damn it. And not just once but twice. He'd tried to reinforce the line between them, make it darker, thicker, harder to cross.

But then he'd looked at her sitting next to him, and the line had disintegrated.

He'd just wanted to console her. He'd just wanted to comfort her. At least, that was what he'd told himself. But the second his mouth had brushed hers, the moment he'd felt her warm, moist breath on his face, the paltry lies he'd told himself evaporated, leaving only a sobering truth.

For a few dangerous minutes he'd forgotten about everything. He'd forgotten about Titan and Kelly, he'd forgotten the blinding needs that had driven him for years. The need for justice. The need to avenge.

He'd forgotten the fact that a little boy's life hung in the balance. That the child's mother was depending on Liam to bring him home safely.

There'd been only Danielle, and a relentless thirst unlike anything he'd ever known. He'd wanted to drink her in. He'd *needed* to drink her in. All of her, not just her pain. The parentless little girl who'd grown up shuffled from foster home to foster home and the gutsy woman, the courageous survivor she'd become. To taste and savor and—

Damn. He really was a son of a bitch.

He wanted to walk faster, but knew she was already going as fast as she could. She was a step behind him, and even though his fingers itched to close around her hand, he didn't trust himself to touch her again. The last time he'd glanced back, he'd seen her scowling at him, clutching the goofy stuffed fish to her chest. She'd looked ridiculously young with her hair wild and untamed around her face, her skin flushed, holding the toy as though it was something dear and to be cherished.

As though it was her little boy.

The realization chilled him to the bone and instantly sobered him of the desire to turn to her and take her in his arms, to hold her tight and kiss the stunned look from her mouth.

He needed to get away from her, damn it. He needed to

be back in his hotel room, where he could be alone with the sleek lines and smooth curves of the bottle he'd ordered from room service. He'd given in to one temptation tonight. He was determined to prove he could resist a second.

"Come on," he said, glancing back at her. "I'm taking you—"

The words died a cruel death. He stopped walking, damn near stopped breathing. Dark spots clouded his vision. He stared through the haze, the whir, at the mob of strolling teenagers and gum-smacking adolescents, laughing families and adoring lovers.

Danielle was gone.

Chapter 9

"What's the matter, afraid?"
"I'm not afraid."
"Then prove it."
"I don't have to prove anything to you. Either of you."
"You are afraid!"

Danielle stared at the House of Mirrors, but barely saw the small makeshift tent. The young woman collecting tickets called to her, to everyone, but the voice sounded faraway, suspended in a tunnel of time and space. There was only a thirteen-year-old Anthony, scowling, even so long ago, with his defiant gold hoop earring and long wild hair slicked back into a ponytail, and Elizabeth, dare in her eyes and holes in her jeans.

The memory drew her, much as the carnival had that hot summer night a lifetime ago, when she and Anthony and Liz had first arrived in Philadelphia. They'd never planned on staying there. They'd wanted to go far, as far as they could get, as far away from North Carolina as possible. They'd been running for weeks. Sleeping in parks and bus stations. Hitching rides with truckers. Picking pockets for bus fare.

That had always been Danielle's specialty. Her lucky sense had always guided her to the safest targets.

California, they'd thought. They'd go west. The land of opportunity and sunshine. No one would find them there. No one would drag them back to North Carolina. No one would make them see Wayne Toliver ever, ever again.

But then they'd made it to the outskirts of Philadelphia, and tired and hungry and dirty, more scared than they wanted to admit, they'd targeted the carnival as the perfect spot to lift a few dollars. Maybe they could get enough to pay for a hotel room. Nothing fancy. Just a room. It didn't matter how dirty it was, as long as it had a bed. It had been so long since they'd slept in a bed.

Even longer since the girls had enjoyed the luxury of dropping off to sleep without the worry of who might try to join them under the cover of darkness.

The carnival had seemed perfect. Lots of people and commotion. Easy to slip around unnoticed. Easy to make an escape.

But then they'd stumbled across the House of Mirrors, and secrets had started to unravel. Determined to show her brother up, Danielle had spun around, searching for an easy target. The tall, older man with the unkempt beard had seemed perfect. He was just standing there, gazing into the distance, not paying the least bit of attention. And his jeans were loose. All Danielle had to do was—

Jeremy Solienti had grabbed her hand the second she'd made her move.

Danielle blinked, surprised to find her eyes had gone misty. Jeremy. She missed him every bit as much as she missed her brother and sister.

The sickly familiar scent of cotton candy almost choked her. Frowning, she checked her mobile phone, then glanced around the crowd, wondering where Liam had gone. After he'd strode away from the Ferris wheel, she'd gone after him, but he'd made it clear he had nothing to say to her, and she wasn't a woman to fall in step behind a man like a good little girl. So she'd taken her own path, let the distance between them widen, and then she'd seen the House of Mirrors and she'd stopped.

Instinct told her to turn away now, to go in search of Liam. He would not be pleased when he discovered her gone. Instead she lifted her chin and moved toward the house, handed a wad of tickets to the attendant, then stepped inside.

The past greeted her like a long-lost lover. The lighting was dim, the air warm. The maze sprawled before her, daring her to choose the right path. She moved forward but found herself bumping against a mirror instead. She turned, tried another path, ran into a miniature version of herself.

"Mommy, look how short you are!"

She spun around and came face to face with another image, this of her impersonating an Amazon queen.

"Dad, when did you get so tall?"

Emotion tightened her throat. Tears stung her eyes. Everywhere she looked, she saw her little boy. He'd loved the House of Mirrors, loved to run from cubbyhole to cubbyhole, smearing his hand up against the images reflected back at him. She and Ty had laughed and laughed.

There was no laughter now. No Ty. No Alex.

She was alone, just as she'd wanted to be. She'd broken ties with her family, determined to live life on her own terms. To give her son a normal life.

Pivoting, she tried to retrace her steps, but the sea of mirrors swallowed her. Everywhere she looked she found only her image staring back at her, her eyes wide and dark.

This was a mistake. The House of Mirrors. The carnival. Leaving her house. She should have stayed home, alone. She should never have left with Liam. She should never have let herself lean, never have let herself want, not for one fraction of one heartbeat.

The quick burst of panic made no sense. It gripped her, circled her throat and squeezed. She tried to breathe, but the air inside the tent had grown warm and stale and sticky, and it stalled at the back of her throat.

Get out, a voice deep inside commanded. *Get out now.* She started to run, but the maze closed in on her. "Please," she whispered.

"Please what?"

The voice was low, dangerously quiet, and it kicked through Danielle with a force that stunned her. She wasn't a woman to gasp, but the small choked sound echoed through the quiet tent. She spun toward the voice, the man, felt herself stagger back against a mirror.

He'd found her, and he was coldly furious. "Liam."

She'd seen him angry with her before. At the beach, when she'd pulled a gun on him for the second time in twelve hours. Just earlier that day, at Sal's shop, when he'd barged in to find Sal with his hands on her. She'd seen the hard lines of warning form on his face. She'd seen the glitter in his eyes. She'd seen the way he moved, protective and threatening at the same time.

But this was so much worse.

He didn't move now, didn't say anything, just stood there in front of a prison of mirrors, his tall, dangerously still image surrounding her like an army about to lay siege. She tried to turn from him, but he awaited her at every corner. She moved anyway, but ran smack into his reflection, tall and imposing. Unmoving.

And then she noticed his eyes. The glitter was there, but it was a flat glitter, dull and uncompromising. The lines of his face were hard, his mouth flat. Gone was any trace of the man who'd slung a softball at the pyramid of milk bottles to win two stuffed animals, who'd gone down on one knee to share one with a little boy he didn't even know. The man who'd stared vacantly over the city, from high in the Ferris wheel. Who'd brushed his lips over hers. Who'd admitted he didn't know what he wanted.

This man knew what he wanted.

"Start talking."

Two little words, but they carried the authority of a man used to being obeyed.

"I don't owe you any explanations," she said, but then he was moving forward, the whole circle of tall Liams closing in on her.

"Do you have any idea?" This time his voice was lower, hoarser. He stopped, halting the encroaching army along with him. "Any idea at all what I thought when I turned around and found you gone?"

She swallowed hard, wanting to step back. But she refused to move. She'd known he wouldn't be happy. She'd known he expected her to be trotting behind like a good little girl. But this... God, no, she'd never expected this. "I didn't think—"

"You didn't think." Acid dripped from his voice. Then another step, this bringing a hundred Liams one step closer. "That's the problem, isn't it? You didn't think. You didn't think the night on the beach. You didn't think this afternoon, and you didn't think tonight."

She lifted her chin. "Just because I'm not playing by your rules doesn't mean I'm not thinking."

"Your words," he said in a silky soft voice. "Not mine."

All those loose ends she'd held together started to unravel.

"Don't you get it?" he practically growled. He lifted his hands toward her, then let them fall to his sides. "I'm trying to help you, damn it. Titan—"

And then, finally, at last, she did get it. She understood his anger, the volatility flashing in his eyes. The glint of something dangerously close to fear—a fear she'd never expected from an FBI special agent like Liam Brooks, who walked unblinkingly through the fire.

Titan.

"You're right," she admitted, and even though she heard her voice falter, she didn't care. "I was so lost in memories that I didn't let myself consider that he could be here."

Laughing, two young boys raced around a corner, barely sparing Liam and Danielle a glance before scampering down the path to the exit she hadn't found—and was no longer sure she wanted.

"It's okay," Liam said, and when she looked back at him, at the Liams surrounding her, she saw that the lines of his face had softened. "I'm here now."

Her breath faltered. Because he was. Everywhere she turned.

"What memories?" he asked, stepping closer.

She blinked. "What?"

"You said you were lost in memories."

The urge to touch him drove her, stripping away the anger and the defenses she'd wrapped so tightly around her only a few minutes before. She lifted her hand, but found only air.

"We used to come to the carnival when we were younger," she said. "My sister and brother and I." She paused but she couldn't look away from his eyes, which were no longer cold and flat, but warm and glowing and surrounding her like a sea of candles. "You remind me of him, you know."

He lifted an eyebrow. "Your brother?"

The smile happened all by itself. "So big and bad and tough, ready to take on the whole world, scared to admit you're afraid."

"I'm not afraid."

Her smile widened. "That's what Anthony always said." And he'd do the same thing Liam just did, kind of puff out like a male peacock. "I always thought he was invincible," she said, letting her mind drift back through the years, "until the night Liz and I tried to get him to go into the House of Mirrors."

Her badass brother had acted as though they'd asked him

to play dolls or dress-up. Horror had drenched his eyes. He'd stepped back from them, thrown up a wall between them.

"He was afraid of mirrors?" Liam asked.

"Not mirrors," Danielle said, and her heart swelled at the memory. "Of closed-in spaces." She and Liz had not realized it until that night. They'd known he carried scars from the night their mother was murdered. They all did. But they'd never noticed how he went out of his way to never be fenced in. "We hid in her closet," she murmured, "while my mother was killed."

Liam swore softly.

"Anthony was almost out of his mind. He was torn between protecting us and protecting her." The memory crested through her like a dark wave. "He couldn't stand being cooped up in there like that, choking on the cloying scent of gardenia that she always wore. He made us promise we would stay hidden, then threw open the door and ran to help."

Liam took a tentative step toward her. "But he was too late."

She closed her eyes, nodded.

"Did he see who did it?"

"I think so," she said, opening her eyes. As long as she lived, she'd never forget finally venturing out of the closet, finding her brother standing over their mother's body. She'd been beaten and strangled. Anthony dropped to his knees and begged her to wake up, but their mother didn't move. Not even when he cried. "The memory is locked so deep inside of him, I don't think it will ever come out."

Liam took a step closer. "And you, Danielle? Are you afraid of small spaces?"

"No. I...I've always felt safest with walls around me." It was only when those walls were gone, when she stood open and exposed as she had that night on the beach, with no one to watch her back, that vulnerability cut through her.

"Then what?" he asked. "What has you so scared right now?"

She angled her chin, tried to deny. "What makes you think I'm afraid?"

His gaze heated, slipped down her body, slowly, lingeringly, then cruised back up. "I'm an FBI agent," he said in that deceptively benign manner of his. "I'm trained to see what others miss."

Her mouth went dry. "And what do you see?"

"A woman who wants to run." He stepped closer. "A woman who keeps glancing around, checking her surroundings, searching for a way out." The lines of his face hardened, condemned. "A woman whose eyes, normally a clear green, are dark and stormy."

Too much, she thought. The man saw too much. She didn't know how he did it—made her feel safe and threatened at the same time. Instinctively she lifted a hand to fend him off, but realized he wasn't close enough to touch. He just looked that way, so tall and dark, surrounding her in an ever-tightening circle.

"Everywhere I look," she whispered, painfully aware of the catch to her voice, "there you are."

"And that bothers you."

She glanced to her right, where the two young boys had vanished around a corner. A corner she could not see, not with all those Liams staring back at her. Watching. Waiting. Crowding.

"It confuses me," she said. It made her heart beat too hard, her blood flow too fast. "It's not real."

He didn't move, just watched her with those steady, penetrating eyes that reminded her of a wise owl, all seeing, all knowing. "You don't think so?"

She swallowed hard, for the first time wishing that she'd trotted behind him the way he'd wanted, that she'd never defied him, never ventured down her own path. Then she wouldn't be standing here in the semidarkness of the House of Mirrors, one woman standing against an army of Liams. "It can't be."

"Why not?"

Because it was too intense, too consuming. Because she kept reaching but, despite the fact she saw him everywhere, she kept coming up empty handed.

Because with Liam she could no longer discern what was real from what was only a shadow of her imagination.

"You walked away," she reminded him, thinking back to the first day he'd barged into her life, when he'd boldly promised to not walk away, not leave her, until her son was safely home. "You told me you wouldn't, but after the Ferris wheel, you practically ran."

He'd left her sitting there, hugging the stuffed fish and staring after him, wondering how in such a short time this man had managed to shred the defenses she'd spent years erecting.

She watched his hands, the way they curled into tight fists. "I had to."

His words were hard, almost guttural, and they should have warned her. They should have prompted her to turn from him, seek the path the boys had taken.

But she couldn't look away, couldn't deny the need to know. "Why?"

For a moment he just stood there, all of him, all those reflected images that surrounded her for as far as the eye could see, standing as still as marble soldiers. Then he swore softly and killed the distance between them.

"So I didn't do this," he said roughly, and before she realized his intent, before her heart could beat, he took her face in his hands and lowered his mouth to hers.

The contact stunned her. The sensation of mouth to mouth. Of hunger. Urgency. Earlier, on the Ferris wheel, it had only been a slight brush. A promise of a kiss, a temptation, a whisper of what could be.

But this was so much more. This was more than just a

promise, more than a temptation. It was a full onslaught, his mouth crushing hers, not with the finesse or restraint she associated with him, but with a blinding urgency that curled her toes and melted her bones. Made her want to cry.

To beg.

She wanted to push away from him. She wanted to twist out of his arms, sever the contact between their bodies, of his hands holding her face, his mouth taking hers, but she could no more have turned from him than she could have resisted the draw of the House of Mirrors.

One of his hands tangled in her hair, and she found herself arching into him, opening for him. A soft little cry rasped from deep in her throat when his tongue swept into her mouth and brushed with hers.

There'd been no one since Ty, no physical intimacy, no hard, male mouth claiming hers, no whiskers rubbing against her cheek, not even a chaste kiss good-night. No one. And now the reality of this man, this kiss, seared clear to the bone, and like a blackboard wiped clean, her mind went blank.

She felt her knees buckle, heard the guttural sound from deep within him. He backed her against a mirror and held her there, pinned between his big body and the cool surface. But she didn't feel trapped. She didn't feel threatened. She felt…everything. She felt every hard line of him, every angle, every ridge. He pressed himself against her and she responded by twining her arms around him, sliding one hand up along his neck, to where her fingers could thread through his hair.

To the world at large, Liam strapped on a shield of control, of indifference, of command. But there was nothing controlled or indifferent about the way his open mouth ground against hers, the tangling of their tongues in an erotic imitation of deeper intimacies. She felt him inside of her, against her. She felt him everywhere, just as she'd seen him.

"And so I didn't do this," he murmured, sliding one big hand down the side of her face and along her neck, to her

chest, where her breasts had grown heavy with a sweet, forgotten need. They ached for a touch they'd not felt in years.

Not true, she amended, drinking in the sensation. His was
a touch she'd never felt before.

But she'd longed for it forever, she realized as his finger-
tips grazed her nipple.

The soft, mewling sound surprised her. The hot curling
ribbon of sensation streaked from her breast down between
her legs. He kneed them apart and she let him in, embraced
him with her thighs and her arms, holding him as tightly as
she could, moving her hands restlessly along his body, map-
ping the feel of him, the size and shape and promise. His
body was big and strong and powerful, capable of crushing
and hurting, but he did neither. In his arms she felt safe. In
his kiss she found a harbor she hadn't realized she'd been
seeking.

Liam, the FBI agent who had materialized in her life when
she'd needed him most, this man of shadows and secrets,
tasted of strength and desperation, of pain and shattered restraint, of a dark denial she recognized too well. He tasted of
need. He tasted of want.

It was the want that got her. The want that penetrated the
haze of desire. The want that she felt, too. That drenched
every pore of her body.

That she had no business feeling.

On a cruel heartbeat the haze crumbled, and reality sliced
in with all its sharp, jagged edges.

"No," she whispered, shoving at him as though he'd been
molesting her rather than kissing her with a passion that left
her breath in shambles. A kiss that she'd been returning.

A kiss, heaven help her, that she'd wanted.

"No," she said again, louder this time, and when she
pushed at him, he staggered back, as though he was nothing
more than a cardboard cutout, rather than more than six feet
and two hundred pounds of hard, driven man.

Trying to breathe, to think, to understand, she dragged the

back of her hand over her mouth, a mouth still moist and swollen and pulsing from the intensity of his kiss. A mouth that felt naked now. Exposed.

A mouth that still wanted.

He stared back at her. All of him, not just the man, but the countless Liams that surrounded her, towered over her, threatening now, where before they'd been protective, seductive.

"No," she murmured again, because there was really nothing else to say. But deep inside she bled. Where there'd been heat and completion a moment ago, now a sickness spread, blotting out every crying need, every throbbing want.

His eyes went dark. "That's why I walked away."

The words devastated her. Because despite everything, she wanted to step toward him, to lift a hand to his face and wipe away the regret.

Instead she turned and ran.

Previously the path had eluded her. Now she navigated the twists and turns, the sharp curves and the deceptive images with a horrifying ease. New needs drove her, not dark and erotic like the ones that had pulsed through her in Liam's arms, but cold and punishing. The need to be outside, away from him. To suck in fresh night air untainted by the scent of man and desire.

She burst out of the house and ran into the swelling crowd. She opened her mouth and pulled in deep breaths, but no relief came, not when all the scents of the carnival jammed into her throat.

"Danielle!"

She kept running. From Liam. From the truth.

From herself.

Alex.

Dear God, Alex. Her little boy was missing. He needed her. And yet there she'd been, in the House of Mirrors, with her body wrapped around that of the FBI agent who'd promised to help her.

He'd helped, all right. He'd helped her see a side of herself that horrified her. A side that needed and wanted, a side that could lean and could fall.

And God help her, if she fell, who would be there for her son?

"Danielle, wait!" Liam was on her then, snagging her wrist to stop her cold. She struggled against him, but he turned her toward him and glowered down at her.

"Don't run from me."

Breathing hurt, so did looking at him. "Don't touch me," she spat. "Not ever, ever again."

She expected his face to darken or his mouth to twist. She expected heated words, maybe even a reminder that he'd not been the only one touching.

She did not expect him to release her. She did not expect an apology.

But that was what he did. "I'm sorry," he said, and the words sounded as broken as she felt. "That was…"

"…wrong," she finished for him.

"Wrong," he agreed.

She put her hand to her mouth again, meaning to wipe away the remnants of his kiss. Instead, she fingered her swollen bottom lip, where a slight throb remained.

"No," he said, and his expression went all soft. "Don't blame yourself. It was my fault. I'm the one who lost—" He stopped abruptly, but Danielle heard what he didn't say, what he could not admit. Not even to himself.

He'd lost control.

So had she.

Moisture stung her eyes. "What kind of mother am I?"

"A good mother," he said without hesitation. "A strong, courageous mother ready to move heaven and earth to protect her son."

A mother who'd, for one blinding moment, savored the taste of a promise she'd taught herself not to want.

"Now, come on." He started to reach for her again, but

before he made contact, he let his hand drop. "Let's get you home."

She'd been fighting him since the moment they'd met, but there was nothing to fight now, not when he offered exactly what she wanted. "We never should have come here," she said, glancing around the bright lights and whirling activity of the carnival, the merry-go-round with its cheery horses frozen in motion, the laughing children going round and round. "I just thought…"

"I know," he said quietly, and something in his eyes told her that he did, that he knew entirely too much about looking for something in all the wrong places. "I saw the way you looked at every child, the way you swung around every time you heard laughter." He hesitated, frowned. "The hope in your eyes."

Too much, she thought again. The man, the FBI agent, whoever he really was, saw too much. "Take me home," she said, and even though she knew better than to let him touch her again, she lifted a hand toward him. "Please."

He brushed by her, not touching her, just heading for the entrance. And this time, unlike after the Ferris wheel, she followed, only vaguely aware of the booths they passed and the hawkers calling out to them.

"No, no, child. You can't leave yet!"

The claim, sharper, more urgent than the other attempts to snag their attention, stopped her cold. She swung around and saw the old woman sitting inside a tent labeled House of Fortune.

Long dark hair, streaked by time and silver, flowed around her face. A face of contrasts, angles and smooth lines, optimism and despair. "You mustn't run out of here without finding what you came for."

Danielle just stared. Leave here was exactly what she and Liam needed to do.

They'd both already found too much.

But deep inside, something stirred, the same niggling instinct that had led her to target Jeremy's pocket to pick. The same whisper that had warned her not to take the drink the man in the Stirling lobby had offered her. Dread crawled down her spine, but she couldn't turn away from the woman. All evening she'd felt as if she needed to be here. All evening she'd forced herself to stay, when she wanted nothing more than to leave. Now, though, awareness vibrated through her. The awareness her siblings had always referred to as her luck.

The luck that had failed her the night Ty died.

Beside her Liam tensed, but she took a step toward the woman, a woman she instinctively recognized as having Gypsy blood flowing through her veins. Maybe it was her features, the mane of dark hair, the bright red and purple clothing. Didn't matter, though, because Danielle knew.

"How do you know what I came for?"

The old woman's gaze, as sharp and distinctive as her voice, gentled. "I see it in your eyes, child. You came for answers."

It made no sense. It was a warm, muggy night, barely cooled by the breeze blowing off Lake Michigan. And yet a chill slithered through Danielle.

"I can give you those answers," the fortune teller promised in a wise, tired voice. "I can give them to you both."

And Danielle knew. Deep in her bones, she knew why she'd demanded that he stop the car. "This," she said, turning to Liam. "This is why we're here."

Chapter 10

"Have a seat." The older woman swept a bejeweled hand toward the chairs in front of a small table draped in purple and red. Magnificent Magdalena, the sign read. "Shuffle the cards."

Danielle felt herself move forward, felt Liam lag behind. Fascination battled with doubt. The deck of Tarot cards glimmered like an icon from the past.

Her mother, she remembered in a heart-stopping flash. Her mother and her aunt. They'd loved the cards of fortune and destiny. Trusted them. Once, Danielle had found them tucked in a drawer and started to shuffle, only to have her mother running into the room and grabbing them from her. To this day, the stricken look in her vivid green eyes lingered.

"These are not toys," she'd said in that gentle voice of hers, and then her aunt was standing beside her, and they were both sharing glances that Danielle didn't understand, but that sent chills up her spine.

Only a few days later her mother had lain dead on the dirty hardwood floor of the living room.

She should turn and leave. Run. She should not flirt with fortune or fate. She knew that. Had learned that.

And yet the grave look in the fortune teller's gaze, the familiarity of the cards, drew her like a magnet.

Slowly she sat. "What do you see in my eyes?"

Magdalena frowned. "Pain," she said. "Yearning."

Danielle's mouth went dry.

"Clear your mind." The older woman nudged the deck closer. "Clear your heart." She glanced behind her to where Danielle felt Liam's solid presence. "Just shuffle."

Liam's hand settled against her shoulder. "You don't have to do this."

The contact electrified even as it soothed. She'd told him not to touch her again, but now, with his palm cupping her shoulder, she made no move to push him away.

"My mother read cards," she told him, dividing the deck into two piles. She picked up one with each hand, then tented them together. "They foretold her death."

She heard his sharp intake of breath, felt him stiffen. "Danielle—"

"Please," she said, continuing to shuffle. "What can it hurt?"

He let out a rough breath. "A lot of things." But then he took his hand away and spun around the chair next to hers and straddled the seat.

As far as surrenders went, it wasn't all that eloquent, but Danielle didn't care.

"When you're done," Magdalena said, "cut the deck into four facedown piles."

Danielle did as instructed. She could feel Liam beside her, his breath, his gaze, but she didn't look, could not look away from the old fortune teller. The rhythms of her Gypsy heritage hummed too loudly, called too deeply.

"Now draw the top card from the far-left pile and turn it faceup here."

It was ridiculous, but her heart's pace picked up rhythm,

thrumming in much the same way it had in the moments before Liam's mouth had come down on hers. When she reached for the first pile, her hand shook. She hesitated, then lifted the card and placed it where Magdalena had instructed.

Wheel of Fortune.

A shiver ran through Danielle. "What does that mean?"

"Not yet," Magdalena said, then instructed her how to lay out the remaining cards. The Three of Swords came next. The Moon. The High Priestess.

Then silence. It was odd how silent the night could fall when the carnival shimmied around them. But a vacuum seemed to envelop them, seal them off from the rest of the world.

Danielle glanced at Liam, found him looking not at her but at the cards. He sat only a few inches from her, yet the distance stretched into miles. Years. Lifetimes.

What do you see in my eyes?

Yearning.

The breath caught in Danielle's throat. There was yearning, all right. Yearning for her son. Yearning for a return to the normalcy of a few days before. And, God forgive her, a yearning for this man, to cut away the dark shadows and secrets that cloaked him.

"Ah, child," Magdalena said, and her voice was low, unbearably weary. "Your destiny is at hand."

The simple statement went through Danielle with unerring precision. "No." Protest screamed through her, but the word came out soft, horrified. She'd have to be blind not to see the pattern in her life. First her mother, then her father. Then Ty. Then her siblings. She'd lost them all, everyone she loved. "I can't lose him, too."

Liam slid a hand to her thigh. Another touch she'd claimed not to want, but could not bring herself to sever. "Danielle—"

"All is not lost," Magdalena said, then stunned Danielle by sliding her arm across the table and clasping Danielle's hand. The older woman's flesh was thin and cool, but beneath it pulsed a strong life force. "Far from it."

Emotion clogged her throat. "I don't understand."

The woman's eyes gentled. "See this card?" She gestured toward the Three of Swords. "It tells me you've come through a period of separation. That your heart was pierced. That you cut yourself off from the world as you knew it, in order to heal."

Around them, the carnival danced on, the bright lights, the milling crowds, but Danielle's world slowed, wobbled.

"And this," Magdalena said, pointing to the Moon card, "warns of hidden enemies and darkness and despair."

Danielle stared at the card, a big yellow ball suspended against a sea of black and supported by a flying owl, and tried to breathe.

Hidden enemies.

"Then how can you say all is not lost?" she asked.

Magdalena smiled. "Because of the priestess." Releasing Danielle's hand, she skimmed her fingers over the card. "The priestess is your strength," she said. "The priestess urges you to trust your intuition. To act on feelings rather than facts." With a soft smile she lifted her eyes to Danielle. "The priestess wants you to reengage with the world."

Danielle tried to breathe but couldn't. Nor could she think. She wanted to deny what the fortune teller said, to shove the cards back at her and laugh, to tell her she shouldn't play games with peoples lives. And yet the very intuition that Magdalena urged her to trust, told her to hold quiet. To accept the prophecy. To trust.

"What about me?"

Lost in thought, Danielle needed a moment for it to register that the question had been uttered by Liam. She looked at him seated next to her, his big body straddling the chair in what should have been a casual pose but somehow wasn't. Because of his eyes, she knew. The fierce glitter. The ominous glow.

"You?" She'd wanted to know this man's secrets, but she'd never in a million years imagined he'd be willing to share them.

He reached for a second deck of cards Magdalena had secured from behind the table. "The FBI isn't all cold, hard fact and evidence," he said, shuffling. "There are special units, units designed to investigate that which cannot be understood."

She knew that. At least she'd heard rumors. But she'd never pictured tall, brooding Liam giving anything other than procedure and protocol a second thought.

That fact that he would, that he did, poked more nasty holes in the picture of him she wanted to draw, that of a driven, isolated man.

Fascination whispered loud and deep as she watched his big hands shuffle the cards with surprising finesse and agility. But then, those were the same hands he'd lifted to her face and slid along her body, and even though they were rough, she'd felt only a heart-shattering tenderness. He shuffled the cards again before he cut the deck and repeated the process. Then she glanced up and felt the breath stall in her throat.

His eyes were closed.

She'd never seen him like this, with his face so fully relaxed. The lines that normally cut deep into his flesh were almost gone, leaving a softness that made her fingers itch to touch. His mouth, which was usually hard and unforgiving but which kissed with abandon and urgency, was relaxed. Even the whiskers along his jaw looked softer, less menacing.

Who was this man? she wondered in some faraway corner of her mind. Who was this man who'd barged into her life and insisted she play by his rules, that he and he alone could bring her son home alive? Who was this man who carried a gun and a badge but kissed like a lost soul and held the Tarot cards in his hands as though they were something to be cherished and revered?

Slowly, eyes still closed, he repeated the process Danielle

had gone through, making four piles, drawing the top card from each and laying it faceup in the pattern Magdalena instructed. All the while he kept his eyes shut, leaving Danielle to wonder what it was he was so afraid of seeing.

In the House of Mirrors he hadn't looked at his reflections, not once. His eyes had been focused solely on her.

The Seven of Wands, a dark card with a yellow cat, came first. Then the tower—a card that screamed violence, desecration and destruction. The Queen of Pentacles.

And still, even after he sorted, he did not look, just let his hands hover over the cards.

Magdalena looked, though. And the sorrow in her eyes deepened, turning the soft green into something primal and ancient. "Child," she said again, but this time there was warmth in her voice. Compassion. Frowning, she laid her hand over Liam's.

It stunned Danielle that he didn't yank away.

"You have suffered much," Magdalena said, and Danielle's heart responded with a painful lurch. She'd known that about him. From the moment she'd seen him across the lobby of the hotel, she'd sensed a deep undercurrent of pain. She'd felt it in his touch. Tasted it in his kiss.

Slowly Liam's eyes opened. "Go on."

Danielle wanted to look away from him, from the stoicism of his posture, the way he was bracing himself, but couldn't. Because even more she wanted to touch.

But she didn't do that, either.

This man had come into her life because of his quest to bring down the shadowy Titan. He was helping her find her son, in the hopes that doing so would bring him closer to achieving his own goal. That was all. She could not allow those lines to blur.

"It pains you when you don't have the answers to the questions you are asking," Magdalena said, fingering the Ace of Wands, which Liam had placed upside down. "But you must remain strong."

Danielle couldn't imagine Liam any other way. Even when he was breaking, the man exuded a strength of will that she'd rarely encountered.

"The odds seem overwhelming," the fortune-teller murmured, running her index finger along the Seven of Wands, "but you are a man of great strength and perseverance." She lifted her eyes to Liam. "Believe in yourself. Walk your own path. That is the only way you will rise above your enemies."

Enemies.

"Who will win?" Danielle leaned closer to Magdalena. "In the end, who will win?"

The older woman's expression grew distant. "That is not for me to say."

"The cards, then," Danielle said. Urgency grew within her. "What do the cards foretell for this hidden enemy that stalks us both?"

The wind pushed the streak of silver hair against Magdalena's face. "He is not here. I cannot say."

"Try." Danielle gathered the cards and pushed them toward Magdalena. "Please."

Liam was still staring at his cards, his index finger tracing the lines of the broken image on the Tower card. "It's important," he said, finally lifting his gaze to pierce the fortune teller. "A matter of life and death."

The little cry escaped Danielle before her heart could beat. "My son's life," she added, and then Liam was reaching for her hand and she was threading her fingers with his.

"Titan," he said. "The man's name is Titan."

Magdalena's eyes darkened. "Titan," she murmured, retrieving the deck and turning it over in her hands. Like Liam, she closed her eyes. Her breathing grew heavier, as though she was entering some kind of trance. "Titan."

Danielle glanced at Liam, found him watching Magdalena. She shuffled, swaying with the breeze as she did so, then sorted the cards into four piles and retrieved the top from each.

The Magician, a black card with a devious-looking rabbit on it, came first. The Nine of Swords was second, followed by the Six of Pentacles. The Eight of Wands.

Anticipation quickened through Danielle, and once again she could see her mother, seated across from her aunt at the kitchen table, their eyes closed as they sorted cards between them. The women had trusted the old ways, trusted the cards.

The Magician, she recalled her aunt hissing when she opened her eyes. *He is near.*

Danielle swallowed hard, pushed the memory aside.

"The Magician," Magdalena said, opening her eyes. "He grows increasingly dangerous."

The quietly spoken words stabbed deep. Danielle felt herself sway, and was grateful that Liam was by her side, holding her hand. She stared at the image, saw what she'd missed before. The rabbit looked harmless enough with its little half smile, but in its hands juggled the sun and the moon and the earth.

The chill started low, spread fast. "Is he going to hurt my son?"

Magdalena's eyes, so sharp and flashing moments before, clouded over. "He has overcome many failures and delays, this one has. Many disappointments. Each has made him more desperate."

Liam swore softly. "And now?"

"This is a man who knows how to get what he wants, how to work behind the scenes and manipulate the world around him. He knows how to hide and juggle. He is a master of control and illusion. Of sorcery and secrecy."

Horror flooded Danielle, not the kind she'd felt in the maze of mirrors after she'd kissed Liam, but darker, more primal, ominous, like an oil spill destroying everything in its path. "Alex..."

"He must be stopped," Magdalena added. "Before he grows stronger."

"But how—" Danielle started to say.

"I cannot tell you that." Magdalena reached for a black shawl draped over her chair. "It grows cold," she said, wrapping the wool around her body, which suddenly seemed much more frail than it had moments before.

"Take this with you." She slid the Magician card toward Liam. "Let it be a reminder."

Instead of picking up the card, he traced the outline of the rabbit with his forefinger.

Magdalena stood. "There is one thing you must remember," she said. "There is one thing you must never forget." The breeze off the lake whipped her silver-streaked hair against the sharp angles of her face. Her pale-green eyes glowed. "Those who walk alone are the first to fall."

Liam walked alone.

Danielle's heart caught on the realization, the sharp rush of truth. She watched him move quietly from room to room within her house, more shadow than man, but for the gun in his hand. He moved with caution, checking each room, each closet, each window, carefully. Deliberately. Much the way he did everything.

Except kiss. When the man kissed—

She broke the thought before it deepened, the memory before it heated, but she could do nothing about the way her fingers found her mouth and skimmed her lower lip.

Outside the last room, she turned away. She didn't need to see him inside, didn't need to see him survey her unmade bed, the clothes she'd left on the floor, the faded lace bra hanging from her dresser. She didn't need to feel the dull blade of longing that cut through her, the one that made her wonder what it would feel like to lean on this man.

"All's clear," he said a few minutes later, joining her in the small foyer.

Light blazed from every room, bright and glaring, but when she looked at him, the shadows had settled back into place. Except she saw so much more now, after their encounter in the House of Mirrors. She saw an intensity that seared through him, a longing she didn't understand.

"Good," she said inanely, because there was really nothing else to say.

He slid his Glock into the holster strapped around his shoulder. "I can stay if you want—"

"No." *Yes.* "I'm fine." *I haven't been able to breathe since Magdalena turned over the Magician card.* "You should get on back to the hotel." *Don't leave.* "Get some rest yourself." *Hold me. Let me hold you.*

His mouth thinned. "You're right."

No, she wasn't, a voice deep inside protested. She was wrong. Dead wrong. "See you in the morning," she said, because she knew that just like all those never-ending images from the House of Mirrors, the draw she felt toward this man was not real. Could not be real. If she tried to grab it, she'd find nothing but illusion.

The priestess urges you to trust your intuition. To act on feelings rather than facts.

Her throat tightened on the memory, the truth. Fighting the fledgling intuition she'd forced herself to ignore for two years, she opened the front door and breathed of the cool night air. She'd trusted before. She'd acted on feelings rather than fact. And in the process Ty had died.

"Call me if you need me," Liam said, but made no move to leave.

"I will." Her heart rebelled at the words. The lie. She would call Liam if she heard from Alex's kidnappers, but for the other needs that pulsed through her, the illusory ones he'd stirred inside the tent of mirrors, there could be no contact with this man. No reaching out. No leaning.

She opened the door wider and looked up at him, deliberately angling her chin. Outside, the branches of the young maple she and Alex had planted last fall danced in time with the breeze, but inside the brightly lit foyer, stillness settled between them like a gauzy veil. She ignored the dark currents humming beneath the surface, just as she'd been doing since they'd left the carnival. They'd not spoken on the way home, had barely spoken since Magdalena had uttered her final warning.

Those who walk alone are the first to fall.

This man had already fallen, she thought with a twist to her heart. Not tonight. Not anytime recently. But once, the tall man with the hard eyes, the one who could walk through the fire without flinching but could barely look inside her son's room, had fallen.

And he'd hurt.

Of their own will, her fingers again found her mouth, trailed over her lips, where only a few hours before Liam had shown her a side of himself normally hidden behind the wall of secrets. He'd shown her the need. The want.

The man.

And just like it had then, the want sent a sharp slice through her.

Because Alex was missing, and that was all that mattered.

"Good night," she forced herself to say, and with a jolt time lurched forward once again.

"Lock up behind me." Liam walked away and slid into his car, backed into the street and drove into the night—for the first time since they'd met not pausing to look back.

Danielle watched the taillights vanish down her quiet tree-lined street before closing the front door and sliding the bolt into place.

FBI Special Agent Liam Brooks walked alone, and that was the way he wanted it.

Frowning, she turned and headed down the hall, not to the feminine sanctuary he'd dominated a few minutes before, where the scent of man and soap and musk no doubt lingered, but to the second door on the right, the one that led to a room brimming with toys and books and memories.

"Alex," she whispered on a broken breath, and damn near doubled over. Alex.

She flicked off the light Liam had turned on, then nudged aside the giant stuffed panda her brother and sister had given her son in honor of his first birthday and continued to the bed. There, she lay with her mobile phone clenched in one hand and the Spider-Man comforter balled in the other, and stared into the darkness for a long, long time. And try as she did to chase aside Magdalena's prophecy of destiny and shadows, danger and salvation, the wise old woman's parting words lingered.

Those who walk alone are the first to fall.

Danielle walked alone.

The thought, the reality, should not have bothered Liam. She'd crafted her life the way she wanted it. She'd carved out a quiet existence for herself and her son. She'd slapped up brick and mortar between herself and the rest of the world, a near impenetrable wall that she used to hold everyone, everything, at a safe, nonthreatening distance. It was a wall she used to protect herself and her son.

Because just as Magdalena had warned, Danielle had fallen.

And she'd hurt. Badly.

She knew what it was like to lose, and to blame herself. She knew what it was to bleed from the inside out.

Frowning, Liam ignored the bottle of scotch and concentrated on the four cards spread on the smooth cherry wood of the hotel dresser. The three tattered postcards of the German farmhouse, a farmhouse he'd actually traveled to Germany to find, to investigate, only to come up empty-handed, glowed like old pals. The newest card, that of the grinning rabbit juggling the earth and the sun and the moon, fascinated.

Titan.

The old woman had been dead-on with her reading. *Dead. On.*

Glancing up, Liam caught his face in the antique mirror,

but rather than seeing himself, he saw Danielle, the stunned look in her eyes when he'd consented to a reading. He'd surprised her but not himself. Some answers came only through throwing conventional wisdom out the window. There were forces at work here he didn't understand, forces that defied logic. He'd accept help where he could find it.

Because he was missing something, damn it. Something fundamental. Something vital. There had to be a link. A reason. There had to be a motive for Titan to want Danielle so badly he'd abducted her son.

Want. Danielle.

The two words twisted, disturbed.

He should never have kissed her. He should never have succumbed to the need that had ripped at him from the first moment he'd seen her, the need that strengthened with every moment they spent together. The need that had boiled over when he'd turned around and found her gone.

Wondered if Titan had stolen her, as well.

If once again he'd been too late.

Swearing softly, his heart hammering too fast all over again, he picked up the phone and stabbed out one of the countless numbers he'd stored in the memory banks of his mind.

"Nothing," Mariah said ten minutes later. "Lennox never said a word about a link between Titan and a woman in Chicago."

Liam turned from the constant drone of CNN and paced the small room. "There's got to be something," he said. Something they were overlooking. "It just doesn't make sense."

Mariah sighed softly, as she always did when about to pull the rug from under Liam's feet. "Maybe," she said. "Or maybe you're looking for links that don't exist."

"They exist." He stared over the lake, watched the light of the moon dance across the choppy dark water. It had been a long shot, but he'd hoped Lennox had said something to

Mariah before his murder, something seemingly innocuous that could not have made sense at the time, but now shone light in a new direction. "Titan didn't just kidnap Alex for the fun of it. The boy is only six years old, for crissakes. He can't possibly pose a threat—"

Mariah sucked in a sharp breath. "Alex?"

The ring of recognition, of disbelief, in her voice echoed through the room like a death knell. "Talk to me, Mariah. What does that name mean to you?"

She was quiet a long moment before answering. "It's probably nothing."

"Tell me, anyway."

"It's just that…" She hesitated, muttered something under her breath. "This is crazy, Liam, but you remember Gretchen, don't you? Jake's sister?"

"We've met." He recalled an image of the striking, brilliant brunette who specialized in deciphering ancient languages. "She was pregnant at the time."

"She has a little girl now," Mariah said. "Violet. She's two."

"That's great, but—"

"Violet's very talented artistically, Liam, and for the past three days she's been drawing pictures. During the night. While she's asleep. Pictures of a little boy."

Everything inside of Liam went horribly still. "A little boy?"

"Alex, she calls him," Mariah whispered. "And she says he's in trouble."

It couldn't be. No freaking way. It just wasn't possible that a little girl in Boston could be drawing pictures of Danielle's son, a boy she'd never even met.

Liam towered over the fax machine in the Stirling's business office, practically willing the image to come across the line. The manager had been amazingly cooperative about opening the center after midnight, but guest accommodation was one of the hallmarks of the luxury hotel, and Liam had definitely needed accommodating when he'd come charging into the lobby.

The phone line rang and the machine started to hum, spitting out a piece of paper one slow millimeter at a time. Liam wanted to yank the damn sheet out, but he forced himself to stand there. And to wait.

Gradually, the image took form.

It was a crude drawing, clearly that of a child, but remarkable in its detail. He saw the feet first, one foot bare, one sporting a tennis shoe, and his blood temperature dropped a few degrees.

One of Alex's shoes had been returned to Danielle.

Then came the skinny legs, the little cargo shorts, the T-shirt with a primitive drawing of a spider-like man, then the face.

Swearing softly, Liam grabbed the single page.

Then he ran.

Chapter 11

Danielle just stared. So did Liam. But whereas she stared at the picture drawn by a child's hand, he stared at her. She stood in the small foyer, with a pool of light spilling around her like a halo. Her eyes, normally a clear, volatile green, were shockingly dark. The roughened edge to her voice told him she'd been sleeping, as she should have been in the middle of the night, but she still wore the same dark jeans and top she'd been wearing when he dropped her off.

"Alex." Clenching the facsimile, her fingers went sheet white. "Dear God, it's Alex."

Liam's gut twisted hard. He was a man who took great pride in being right. But here, now, hearing the horror drench her voice, he found only the slimy, sludgelike feeling of dread.

She looked up, pierced him with her gaze. "Where did you get this?"

It should have been an easy question. "Come on." He put his hand to the small of her back and steered her toward the kitchen. "I'll explain."

Darkness poured in from the windows, isolating them from the world beyond and creating a disturbing intimacy he did not want to feel. Danielle Caldwell was a tough, gutsy woman. She didn't cower. She didn't crumble. She lifted her chin and faced every challenge life cast her way. But now, with the hour past midnight and the drawing of her son in her hands, Liam sensed a vulnerability that ripped at him.

He didn't want to sit at the old round table, where a vase made of purple-stained Popsicle sticks held daisies past their prime. He didn't want to coldly and logically explain something that made absolutely no sense. He didn't want to be the impersonal FBI agent, the one who walked alone.

He wanted to be just a man, to draw this woman into his arms and hold her, to promise her everything would be okay.

But he couldn't do that, not any of it, so he pulled out an old kitchen chair and robotically helped her sit, then flipped around the one beside her and straddled it to start to explain.

The postcard stopped him cold.

"Where did you get this?" he asked, and though he tried to be matter-of-fact, the question tore out of him.

Danielle glanced at the clutter of bills and catalogs across the table, where the deceptive image of a pastoral German farmhouse graced a postcard. "It came in the mail," she said dismissively. "Yesterday, I think."

Liam swore softly. He untucked his shirt and wrapped his hand in the wrinkled cotton, then reached for the card with a Chicago postmark, turned it over and saw the words. Four of them, simple, seemingly harmless.

"I'll be seeing you."

His vision blurred, and any doubt he'd tried to harbor, any figment of hope he'd tried to manufacture that Titan was not after Danielle went up in flames.

Don't stare, Danielle remembered one of her foster mother's lecturing, over and over and over. She could still see the June Cleaver wannabe, in her prim little high-necked pink dress and expensive pearls, her neatly coiffed frosted hair, scowling at Danielle, who couldn't stop watching a young mother cooing to her newborn baby. It's not polite, Mrs. Watters had snapped. It makes people uncomfortable. It shows bad breeding.

But Danielle hadn't cared then, and she didn't care now.

The woman who'd arrived thirty minutes before wasn't beautiful, not in a classical sense. Her features were a little too sharp, her eyes, an amazing shade of blue, a little too intelligent.

Arresting, Danielle realized. The woman, with her long, silky mane of dark hair, was arresting.

That was why she stared, she reasoned. That explained the odd hum that had started deep inside, the moment Gretchen Miller had walked through her front door, followed by a tall man with wavy brown hair. Her husband, Danielle had learned. Kurt. And propped on his hip with her chubby little arms thrown around his neck, he'd held a miniature version of his wife, little Violet.

The child who'd drawn the pictures of Alex.

She'd been in the news, she recalled. Not the daughter, but the mother. Gretchen. The woman who'd graciously flown out from Boston that morning. She was one of the Proteans, a woman born not of love, but genetic experimentation. Several years back the shocking story had flooded the airwaves. There'd been rumors and allegations, a stark fear that there could be more than the original six. For a while, everyone who'd been adopted in the mid-seventies was suspect.

That explained the blast of familiarity, Danielle reasoned. The strange echo, the swirling sense that she'd met Gretchen before. That she knew her, had always known her.

"I didn't think much of it at first," Gretchen was saying. She sat on the denim sofa, her elegant cream traveling suit making the newest piece of furniture Danielle owned look shabby somehow. "Violet is always drawing things. She's quite talented."

Danielle glanced at the little girl who sat wedged between

her mother and father. She fiddled with an old Rubik's cube Alex had found at a flea market. Her hair was lighter than her mother's, but her eyes were the same unusual, striking shade of blue.

"But then she started waking up agitated," Gretchen said.

Violet looked up. "Awex wants to come home," she said in her little-girl voice, but her eyes suddenly looked ancient. Wise.

Danielle moved to kneel in front of the little girl. Her heart was beating so fast she could barely catch her breath. "Where is he?"

Violet frowned. "On a cot."

Danielle's breath stalled, but before she could say anything, Liam was standing beside her, tall, strong, solid, gently laying a steadying hand on her shoulder.

"Has she done anything like this before?" he asked.

"No. Never. I mean, she's always been extremely talented, but the pictures didn't start until the morning after—" Gretchen broke off, shot a sharp glance at her husband.

"After what?" Liam asked, and Danielle had to fight the urge to lift her hand to his, link her fingers with his, feel his strength, the life force that flooded a room the second he walked inside.

Gretchen worked her lip. "It's nothing, really. It's just…" She again glanced at her husband, her expression screaming discomfort.

"A few days ago Gretchen thought she heard Violet scream," Kurt said. Warmth filled his voice, a deep, soothing, Texas drawl. "She ran upstairs, certain something terrible had happened, only to find Violet drawing quietly in her room."

The hairs on the back of Danielle's neck bristled.

"When was that?" Liam asked. "What day?"

Gretchen and Kurt exchanged glances. "Three or four days ago?" Gretchen said. "Monday, I think?"

Danielle absorbed the information like a blow. "That's when Alex was kidnapped," she whispered, not even trying to hide the ripple of horror.

Liam knelt beside her and quietly slid an arm around her waist, drew her against him.

It was all Danielle could do not to sag.

Quiet spilled into the room. Danielle looked at the picture on her coffee table, the crude drawing of her son, with his tennis shoe missing and his favorite T-shirt sagging on his chest. "Is he okay?"

The question practically burst out of her.

Little Violet nodded sagely. "He just wants to come home," she said. "I told him my daddy would help since he doesn't have one."

The room started to spin. "Oh, God," she murmured, and Liam pulled her tighter against him.

"And Miss Caldwell," Violet said.

It took effort, but Danielle stitched together the threadbare edges of her composure and smiled at the little girl. "Did you remember something else, sweetie?"

Her little lips trembled. "He wasn't mad."

Danielle blinked. "Wasn't mad?"

"Awex," she clarified. "When he didn't get the Spidaman shoes." She set down the cube, all the colors perfectly aligned. "He heard you crying in your room and feels real bad about the fit he threw." She paused, frowned. "He knows you woulda gotten him the shoes if you coulda."

And Danielle couldn't do it one second longer, couldn't just kneel there on the old braided rug and pretend she wasn't unraveling, thread by tattered thread.

"Oh, God," she cried on a broken sob, then turned into Liam's chest and absorbed the feel of him, the clean soapy scent of man and strength, the dangerous luxury of feeling his arms close around her and hold on tight.

"You need to eat more than that."

Danielle glanced at the bowl of chicken noodle soup Liam had heated up, and felt her stomach lurch. "I'm not hungry."

"That doesn't mean you don't need your strength," he said, studying her from across the table. He'd practically inhaled the bowl he'd fixed for himself, then he'd just sat there, staring at the postcard of the German farmhouse. She wasn't sure how much time had passed, didn't realize he'd been aware of her or her movements.

"Maybe later." She stood and carried her bowl to the sink. He was right. She did need her strength. *Alex* needed her strength. But every time she'd brought the spoon to her mouth, she'd almost gagged.

Gretchen and Kurt and their adorable daughter had stayed for the better part of the afternoon, before heading off to catch a flight back to Boston. Now the shadows of early evening crept in the window, replacing the bright light of late afternoon.

She should ask Liam to leave. She knew that. He'd been at her house since shortly after midnight, when he'd simultaneously banged on her front door and called her from his cell phone.

He looked tired, sitting at her kitchen table, with the light from the overhead fixture glaring down on him, emphasizing the tight lines of his face and the dark whiskers crowding his jaw. He wore the same clothes he had the day before, but with the sunrise she'd convinced him to at least take a shower.

Funny that the scent of man lingered, even though she knew the bar of soap he'd held in his big hands had a light lavender fragrance.

"When are you going to tell me about the postcard?" she asked, returning to the table. She hadn't thought much of it when she'd found it in the mail, had almost tossed it in the trash. Now she realized what a grave mistake that would have been.

He looked up at her. "It's from Titan."

She'd figured as much. "How can you be sure?"

"Because I have three others in my hotel room." His mouth twisted. "One was found in Senator Gregory's room after he died," he said. "And one appeared in my room a few days later, with your name scrawled on it."

The chill started low, spread fast. "And the third?"

All afternoon Liam had been quiet. Guarded. Almost withdrawn. He'd shown very little reaction, even when Violet Miller spoke of things there was no way she could know. He was a man of great passion but of great strength, as well. And it was the strength that was normally in control, the strength that kept him still and stoic no matter how grave a situation became. He hadn't even flinched when she'd pulled a gun on him twice.

There were cracks, she knew. The strength was real, but the stoicism was not. It was just a defense, a shield to conceal the passion boiling deep inside, the passion that for some reason he tried to deny.

There was no denying it now. She saw his eyes flash and his nostrils flare. His head snapped back and his expression went stark, as though fending off a quick pain.

She'd seen the expression before, on a big beautiful Great Dane who'd broken away from a young girl along the shore of Lake Michigan and chased after a wild goose. The dog had run full throttle, so focused on his prey that he'd been oblivious to the busy lakeside road, until he'd charged straight into traffic.

The woman driving the red Volkswagen had tried to avoid a collision. She'd swerved, slammed on her brakes. But the car clipped the dog anyway and sent him sprawling to the side of the road.

Danielle had seen the horrible incident unfold, had screamed and started to run in those final long seconds before impact. She'd seen the flash of panic in the dog's eyes, the way its head had snapped back, the moment of awareness before the car made contact.

It was a look she'd never expected from the tall, imposing man who'd walked into her life only a few days before, who'd held her up, held her together, even when she'd tried to push him away. The man who'd tracked her down in the House of Mirrors, whose image had surrounded her, buoyed her, the man who'd kissed her senseless, then pretended the whole thing had never happened.

"Liam." She reached for him, but before she could touch, he swore softly and pushed back from the table, striding past her and into the family room, yanking open the sliding glass door and disappearing into the night.

Leave him alone, the voice of reason whispered. Let him lick his wounds in private. Don't poke. Don't prod. He's a grown man. He can take care of himself. He'll survive, just like the big beautiful Great Dane had survived.

The priestess urges you to trust your intuition. To act on feelings rather than facts.

It was all she could do not to run. She found him standing on the edge of her small patio with his back to her, staring out toward the remnants of the setting sun. He stood completely still, but she heard the breath sawing in and out of him, as though he'd just run a great distance at a great speed.

"Liam." Even though logic told her not to take another step, she closed the distance between them and laid a hand to his shoulder.

He flinched.

The simple gesture should not have surprised her, should not have wounded her, but somehow it did.

Slowly he turned to face her.

And once again nothing prepared her for his stark, ravaged eyes, the miles of pain staring back at her.

"Her name was Kelly," he said.

She swallowed hard, reminded herself to breathe. "Who?" she asked, though deep inside she already knew. "Whose name was Kelly?"

The breeze whispered through the old trees dotting her

backyard, the maples and oaks, nudging the abandoned tire swing into a slow sway. "My wife," he said, and her heart damn near stopped. "She was my wife, and I killed her."

Danielle wasn't sure how she stood there, not moving a muscle, not flinching, not staggering back, not stepping closer. She wanted to turn from him, to run while she still could. Even more, she wanted to put her arms around him and draw him to her, hold him, give him something she instinctively knew he had not received.

Comfort.

She did neither, just stood there, trying to breathe through the flood of horror. God, Magdalena had been right. This man had suffered much. Too much.

The sun sank lower, the swirling streaks of purple and crimson growing darker with each heavy beat of her heart. And suddenly it all made sense, the disturbing aura that surrounded him, the secrets and shadows dwelling in his eyes, the flashes of passion he tried to deny. He'd allowed himself that passion once. He'd given in to it...

...and it had destroyed his wife, himself.

"No," she whispered, and the need was too great. She stepped closer and even though she saw the wince, she lifted a hand to his face. "You didn't kill her."

She wasn't sure how she knew. She just did.

"Yes," he said very slowly, very coldly, very deliberately, "I did."

She let her fingers roam his face, taking in the feel of him, the texture. "You're not capable," she said. "There's violence in you, but it's directed at the darkness." She paused, reminded herself to breathe. "You try to hold the ugliness at bay, to erase it, to destroy it."

"You don't have a damn clue what you're talking about."

"Yes, I do." For the first time since the night Ty had died, she went with the feelings inside, the ones that had guided her and directed her for so many years. The instinct that had brought her and Liz and Anthony to Jeremy. The intuition that had saved her life, all their lives, more times than she could remember.

"There's too much goodness in you," she whispered, and her heart bled on the words. "Magdalena was right. You're a man of strength and passion." She stepped closer, felt her throat go tight. "Of gentleness." Of a tarnished nobility that ripped at her. She'd felt it in his touch, his kiss. His restraint. "Honor," she added. "Loyalty."

Liam's eyes were glowing now, hot, like the fading embers of the sun on the western horizon. "If that was true, my wife wouldn't be dead."

"That's the guilt talking," she said, because she, too, knew what it was to lose someone you loved. "I've been in your shoes," she told him, wondering when she'd stepped out of those shoes. When she'd opted to start living again. "When Ty died. I've stood by the grave of someone I loved and felt the sharp sting of guilt." She hesitated, swallowed hard. "I've dropped to my knees and cried."

A little muscle in the hollow of his cheek began to thump, and she knew she'd encroached upon murky waters.

"Have you, Liam?" she asked quietly. "Have you cried?"

He tore away from her with a ferocity that staggered her. He strode deeper into the night, toward the empty tire swing.

She followed, said nothing, just once again laid a hand to his back.

Time slowed, the sounds of the night wobbling like a record played on the wrong speed. Crickets and cicadas and toads served as the sound track, the neighbor's basset hound the accompanist.

"We were supposed to go away," he said, and his voice was low, as remote as the faint roar of an airliner overhead. "For just a weekend. To reconnect."

Danielle let her fingers widen against his back but resisted the urged to slide them down his arm.

"She thought I cared more about my job than her."

She closed her eyes, absorbed his pain.

"And maybe she was right." Swearing under his breath, he shoved at the old tire swing. "I had my teeth in a new case," he said, then spun toward her. "Titan."

The small sound of surprise escaped before she could stop it. "Titan?"

"Several of his signature black-market drugs started appearing in the inner cities. Squeaky-clean high school kids and junkies alike began showing up in emergency rooms with symptoms the medical community had never seen before. Several died. Rumors ran rampant."

Danielle drew a hand to her throat. "What kind of rumors?"

"Of designer drugs," he bit out. "A high unlike anyone had experienced before. Addiction from just one hit. A craving that overrode caution and sanity and logic. The kind of blind need that drove even hardened men to their knees."

And Liam, this man of honor and integrity, had found himself square in the middle of the investigation. It must have driven him wild, she realized, filling him with an equally strong craving, not for a hit of an illegal substance but the justice that defined him. "My God."

"I couldn't walk away," he said, and this time his voice was thicker. "I knew Kelly was lonely. I knew she felt neglected, but Christ, I just couldn't—" He looked toward the old oak at the back of the yard. "Then she turned up pregnant."

The dread came hard and fast, crawled over her and through her.

"She told me it was her or the job," Liam said, still looking off into the night. "She told me I had to choose."

"But you didn't know how," Danielle supplied for him.

He turned back toward her. "I'd made a commitment to her," he said. "A commitment I took seriously. I wasn't going to be like my old man."

Danielle braced herself. She'd known better than pushing and prodding Liam, but here they were, and just as he'd been unable to turn away from the Titan investigation, she was unable to turn away from the questions. "Your old man?"

"It was important to me to be a good husband," he said, and again his eyes flashed. "It was important for me to keep promises I made."

Because clearly his father had not. Danielle looked at him standing there by the swing, Liam the FBI agent, the man, but for a fleeting heartbeat she saw a new Liam, the boy, the son of a father who'd let him down in the most fundamental ways imaginable. A boy who'd grown into adulthood, driven by demons of his childhood, determined not to repeat the sins of his father.

"You do," she said, wanting so badly to touch him that the ache squeezed her heart. But now was not the time. "You keep your promises."

"Not to Kelly," he said. "She had it all planned, the weekend at the beach, just the two of us and the child growing within her."

Obviously, her plans had never come to fruition. "What happened?"

Liam scrubbed a hand over his face. "There was a break in the case, a new lead to follow." He paused, looked down at her with such aching earnesty she wanted to weep. "I could have let my partner, Lennox, follow it. I should have. He would have. He volunteered to."

"But you couldn't."

"I knew the danger," he went on. "Two agents in Europe had already lost their lives over the case," he said, then swore softly. "I thought I was invincible. I thought I was better, stronger, smarter."

"Liam," she whispered, and this time she allowed herself to touch him. Just his hand, her fingers brushing the backs of his. "You are."

"I worked late." His voice droned low, as distorted as the crickets and cicadas. "It was after midnight when I left the office. I was tired, barely able to keep my eyes on the road."

Those eyes were dark now, bottomless, and in the deepening shadows they glistened. "I smelled the smoke first, but didn't think much of it. Until I turned the corner and saw the barricade of police cars and fire engines."

She slid her fingers among his, curled them tight.

"They wouldn't let me pass," he said, "and God help me, I knew. I got out of the car and ran toward my house, the sirens, the flames…"

But it was too late.

"They wouldn't let me inside. I kept shouting that my wife was in there, that she needed help, but then they pointed to the black body bag, and—"

Danielle didn't stop to think. She didn't stop to consider. Flimsy things like consequences didn't matter, not in the face of what this man had been through. "It wasn't your fault," she said, pushing up on her toes and putting her arms around him. She dug her hands into his back, held him as close as she could. "There was no way you could have known."

"But I should have," he ground out. He stood stiff and unyielding, neither accepting nor rejecting her comfort. "I should have."

She didn't want to release him, didn't want to let go, but the need to see overrode the need to touch. "It was a terrible tragedy." She pulled back to look him in the eyes. "But Titan is to blame." Finally she knew why his vendetta against the man, the syndicate, ran so deep. "Not you."

He stared down at her, but Danielle wasn't sure what he saw. "I could have saved her," he said. "I could have saved her and our baby, if only I'd come home on time."

"You don't know that," Danielle countered. "Maybe she would have lived that night, or maybe Titan would have taken you down, too."

The thought, the very real possibility, chilled her to the bone.

"It's not for us to play God. None of us knows when our time is up."

He muttered something under his breath. "Titan's time is up," he vowed. "So help me, God, that bastard is not going to get away with all the lives he's destroyed."

And the ones still on the line. She closed her eyes, saw her son as he'd been the last morning she'd seen him, eating his Lucky Charms and talking about the carnival she'd promised they could attend that weekend.

"The postcard came two days later," he said abruptly, and she opened her eyes. "It was the first. The quaint little farmhouse seemed so serene, innocuous. Until I turned it over and read the message. 'My deepest sympathy.'" Liam swore softly. "He slunk away after that. Like a coward, he pulled up his U.S. operation and retreated to Europe."

"Until now," Danielle whispered.

"Until now."

She swallowed hard. "I trust you," she said, and the realization scraped deep. She did trust this man, wholly and irrevocably.

And that scared her to death.

"You shouldn't."

The rough edge to his voice should have warned her. The glitter in his eyes should have prompted her to turn away.

Neither did.

"But I do," she said to a sudden burst of warmth. "I trust you to bring home my son, and I trust you to bring down Titan."

There was a light in his eyes now, fierce, glittering, as mercurial as the moon. "All these years," he said in a low quiet voice. "All these years I've waited and planned, laid traps, living for the day Titan made the mistake of again crossing my path."

The wind gusted around her, but Danielle stood very still, not even moving to swipe the hair back from her face.

"But I wasn't really living," he said. "Not here." He drew his hand, and hers with it, to his chest. "Not inside. There I was every bit as dead as Kelly."

The warmth came first, a glow against the inside of her palm, followed by the steady thrumming of his heart.

"That was the way I wanted it," he said. "That kept me strong, focused."

Suspended.

"I was ready," he said, his voice pitched low, rough. "Eager. Excited, even. When Senator Gregory turned up dead and I went to New York and found the links to Titan, I was ready." He paused, and once again his eyes flashed. "But God help me, I wasn't ready for you."

The breath stalled in her throat. "Me?"

"You're dangerous. You could ruin everything."

The pain was fast and brutal. It cut through her, followed by an equally violent rush of denial. "I would never hurt you."

He laughed. It was a dark sound, distorted, torn from somewhere deep inside him.

"It's not me I'm worried about," he said, then stunned her by taking her face in his hands. "Do you have any idea?" he asked. "Any idea at all what it does to me to hear you say you trust me to bring home your son, bring down Titan, when, like a son of a bitch, all I can think about is putting my mouth to yours and making the rest of the world go away?"

Chapter 12

The night deepened, thickened. The last light of the sun had faded, leaving only the purple hues of darkness spreading across the sky. No moon yet. No stars. Just shadows.

And Liam.

Danielle savored the feel of his big hands on her face, rough yet gentle at the same time, much like the man himself.

"You're so beautiful," he murmured, "standing here in your backyard, with the wind in your hair and promise in your eyes."

Her heart knocked against her chest, sending her pulse thrumming in time with the cicadas. Her yard wasn't fenced, but she felt the edges closing in on her, the trees, big and beautiful, turning into prison wardens. The urge to turn away, to break contact and run, streaked in from somewhere deep, somewhere that had not seen a man look at her like this in years.

Ever, she silently amended. No man had ever looked at her like this, not even Ty. Theirs had been a simple love, a young love. Uncomplicated. Joyful.

But there was nothing simple or uncomplicated about this man, or the unsettling murmurs he unleashed within her.

Her throat was like cotton, but she managed his name. "Liam."

Even in the darkness his eyes glittered. "You make me feel alive." His thumb rubbed the length of her bottom lip. "For the first time in years I want to taste and touch, to take—"

The breath jammed in her throat. Great passion, she remembered thinking, but not even that awareness had prepared her for this. Because she wanted, too. Heaven help her, she wanted. So much. Not just the physical, either. The wants this man stirred in her had more to do with the soul than the flesh. She wanted to patch him back together, to strip away the darkness that surrounded him and bare the person inside, the real person. The man who had fallen. Who had hurt. Who still hurt.

"Wanting to kiss me doesn't make you a bad person," she said quietly. It only made him human.

"The hell it doesn't." The words were hard, laced with self-recrimination, but he didn't take his hands from her face, didn't sever the touch. "You're vulnerable," he said. "You're in trouble. You need me, not in your bed or your body, but to bring home your son. You need the FBI agent, not the man who's forgotten what it's like to be with a woman, to look at her and want her naked and in bed."

She wasn't sure how she stayed standing. She did need, but he needed, too. "Liam—"

With his hands on her face, he urged her closer. "Yesterday you asked me what kind of mother you were—"

"—and you told me I was a good mother," she reminded him. "Strong. Courageous. That I was only human."

His mouth flattened into a hard line. "Don't you see? It's not you, damn it. You're not the one in question. It's me."

"You're being too hard on yourself."

"Am I?" This time when his thumb skimmed her lip, it

dipped inside her mouth. "Do you have any idea what I want to do to you right now?"

She gazed up at him, saw the answer in his eyes. Felt it quicken through her. "Kiss me."

A hard sound broke from low in his throat. "That's just the beginning, honey." He hesitated, almost seemed to drink her in. "You're hurting and in trouble, out of your mind with worry over your son, but here I am, touching you, imagining what it would be like to take you right here and right now, to see you standing naked in the night, to feel you, touch you, taste you. To be inside of you."

The melting started deep within her, slow at first, then picking up speed with every beat of her heart.

"But I know what will happen if I do," he said, and before she could blink, he dropped his hands from her face and stepped back, packed the man away all neat and tidy, locking him behind the hard veneer of the FBI agent. "You're not mine to have," he said very coldly, very matter-of-factly. "You're a temptation, a complication I can neither afford nor want."

"But you can't go, either, can you?" she returned. It wasn't hurt that drove her, she assured herself. It wasn't the sharp sting of rejection. It was just the plain and simple truth. "You can't walk away, not until your job is done and my son is home."

But then he would, she knew. Then he would.

His lips curled into a cruel mockery of a smile. "It won't be much longer," he said. "The tide is about to turn. I feel it in my bones." Then he spun and walked inside the house, leaving her standing there in the darkness of her backyard, staring at a truth she wasn't ready to see.

She'd never known a man who could stand so very, very still, for so very, very long. She'd never known a man who could withdraw so completely, who could be present in body only. Who could go hour after hour without uttering one word.

Her brother certainly couldn't. Anthony had too much of their mother's hot Gypsy blood pumping through his body. His temper was legendary. He could brood but he wasn't one to keep what he felt inside. It exploded out of him with a force that could frighten.

Ty hadn't been volatile like her brother, but lively. Jovial. Always one to clown around, make jokes and play tricks. That had been part of the appeal, part of the fascination. He'd been so fundamentally different from everything she'd known.

It was also why she hadn't married him.

Theirs hadn't been that kind of relationship. They'd cared for each other, but their love had been a young, fun love, a carefree friendship. He'd lit up her world, but he hadn't rocked it, hadn't sent her heart into a dizzying tailspin.

And Jeremy, he was the closest thing to a father she'd ever had, and like her brother, like Liam, he was an intense, passionate man. But unlike Liam, he didn't hold back. He laid what he thought, what he wanted, right out on the line.

But Liam... He'd barely said two words since turning his back on her several hours before. He'd stayed, just as she'd challenged him to do, but she might as well have been alone. He'd stared at the postcard for a long time, then he'd taken up residence at the window, with his back to her.

And she hated it. She hated the wall of tension stretching between them, the silence that pulsed as thickly as the night.

"I don't understand," she said, exhausted from turning over all the stones in her mind. Different pieces to the puzzle hid beneath each of them, but none of them went together.

Slowly Liam turned toward her. "Neither do I."

Surprise hit like a quick chop to the throat. She'd wanted him to look at her, to talk to her, but now that she saw him, the lines of his face and darkness in his eyes, her breath faltered.

"Sometimes it's best not to even try," he added.

Safest, maybe. But not best.

She glanced at the coffee table, where crude but distinct drawings of Alex sat in a neat row. "That little girl saw him." The chill swept over her once again. When Violet talked of Alex, it was as though she'd been there with him. Trapped. Alone. Except she woke up safe and sound in her own bed.

Alex did not.

"She's never met him, never seen him before. She lives halfway across the country. But she knew."

Liam stared at the pictures. "Not everything can be explained," he said quietly, and finally the edge to his voice was gone. "That doesn't mean it can't be real."

It was hard, but she bit back the sound of frustration. Do you hear yourself? she wanted to ask. But didn't. Throwing his hypocrisy in his face wouldn't get them anywhere. They were talking again. For now, that was enough.

"What do we do next?" she asked, and before she could stop it, a yawn slipped free.

"Get some sleep," Liam said, then stunned her by crossing the room and squatting down beside the sofa. "You're exhausted." He reached for the wine-colored fleece blanket Liz had once given her for Christmas, then draped it over her legs. "Staying up all night isn't going to bring Alex home any faster."

Fatigue pulled at her, but she didn't want to close her eyes. Didn't trust herself to let go. "You make it sound so simple."

His smile was so subtle, so pained, she almost missed it. "Not everything has to be complicated."

The old anniversary clock showed the hour pushing toward three. He should be tired, he knew, and maybe he was, but when he'd turned from Danielle and walked into the house, he'd turned off all feeling, as well. Mental, emotional and physical.

Now there was only restlessness. He wanted to pace or prowl. Wanted to go for a long, hard run. But she was right, damn it. She was right. He couldn't walk away, no matter how badly he wanted to.

No matter how badly he did *not* want to.

Frowning, he turned toward the sofa, where finally she slept. She'd fought him, resisted him, but in the end the fatigue shadowing her eyes had won. She lay there now, her features softer and more relaxed than he'd ever seen them, making her look younger, achingly vulnerable, with dark hair spilling around her face and her mouth slightly open.

The need to touch her slammed in hard and fast, just as it did every time he saw her. Earlier that night he'd indulged. Earlier, he'd touched and felt. Too much. He'd slid his finger inside her mouth and felt the moist heat there, had imagined the moist heat he might feel somewhere else.

There was desire, too, not just the desire to have her naked and twisting in his arms, but to tear away the last of her defenses and bare the woman inside, the courageous woman who'd been hurt and abused, neglected, abandoned, but who never gave up. Who met life head-on.

The woman who made his heart thrum and his blood heat.

"Don't go," she murmured, thrashing in her sleep, and the urge he felt to slide beside her, to pull her to him and hold her tight, to make promises he could never keep, almost gutted him. "Come back…Alex."

Alex.

The softly spoken name was all the permission he needed. When he'd thought she was dreaming of him, Liam, he'd forced himself to stay away from her. Refused to let himself touch.

But she wasn't dreaming of him. She was dreaming of her son, and the pain in her voice, on her face, was real. No matter how well he'd trained himself not to think, not to want, not to indulge, he couldn't just stand there and watch her suffer.

"He's coming home," he promised, sliding down beside her. She moaned softly and turned into him, buried her face against his throat. "He's coming home," he promised again.

And then Liam would have no choice.

He would leave.

Dawn whispered through the miniblinds. Liam blinked gritty eyes against the soft intrusion of light but couldn't bring himself to leave the sofa. Soon he would have to. Before she awoke, before she stretched lazily and found him holding her, running his hands idly through her long, tangled hair.

But not now. Her breathing was still deep and rhythmic, her body languid. They'd been this way for hours, hours during which Liam had occasionally nodded off, only to force himself awake before the images in his dreams became too strong, too real. Images of Danielle, in his arms as she was now, but naked and wanting, urging.

Just the thought had his body going hard all over again.

The ringing of his mobile phone changed everything. In an instant Danielle was awake, jerking upright with her eyes wide and drenched with dread. He sprang into action, disentangling himself from her and reaching for the small phone sitting by the hand-drawn pictures of Alex.

"Brooks, here."

"Liam, thank God I reached you. It's Gretchen."

His heart, hammering cruelly from the abrupt invasion of sound and sensation, damn near stopped. "What is it?"

Danielle was by his side, tugging on his arm, watching him with those wide, imploring eyes of hers. He knew she wanted him to share the conversation with her, let her hear, but until he knew what Gretchen had to say, there was no way in hell he would let Danielle listen.

"There's another picture," Gretchen said. "I found it just now."

"Of Alex?"

Danielle's grip on his arm tightened, her short fingernails digging deep.

"No," Gretchen whispered. "Of a hospital."

He stiffened. "A hospital?"

Danielle grabbed his wrist, pulled the phone toward her face. "Is he hurt?"

"I don't know," Gretchen said. "Vi doesn't know why she drew the picture. She just keeps saying over and over that it's cold and empty, that there's no one there to hear the cry in the dark."

Once, the upper-north-side building had teemed with activity. Lives had begun there, others had ended. Tears had been shed, some in joy, others in sorrow. Prayers had been uttered in the incense-laden chapel, some answered, others seemingly unheard.

Danielle whispered her own prayer, tried to ignore the tightly coiled band of dread and fear and horror that wrapped tighter around her throat with each beat of her heart.

By her side, holding her clammy hand as he'd been doing since the moment they'd disconnected from Gretchen, Liam surveyed the landmark hospital that had lost its battle with the cancer of funding. The old structure, abandoned to time and fate, endless zoning requests and heated redevelopment arguments, stood stark and desolate against the dove gray sky of early morning.

Dark clouds gathered on the northwest horizon. Thunder rumbled quietly, the silent echo of drums on a faraway battlefield. There would be no sun this morning, not until noon passed and the gathering storm washed the sky blue.

"Come on," Liam said, leading her toward the south entrance. He moved with a stealth that fascinated her, this bold man who cut through life like a sickle through the harvest. She was seeing the highly trained graduate of Quantico, she knew, the FBI agent who could find her son.

The man who could bring her—

No. She wouldn't let her thoughts go there.

Secured doors barred their entrance, and with a wrench of her heart, she thought of her vibrant sister, Liz, who'd not met a lock she couldn't jimmy through sheer concentration, and of Anthony, who could deactivate the most elaborate security system through nothing more than acute force of will. They'd made quite a trio, with Danielle's ability to sense danger before it snared them guiding the way.

But her siblings weren't here now. There was just Liam and her, and the swishing of a cool breeze blowing in ahead of the storm. And Alex, she silently amended. Please, God. Alex.

"Through here." Liam guided her to the gaping darkness behind a shattered window. "Kids," he amended. "Come midnight, this is probably quite the place to be." He brushed away the shards of glass. "When I was growing up, spending the night in the abandoned St. Mary's Hospital was tantamount to a badge of courage. If you could withstand the morgue—"

The intuitive chill hit her the second she slipped inside the darkened corridor. She went absolutely still, the sickly sensation washing over her and through her.

The morgue.

"No," she whispered, but wasn't sure the word made it past the wedge of horror. Dear God, no.

Liam was beside her in a heartbeat, sliding his arm around her waist and drawing her to his side. "Jesus," he muttered, "I'm sorry."

She looked up at him slowly, blinked to bring him in focus. Once, the hall would have been bright and white and sterile, but now only shadows remained, the faint, nauseating smell of leftover antiseptic.

Sadness swept in on a nonexistent breeze. It pressed down on her like an oppressive weight making each breath a battle. Sorrow crowded her throat.

"Liam," she whispered, and all the lectures she'd given

herself, the new cardinal rule she'd created during the long, still hours of the night, didn't matter. She reached for him, grabbed his hand and held on tight.

Because deep in her bones, she knew. The inner voice she'd tried to silence clamored loudly. "There's no one alive here."

He swore softly. "You don't know that, honey."

She swallowed hard. "Yes, I do."

Last night he'd run his hands through her hair. She knew he thought she'd been sleeping, and she should have been, but the gentle sensation had awakened her. She'd lain there, acutely aware that she should spring to her feet and demand that he not touch her, that he leave, but it had been too long since someone had touched her, since she'd let someone, and the sensation had turned her warm and languid.

Now those hands tightened around hers. "We have to look, anyway."

At one time, she would have fought him. Now there was only the cold echo of acceptance. "I know."

They started on the ground floor, quietly canvassing the corridors. He guided her through the hallways, much as he'd guided her through the past few days. Warmth greeted her in some rooms, a chill in others. No one lived within the deserted facility, but auras lingered, those of happiness and laughter, of tears and joy and devastation. Of exhaustion and exhilaration. Of dedication and despair.

From floor to floor they went, guided by the beams of two flashlights. Not much light seeped in from outside. From the droning of the wind and the increasingly loud growl of thunder, she knew it would rain. Soon the storm would break.

And then there was only one place left to check. The one place they'd been avoiding.

"We have to," Liam said, and though she knew that, her heart rebelled at the thought, the reality.

"I know." She held his hand tighter. "I know."

She'd been instructed to keep Alex's abduction to herself.

She'd been ordered to tell no one. She'd been warned of the consequences. But as Liam led her down the darkened stairwell toward the basement morgue, she couldn't imagine going through the past few days and nights alone. He'd buoyed her when she'd wanted to fall, supported her when she'd started to crumble. He'd given her his strength and his faith, and in the process she'd found herself starting to lean.

The fall would be long and hard, she knew. And he might not be there to catch her. He would want to, but she'd learned enough about FBI Special Agent Liam Brooks to know that rarely did he indulge himself in what he wanted. Duty, honor, a burning sense of responsibility and guilt—that was what drove him.

But here, now, he was holding her hand, and for the moment that was enough.

Complete darkness blanketed the basement. Liam directed his flashlight down the long hall, and Danielle did the same. She swallowed hard, braced herself for what the two narrow beams of light would reveal.

Death. So much of it. Like a slimy sludge it crowded in from the ceilings and the walls, pushed up from the floors. She'd always been sensitive to auras, had read people and places with an accuracy that had creeped out even Liz and Anthony.

That was how she'd first detected the secrets circling Liam. His was a dark aura, one of blackness that covered him like a thick cloak.

But in the days and nights since then, the cloak had parted on occasion, revealing the widower, the son of an abusive father, who'd grown up determined to be a better man, a better husband, but who'd been unable to protect his wife from the ugliness that was Titan.

The aura swirling beneath the cloak, tattered and bruised but still intact, much like Liam himself, was red and vital, that of strength and passion. Just as Magdalena had said.

There was a primal energy, a pulsing life force of both mind and body.

And it was that aura that drew Danielle, even as the ever-present cloak of darkness warned her away.

In the basement the first room was large and spacious. Most of the contents had been removed, but a few stainless steel tables remained, coated in dust not blood. Against the back wall a row of stainless-steel doors concealed the vaults behind. Liam ran his flashlight over them, one at a time.

"No one's been here," he said.

She tried to tear her gaze from the vaults, but thoughts of what could be behind any one of the doors paralyzed her. "How can you be sure?"

He directed his flashlight toward the floor. "No footprints."

Behind them, where they had walked, a faint trail announced their presence. Ahead of them, where they had yet to venture, sprawled an even thicker coating of dust and neglect.

The breath left her body on a violent rush. Alex, her little boy who put on a brave face but insisted upon sleeping with a night-light on, did not lie cold and abandoned in one of those sterile, impersonal vaults.

She sagged against Liam, didn't care that she leaned.

"I've got you," he said quietly, and as she absorbed the warmth of his body, the solid, steady strength, she knew that he did.

"He's not here," she whispered brokenly.

"No, he's not," Liam said, guiding her from the grotesque room and back to the hall.

More rooms awaited them, and in each they found the same. Darkness, shadows, neglect and decline. Until they reached the last room on the left.

Danielle sensed the difference before Liam led her inside. Her heart lurched. Her throat tightened. Her lungs rejected the oxygen she tried to draw in. She felt a chill and warmth at the same time, one starting from within, the other encroaching from without.

"Alex..."

There's no one here alive.

Dread gripped her, but a bone-deep love, born of late-night lullabies and bedtime stories, grubby hands and skinned knees, finger-paintings and Popsicle stick vases, overrode the moment of paralysis. She surged ahead of Liam and burst into the small dark room, ran the beam of her flashlight along the sparse contents, the small table, the broken chair, the cot with a dingy white sheet pulled tightly beneath a pillow.

And the shoe.

She swayed. Or maybe that was the room. Or maybe it wasn't a sway at all, but a violent cessation. For a moment everything froze, time, space, her heart. Then it jolted forward, faster, faster. Spinning. Darkness gave way to a flash of light, then a thick, cloying haze of gray.

Gardenias.

She smelled gardenias.

And voices. The echo of children's voices swirled around her, close, yet impossibly far.

I don't have a daddy.

Everybody has a daddy.

I don't. My daddy went to heaven.

Everything blurred then. The room, the voices. The past, the present. The future. Danielle felt herself lean, felt the ground slide from beneath her. Felt her knees hit the cold linoleum tiling. Felt the horror swarm the back of her throat.

"Jesus God," Liam swore, and then he was there beside her, on the floor, crushing her in his arms and cradling her to his chest. One of his hands sprawled against her back, the other stabbed into her hair.

The sensations assaulted her. The need consumed her. She grabbed on to him with a force that stunned, held on with an intensity that staggered. "He was here," she whispered into the soft cotton of the oxford-shirt covering his chest. "He was here."

"Shh," Liam soothed, pulling her into his lap. There he rocked her, just rocked. "Shhh."

Deep inside, something broke and gave way. The sobs came then, deep, wrenching, torn from that dark place where she buried everything—memories of her mother, of Ty, of the unbreakable unity that had once knitted her and Liz and Anthony together. Once, she would have tried to deny the emotion, the fear. Once, she would have lifted her chin and pretended she was fine. Now she buried her face against Liam's throat, not giving a damn about the tears she smeared against his skin.

"It's okay," he kept murmuring, over and over and over. His voice was soft but rough, gentle yet bruised. It rasped from low in his throat and flitted around her like the kiss of a butterfly's wings. "So help me God, everything's going to be okay."

Logic, the cold, hard voice of fact and reason that had kept her alive and sane, rejected the promise. But the voice she'd tried to smother all those years before, starting the rainy night when she'd held Ty's battered body in her arms while his blood spilled into her lap and his last breath rattled from his chest, the voice Liz and Anthony had called her luck, her salvation, whispered through her like the first warming breeze of springtime giving a wake-up call to the naked branches of the oaks and elms and maples.

"Trust me," Liam whispered through the darkness. "Trust me."

She didn't want to go home. She didn't want to step foot in the house she'd shared with her son, the house that should have been ringing with the joy of little-boy laughter or the ping of video games. She didn't want to be alone with the memories.

But even more, she didn't want to be alone with Liam.

Because somewhere along the line, he'd done the impossible. He'd earned her trust, and now that he had it, she could no longer trust herself—or the need that twisted through her. It was dark and greedy and primal, not a need of the body, but deeper, more fundamental.

She watched him ease down the semilit hallway of her house, with his back to the wall and a gun in his hand. It was the farthest apart they'd been since he'd turned from her in the yard and walked inside. The urge to go to him, to sink into his arms and let him hold her blindsided her.

It also sobered.

Because it was wrong.

Swallowing against the tightness in her throat, she looked at the small tennis shoe in her hand. The one she'd found on the floor of the deserted room in the hospital. And she remembered.

She'd promised herself she would never lean again. Never make herself vulnerable to the piercing ache of loss. Whatever she felt for Liam, whatever draw, no matter how powerful, wasn't real and wouldn't last. It was just basic human need, the need for comfort, for solace. For hope.

But it was also a need she could not succumb to, no matter how much she longed to return to his arms.

It was a need that shamed her.

He was a man consumed by shadows. She was a woman who'd vowed to give her son a life free from that dark place—days and nights of happiness and laughter, of sunshine and bright, vibrant light. It was as simple as that.

"All clear," Liam said, stepping from the doorway of her bedroom. He walked down the hallway toward her, a big man who moved through life without disturbing the world around him but who disturbed her on so very, very many levels.

"You're exhausted," he said. "Why don't you lie down for a while. I'll fix us something to eat."

"No." The word shot out of her, strong, hard, because in

truth, there was very little she wanted more than what he suggested. Only to have her son home, safe and sound and nagging her to go play ball. "That's not necessary."

Liam's expression hardened. He stopped and lifted a hand toward her, let it fall in the moment before contact. "If you're worried about what I told you last night, don't be. I'm not going to jump your bones the second you close your eyes."

The words were crude, not at all the quiet murmurings of the man in the basement of the hospital, and they stung.

"I just want to be alone," she told him. *Needed* to be alone, because what she wanted was so much more dangerous.

"Danielle," he started to say, but then his cell phone rang. He swore softly and clicked it on. "Brooks here." He was silent a moment, his expression completely unreadable. Then he let out a rough breath. "I'll be right there."

"Problems?" Danielle asked when he disconnected the line.

He shoved a hand through his hair. "My commanding officer is in town. He wants to meet with me ASAP."

Relief nudged against a quick swell of disappointment. "Then you'd better go."

His gaze lingered on her a long moment before he answered. "I'll be back," he said, then without another word, he strode past her and walked out the door.

Danielle closed her eyes and let her head loll back against the wall. The house had been quiet before, but now the silence screamed at her. She wanted to run to the door and open it, call after him, ask him to take her with him or to hurry back.

The roar of an engine broke the absence of sound, followed by a quick shriek of tires.

Frowning, Danielle turned and walked down the hall to her son's room. There she lay down on his bed and held his shoe to her chest, and stared at the white walls for a long, long time.

* * *

"I'm not chasing shadows, damn it." Standing outside Soldier Field, Liam stared at the tall, impeccably dressed man with the thinning gray hair, and reminded himself not to lose his cool. "I have reason to believe Titan has struck again."

"You're on leave," Rod Bankston reminded him. The older man scowled at Liam, his slight jowls dragging at his face. "You said you wanted a few days R&R."

"I haven't broken any laws," Liam pointed out.

"No, just your word."

It was a low blow and both men knew it. "I did what I had to do," Liam said coldly. It was one thing for Bankston to disapprove of his actions, another to attack his character and motivation. "I won't apologize."

Bankston slid his hands into his pockets. "I don't want your apology. I want to know what the hell is going on."

Liam looked away from the man he'd trusted and respected for almost ten years and stared at the imposing facade of the Chicago football stadium.

His desire to bring down Titan was no secret, but he'd made damn sure to never let Bankston or anyone else know about the fire that burned inside, the one that had started the night Kelly died. Deep in his bones he knew Titan was responsible, but it was a belief he never voiced, even when it torched everything inside of him. If anyone had known, anyone had suspected, Liam would have been yanked from the case so fast he wouldn't have had a chance to blink.

And that he could not allow to happen. Titan was his.

Now he drew a rough breath, wondered how to explain. The only tangible link between Titan and the senator's murder were the postcards—the one Liam had received after Kelly's death, the one found in the senator's hotel room.

It was a link that damned, in more ways than one.

"I received a tip," he said, then checked his watch, working hard to keep the impatience from his face. The need to get back to Danielle ate at him like acid. He didn't like the way she'd looked when he'd left. He didn't want her alone. It was irrational, but unease spread through him like a cancer, deeper and colder with each minute that dragged by.

"While I was in New York," he continued, then went on to straddle a very thin line.

"I'll give you forty-eight more hours," Bankston said at the end of Liam's story. "Bring me a hard link to Titan and I'll give you all the support you need."

If he didn't, if he couldn't, Bankston would order Liam to cease and desist.

And that was something Liam would never do. He'd leave the Bureau first.

The two men said a curt goodbye, then Liam forced himself to walk to his car when he wanted to run. His heart was pounding and a film of sweat cased his hands, reminding him of his training days, when he was wet behind the ears and too damn eager to please, still trying to learn the difference between reality and tests.

Maybe there was no difference, he thought now, clenching the steering wheel in his hands. Maybe reality was the test. Maybe that was the riddle he'd failed to figure out all those years before.

A smart man would whip the car around and go back to his hotel. A smart man would sever the pull he felt toward Danielle, the one that grew stronger with every moment they spent together—and those they didn't spend together. A smart man, a good agent, would focus on the case without the distraction of the woman.

Liam kept driving north, toward the quiet working-class neighborhood where he'd left her, close to two hours before. He picked up his cell phone and jabbed out her number, swore under his breath when she didn't answer. Frowning, he took the turn into her subdivision a little too fast, had to slam on his brakes at the unexpected flood of cars stopped in the street.

Then he saw the dark clouds puffing against the sky.

Odd, was his first thought. The storm had passed hours before, leaving a ridiculously blue sky in its wake. There'd been no mention of a second front. No clouds marring the downtown skyline. And yet—

His heart stopped. Memory slammed in. Reality sliced.

Those weren't clouds.

It was smoke.

Chapter 13

Big, dark clouds billowed against the late-afternoon sky. Liam jerked his car around the spotless SUV stopped in front of him, swerved around a fire hydrant and onto the sidewalk. He gunned the engine, plowed over a bike on its side, mowed down a small bed of dying daffodils.

Danielle.

Memories crowded in, kicked his heart into a painful rhythm. Dark spots clouded his vision. He clenched the steering wheel hard and ignored the older man shaking his fist at him.

Danielle.

Around the corner a trio of police cars blocked the street. Liam slammed on his brakes and threw open the door.

Danielle.

The sounds droned in his ear, the sirens and horns, the shouting, the sickeningly familiar crackle and hiss of the fire, the shouting of a man in uniform for him to stop.

He ran.

Maybe it wasn't her house. Maybe none of this was real.

Maybe he'd nodded off and this was just a nightmare. Maybe this was the price he had to pay for coming back to life.

But then he saw her house, the quiet little white frame house that she'd turned into a home, surrounded by a ring of men in thick black-and-yellow water-resistant coats, pointing giant hoses toward her roof where flames licked toward the sky.

Danielle.

The past sucked him back even as he fought his way forward. There was no sun, not anymore. No bright-blue sky standing in stark contrast to the smoke. Only darkness as black as night. No clouds, no stars, just the smoke staining the horizon.

Kelly.

A barrel-chested police officer moved to block Liam's path. "Hang on there, sir."

Liam jabbed his hand into his pocket and pulled out his wallet, flipped open his badge. "FBI."

The officer narrowed his eyes. "This is just an ordinary house fire, sir."

"Like hell," Liam growled, pushing past him. The truth chased him every step of the way.

Titan.

"Danielle!"

"I'm sorry, sir," another man said, this one taller and wearing a fireman's helmet. "You can't go any closer."

He grabbed the man's arms, stabbed him with his gaze. "There was a woman…" He tried to breathe, to suck in oxygen, but smoke burned his lungs. "Inside."

The fireman shook his head. "I don't know about that, sir."

Liam pushed around him, tried to run.

"You can't go in there!" There were two more firemen, and they were all fighting to restrain him.

"Danielle!" he shouted, but the greedy roar of the fire absorbed his words. He shoved with superhuman strength and broke free, then lunged toward the thick smoke pouring from the open front door. No flames there. He could get inside, find her. She'd be in her room. Maybe the bathroom, in a tub of water, trying to breathe. Or—

God no.

Titan could already have her.

When he pushed forward, something hit him from behind and drove him to the ground. He rolled, found himself pinned down by one of the fireman. "Are you freaking out of your mind?"

Worse, he thought to himself. "Why won't you listen to me? There's a woman—"

She emerged from the thick cloud of smoke, and the world around him tilted, blurred. Stopped. "Liam!"

He blinked hard, but she was still there, running toward him, her movements painfully slow. Her hair was wild and tangled around her face. Dark smudges stained the pale flesh of her skin. And her eyes were huge, dark. Horrified.

"Danielle." Her name scraped his throat on the way out. He shoved at the fireman holding him down, but before he could roll to his feet, she was there, on the wet grass beside him, pulling at him, urging him to her, wrapping her arms around him and holding on with a force that staggered him.

"It's okay, honey," he whispered, forcing himself to be gentle when there was nothing gentle inside of him. He pulled back and took her face in his hands, ran his fingers along the dark stains on her cheeks, thanked God when the motion wiped them away. Not bruises, just soot. "Are you all right?"

She nodded. "I wasn't inside."

Her words registered through a wobbly tunnel of time and memory. "You weren't inside?"

"I got a call," she said. "Told me if I wanted to see Alex alive, I'd get out of the house."

Liam absorbed the words, the implications. She'd been warned. Titan hadn't wanted her hurt. Just scared. "God, baby, I'm so sorry," he said, smoothing the hair back from her face. "I should have been here."

She buried her face against his throat, pressed her hands into his back. "You couldn't have known."

But he should have. God, he should have. He was a highly trained FBI agent. He'd been tracking Titan for years. He knew the man's modus operandi, his penchant for playing twisted mind games. His love of striking when least expected. His desire to watch Liam squirm. Make him suffer. Make him pay.

Which meant Titan knew. Titan knew Liam was in Chicago. Knew Liam had figured out his involvement in Alex's kidnapping. Knew Danielle had become more than just a case.

It also meant Liam was getting close.

"He's mine," he gritted out against her smoky hair. He tangled his hands through the thick strands, held her as closely as he could. "That bastard is mine."

He just stood there. Danielle watched him, itched to do something, anything to break the horrible silence, the excruciating stillness. She'd known that Liam was a man of great control. That he had an uncanny ability to bottle everything up inside him, to shove the ugliness down deep and wrap the darkness around him.

Knowing didn't prepare for witnessing the aftermath.

He stood at the window of his hotel room, with his back to her. Beyond, the darkening twilight sky sprawled endlessly, melding at the horizon with the azure hues of the lake. In the distance a few brightly colored sailboats remained, silhouetted, gliding serenely across the placid surface.

Restless energy surged through her, but she remained seated on the edge of the Louis XIV bed. She didn't trust herself to move, not when she knew if she did, she would go to Liam, put her hands on him, force him to look at her.

To confront the darkness that consumed him.

They'd stayed at her house until the flames had been extinguished and she'd answered all the officers' questions. The fire itself had been small, mostly contained to the roof and garage, but the water damage made her home uninhabitable.

Through it all, Liam had never left her side. Never stopped touching her. A hand in hers, a palm at the small of her back. But other than a barked word here or there, he'd said very little. His eyes were distant, his face a grim mask she barely recognized.

At the hotel she'd been greeted by the property's celebrated owner, Derek Mansfield, who'd insisted she stay at the Stirling as long as she needed to. Cass, his police detective wife, had supplied three bags of necessities—jeans and tops, underwear, makeup and lotions, shampoo, everything Danielle would need to get through the coming days. There was even a bag of clothing for Alex.

Because still no one knew he was missing.

Danielle had quickly fabricated a story about him visiting her sister in Philadelphia.

The ache in her chest deepened. It amazed her that she could function for the world at large, while horror gnawed away at her, moment by moment, like destructive acid. Her little boy. God, she hadn't been separated from him for more than eight or ten hours since his birth.

Now it had been almost a week.

She should have gone to the room Mr. Mansfield had provided, three floors below Liam's. There she could be alone. There she could have sunk to the floor of the shower or curled up in the bed and let go. She could have screamed into her pillow or pounded her fists against the mattress. She could have cried the tears she'd been fighting.

But when the elevator had dinged at her floor and the doors had slid open, she hadn't been able to step into the hallway, nor could she when she'd looked into Liam's eyes and seen hell.

They wouldn't let me pass. His words from the night before haunted her. *I kept shouting over and over that my wife was in there, that she needed help, but then they pointed to the black body bag and—*

Caution told her to leave it alone. Leave him alone. But caution had never come easily to her. She'd wrapped herself in a blanket of it for the past two years, but that blanket was singed and tattered now, threadbare. It no longer shielded her from the hot Gypsy blood that ran through her veins.

The need to touch consumed her. The need to strip away the aura of darkness and bare the man inside, the one who still blamed himself for his wife's death. In a fire. Set by Titan.

The priestess is your strength, the old fortune teller had promised. *The priestess urges you to trust your intuition.*

That intuition was shouting now. Screaming. She couldn't just sit there and watch Liam unravel, not when she knew his involvement in her life was accelerating the process. He'd been her rock from the moment he'd shown up at her front door.

Now it was her turn.

Frowning, she glanced at the sidebar across from the bed, where four postcards sat in a neat line and a bottle of fine aged scotch stood tall and barely touched. Too easily she could see him here in this room, night after night, pacing, standing at the window, fingering the postcards, consumed by a fire that burned hotter and more deadly with every passing day, a fire that had already claimed at least one life.

A fire dangerously close to consuming another.

Quietly she crossed to him, stopped just short of touching. "It wasn't your fault."

The muscles in his back went rigid. He'd showered after she had, emerged from the bathroom with a pair of faded jeans hugging his hips and a wrinkled white button-down, untucked and unbuttoned. It was a completely casual look, but it only emphasized the hard lines of his body.

"Liam." Her voice broke on his name. Her heart broke on his silence. "There was nothing you could have done."

He spun on her so fast her heart didn't have a chance to beat. "Nothing I could have done?" His eyes flashed with an intensity she'd never seen, not even from him. "I'm a trained agent. I should never have left you, not when I know what Titan is capable of."

"I'm not Kelly," she said quietly, then, trusting the intuition that flowed through her, she lifted a hand to his face. He hadn't taken the time to shave, leaving his whiskers thick but surprisingly soft. "This isn't the past."

He brushed by her and strode barefoot across the small room. At the sidebar he grabbed the scotch and twisted off the cap, brought the sleek bottle to his face. But he didn't drink. He breathed. Deeply.

He said nothing.

She watched him, the rigid lines of his body, the misplaced curl of damp hair at his nape. It made him look boyish and vulnerable in a way she'd never imagined possible.

"You don't want to do that," she said above the rapid-fire beating of her heart.

"No?" He pivoted toward her, scorched her with those hot eyes of his. "You sure about that?"

"It's not the answer."

"Funny," he bit out. "I don't recall hearing a question."

Darkness crept in through the window and swirled around the room, but she made no move to flick on a lamp, and neither did he. "That's not true," she whispered. "You live the question. You've lived it every day for the past three years."

A hoarse sound broke from low in his throat and squeezed the breath from her lungs. "What question?"

The same one that had chased her from Philadelphia to Chicago, the question that had prompted her to turn her back on everything she knew and loved. The question whose answer could only lead one place.

"How do you live with yourself?" Her voice was soft, but the words echoed through the room. "How do you forgive?"

He swore softly. "You don't know what you're talking about."

"But I do," she said, turning her back on the unnatural caution that had defined her for too long. She crossed to him and lifted her hand to the bottle clenched in his, capped it, then curled her fingers around his. "You're not the one who needs to be punished."

He staggered from her, the gulf between them widening, bridged only by their outstretched arms, the bottle they held.

"You don't want this and we both know it," she said. He was too strong for that. Too honorable. Drinking was the easy way out. It dulled the senses this man kept finely sharpened.

"If you did, this bottle wouldn't still be full."

The muscle in the hollow of his jaw twitched. "You don't have a damn clue what I want."

Nothing could have stopped her, not even the warning shrieking through her veins. The need was too great. The pull too strong.

"Yes, I do," she whispered, then closed the gap between them and pushed up on her toes, lifted her mouth to his.

There was a sharp hiss of breath between them, a low mutter, then the bottle dropped to the rug beneath them and his lips found hers.

This time the ragged little cry was hers.

Magdalena had warned her. Magdalena had warned that he was a man of driving passion, and deep in her bones Danielle had known as much, even while he'd stood behind the wall of his control. But all that was gone now, just as she'd hoped. His arms went around her like steel bands, much the way they had when she'd run across her yard to him, when she'd dropped down on her knees to hold him. She'd wanted his mouth then, needed to taste him, to absorb the strength and ferocity that defined him, to assure herself that she was alive, that he was alive, and somehow, some way, they were going to come through this nightmare intact. Together.

She tasted all that now, and more. His mouth slanted against hers greedily, the whiskers of his jaw scraping against her in a way that affirmed he was real and vital, that he *was* holding her. That he needed her as badly as she needed him.

And she did need him. The realization staggered her, but she couldn't fight it anymore, not when she tasted the ashes of his restraint, the sweet warmth of promise. She twined her arms around him and pressed into him, absorbing every hard, hot line of his body. Her hands itched to cruise along his flesh, to feel every inch of him, as though in doing so she could magically heal them both.

For now she contented herself with pressing her fingers against the planes of his back, concealed by the soft, wrinkled cotton of his shirt.

"Danielle," he murmured against her open mouth, then changed the angle of his kiss. His mouth was hot against hers, demanding, urgent.

It was the urgency that got her, the urgency that swept through her with the same intensity the fire had swept through her attic. She felt the flames lick through her, lick deep, lick from her breasts down between her legs.

"I'm here," she whispered, bringing her hands to the front of his shirt, so she could slide it back, down his arms. His skin was hot to the touch, driving home just how alive and vital he was. That the moment was real, not one of the dreams that had destroyed her sleep since the second he'd walked into her life.

She'd forgotten. No, not forgotten. She'd never known this kind of passion, this kind of blinding need. She'd never craved like she did now, as though she would simply shatter if this man didn't touch her. Hold her.

Need her.

As she needed him.

"Don't stop," she murmured, shoving the shirt from his

body. And then there was just his chest, all big and hard, with smooth muscles and springy hair. She lifted a hand to the flesh there, let her fingers explore a flat nipple. "Don't ever, ever stop."

Not just kissing her, not just touching her, but being there, standing strong and unyielding no matter how hard she pushed. How hard she denied.

He tangled his hands in her hair, urged her head back, dragged his mouth along her jawbone. "You have no idea," he said huskily. "No idea what I thought when I saw that smoke."

But she did. She knew, because she'd seen it in the decimated look in his eyes, tasted it in the ferocity of his kiss. "None of that matters now," she said on a shattering wave of warmth.

"The hell it doesn't," he gritted out, and then he was gone, ripping away from her, pulling away with such force that she fell back against the bed.

She lay there, staring up at him through the haze of passion and shadows, trying desperately to breathe. "Liam—"

"Shh. Not another word."

Hurt broke from her heart and filled her throat, tried to flood her eyes. A bone-deep cold replaced the glowing embers of heat. "Don't push me away," she said, and her voice broke on the words. "Don't pretend this isn't what you want."

"I'm not pretending."

The slice of pain was like a knife across her throat. Slowly, dazed, she lifted a hand to her neck, fully expecting to feel the warm, sticky trickle of blood against her fingers. "No?" she asked. "Then what would you call it?"

Dangerous. That was what Liam called it. That was what he called her. He stared down at her, sprawled on the dark purple comforter, with her hair, damp and tangled, spread around her. She wore simple clothes. There was nothing sexy or erotic about them. Just a crimson scoop-necked T-shirt and a pair of loose-fitting black pants. But in them, she looked like a centerfold torn straight from the pages of his darkest fantasies.

The breath sawed in and out of him. He tried to slow it down, to cage the beast he'd mistakenly let loose, but he couldn't look away from her. She made a beautiful picture lying there on his hotel bed, staring up at him through those fascinating sea-green eyes that had captivated him from the first moment he'd seen her, not big and bruised as they'd been at her house, but flashing with challenge.

He was a strong man. He'd trained himself not to feel, not to want. And not just after Kelly's death, either. He'd started the training early on, sometime in his early teenage years, after he'd begun to stand between his mother and his drunken father. He'd promised her, promised himself, that he would never let anything control him like that. Own him.

Destroy him.

Clenching his jaw, he glanced down at the elegant rug, where the bottle of scotch lay untouched, then back at Danielle.

She pushed up on her elbows. "I never took you for a coward," she whispered.

He felt the muscle clench in the hollow of his cheek, the need begin to boil. "Don't push me, Danielle."

Her eyes flashed. "Why not?"

Because he was only freaking human. "I'm trying to protect you, damn it."

"Protect *me?*" Rather than stinging, the question was soft, gently probing. "Or yourself?"

He winced. "This isn't about me."

Through the shadows, a sad smile played with her lips. "Are you sure about that?"

"Yes," he said, and prayed that he was right.

Her gaze flicked to his groin, where the hard evidence of his desire lingered. "I don't need your protection. I need—"

Her words died abruptly. Violently.

So did the fire in her eyes.

He'd seen devastation before. He'd seen its human toll. He'd seen the dull, glazed look on survivors. He'd seen it on others and in the mirror, but until this moment not on Danielle, this gutsy woman who kept her head high long after most women, most men, would crumble.

And he couldn't stand it. Couldn't ignore what he saw, not when it reached inside of him like a claw and twisted.

"What?" he asked in a voice no longer hard with restraint, but gentle with remorse. "What do you need?"

Three days after the fire that had destroyed his home, he'd been allowed back inside. He'd walked among the ruins of the comfortable two-story, kicking through the debris, squinting to recognize the charred remains. The fire didn't have to touch directly to destroy. The heat could do the trick. He remembered seeing one of Kelly's silk floral arrangements, still jutting up from an urn she'd found at a flea market, but only the stems remained. The flowers had been completely incinerated.

But it was the pictures he thought of now, the photo albums he'd found in a pile of sooty water. He'd squatted down and flipped through the collection of pictures spanning years and miles and lifetimes, only to discover the heat had melted away the images. The colors dripped and blurred, fused together, leaving nothing.

This was the first time he'd witnessed the effect up close and personal. His question, born in unrefined sincerity, stripped the frozen mask from Danielle's face. But rather than leaving an undiscernable blur, it etched her features in sharp relief. Gone was the haze to her eyes. Gone was the alabaster quality to her cheeks. Gone was the slight part to her lips.

The tears stunned him. They flooded her eyes with emotion. Her skin flushed. Her mouth fell open, her bottom lip started to tremble.

And, God, he knew. This was Danielle. This was the

woman from deep inside, the woman she shielded and protected, the one she'd buried so many years before. It was the
girl who'd lost her mother and her father at an unbearably
young age, who'd been shuttled from foster home to foster
home, who'd lived on the streets, survived ugliness someone
so young should never see, the woman who'd born a child
and lost a lover, said goodbye to her siblings and tried to start
her life over again.

Deep inside, where the vulnerable little girl had grown into
a tough but vulnerable woman, the hurt lingered, and the need
still burned.

"I…" Her mouth worked, but little sound came forth.

Her voice was hoarse, and it destroyed what little restraint
he had left. "Danielle," he said, then lowered a knee to the
bed. "Hey."

She gazed at him through eyes huge and dark and devastated. "I can't do this anymore," she whispered hoarsely. "I
can't pretend I'm okay when in truth I'm dying inside."

Beyond, dusk had given way to night, leaving the room in
shadows. But he didn't need light to see the truth, not when
it slammed into him like a crowbar to the skull. All afternoon
she'd been tough and brave, dealing with facts, focused only
on how the fire had impacted him. The memories it had
dredged up. The emotions it had stoked. But now he realized
all that had been a smoke screen. When the need was his,
she could reach out, and she could help. Heal.

But when the need was hers, she denied it.

"I need my son back," she said, finally answering his
question. "I need to feel alive."

Because like him she'd fallen, and she'd hurt. Like him,
she held herself responsible for the sins of the past.

"I think you do, too," she whispered, and her raw honesty,
her courage, punished him. Sprawled there on the bed,
propped up on her elbows with her hair falling into her face
and her eyes trained on his, she was letting him see the vulnerability she so skillfully hid from the world.

"Foolish woman," he muttered, but he didn't pull back as he should have. No power on earth could have made him turn from her now, deny the truth that scorched everything he was. Everything he'd taught himself to be. Not when she looked at him as if she needed to feel his touch as badly as he needed to feel her.

"You are alive," he murmured, lowering himself to her, taking her face in his hands and returning his mouth to hers. "You're alive and you're beautiful."

She pulled him down with her, twined her arms around his neck. "Show me," she whispered. "Make me remember what it's like to feel alive."

Chapter 14

She'd picked the wrong man for the job, but when he tried to tell her that, Liam's thoughts blurred and the words refused to form. He slanted his mouth against hers, drank in the taste of her, the intoxicating mixture of courage and vulnerability, and knew that even if it killed him, he would find a way to give her what she wanted. To show her, help her remember what it was like when the darkness parted and the light poured in, when physical sensation brought pleasure and not pain.

He started with his hands, let them roam the curves of her body, exploring, memorizing. She was soft and yielding, and wherever he touched, she arched into him.

"Like that," she murmured, echoing his movements with her own hands. They skimmed along his back, rode lower to slide over the back of his jeans, and pressed.

He wanted to go slow. He wanted to give her tenderness. He wanted to kiss and touch and taste every soft, smooth inch of her. But her jerky movements made it clear she did not want the same thing. She twisted beneath him, reached for one of his hands and dragged it to her chest.

He needed no more urging than that. He let his fingers play over the soft swell of a breast, let them skim across the hard tip of her nipple. All the while he kissed away her tears, using his body to make promises he knew he wasn't capable of keeping.

But wished desperately that he was.

There hadn't been many women in the past three years, none at all for the past two. And with the few there had been, in those dark months following the fire, his senses had been too dulled to take in what was happening. Too dulled to savor or enjoy. Too dulled to care about anything beyond the moment.

There was nothing dull now. Every sensation was razor sharp, every desire, every need, every sigh. He kissed her deeply, losing himself in the way she kissed him back with the same urgency that burned through him. He wanted to leave his mouth on hers forever but even more, he wanted to slide it along her jaw and her throat, keep on going, never stop.

She cried out when he abandoned her breast and reached down to help when his hand found the hem of her shirt and he yanked it over her head. With her eyes on his, she rid herself of her bra, baring herself to his eyes.

The sight knocked the breath from his lungs. She was beautiful. Her breasts were full and ripe, her nipples wide and dark, pebbled. His hands wanted to touch, but his mouth found them first, bestowing on them a soft little kiss, then a long, slow swirl of his tongue, and then he opened his mouth and began to suckle.

A kaleidoscope of color and sensation assaulted him, some dark, some swirling, a few tinged with the unfamiliar glow of pastels. She writhed beneath him, held a hand to the back of his head while he suckled harder, deeper.

"Yes," she whispered, and then her thighs fell open and

he settled between them. In the same instant she had her legs
wrapped around his and her hips tilted up to him.

He wasn't going to last. The thought stunned him. He was
a grown man. He was no novice or stranger to sex. But the
need he felt for this woman surpassed anything he'd ever felt.

"Hang on, honey," he muttered, kissing his way to her
other breast.

She found his zipper and slowly slid it down, then reached
for his waistband and pushed, leaving the length of him to
spring free.

On a moan, he lifted his hips and helped her, kicked off
the jeans once they passed his knees. And then he was easing
the soft knit pants from her body. He reached for her panties,
found they were already gone. There was just Danielle, warm
and wet and completely ready for him.

"Now." She tilted up toward his hand. "Please."

He slid a finger inside, then another, matching her rhythm
with his own. Sensation blanked his mind. He had his mouth
on her breast and his hand between her legs, but it wasn't
enough. Wasn't anywhere near enough.

"You're alive," he said again, lifting his head to look at
her, drink her in. Her eyes were crystalline green and languid,
and in them he knew a man could drown.

Knew he'd already done so.

Knew he should try to end this, that this was a barrier he
should never cross. But he could no more stop what was
happening between them than he could rip out his own heart.

With a violent movement, he yanked the comforter back
and pulled her with him up to the pillow, then dragged her
hand above her head. "Very, very alive," he murmured, linking her fingers with his.

She reached for him, guided him to her. "Prove it," she
whispered, arching her hips.

And he could hold back no longer, not with Danielle slick
and naked beneath him, arching, urging, wanting. Because he

wanted, too. He wanted to feel her close around him. He
wanted to feel himself inside of her. He wanted to feel alive.

"Maybe this will help," he said, returning his mouth to
hers as he pushed inside. She cried out against his open
mouth, tilted up to accept him. She was small and amazingly
tight, but warm and wet, and after only a brief hesitation she
opened for him, allowing him deep. He wanted to stay there,
buried inside of her heat, her warmth, but the urge to pull
back and drive in again was too strong. He did, over and over
and over, while her fingers dug into his back and her body
welcomed him.

"Yes," she whispered, and he felt her tighten, felt her
tense, felt her fall apart. Little spasms shook her and allowed
him deeper, and then he was the one whispering, "Yes."
Except it wasn't a whisper. It was a shout.

He was alive.

She was alive.

They were alive.

And there in the shadows of his hotel room, for the first
time in three years, light cut through the darkness.

Nothing mattered in the darkness of Liam's bed. Time lost
meaning. Consequences held no relevancy. There was only
the heat of his body moving over and under hers, the gentleness of his hands, the promise of his kiss. She moved with
him in forgotten poetry, welcomed him, gloried in the sensation that drenched her.

During the long months and years since Ty had died, she'd
not allowed herself to feel. Not allowed herself to want. And
in doing so, over time, the absence had become the norm,
and she'd forgotten. She'd stopped wanting.

Until Liam.

With Liam she remembered and she wanted. Even more,
even worse, she needed. She needed to feel his touch. His
possession. She needed to feel his hard mouth slant across
hers, his callused hands cruise along her body. But nothing

had prepared her for the deliriously erotic sensation of his mouth closing around her nipple. Her mind went blank at the sensation, and there was only a swirling need, a greed, a blinding desire for him to never, ever stop.

Because as long as he touched her, as long he kissed and fondled and needed, she didn't have to think. And if she didn't think, she didn't have to remember. And if she didn't remember, she didn't have to bleed.

And if she didn't bleed, then she could keep right on pretending the dark beauty of the night was real and that it wasn't wrong. That it could last forever.

He awoke to the lingering scent of smoke and the muted sound of running water. He lay sprawled on his back, blinking against the intrusion of early-morning sunlight. It poured through the curtains and illuminated the twisted sheets on the big bed.

His body still burned. They'd made love countless times during the night, but the more he'd touched, tasted, the more he'd wanted. If he closed his eyes, he could still see Danielle writhing beneath him or straddled over him.

But she was gone now, the mattress beside him empty.

The loss cut more deeply than he'd imagined possible.

Frowning, he rolled from bed and crossed to the bathroom, quietly pulled open the door. And saw her. Not standing naked and languid beneath the spray of the shower, but sitting on the closed lid of the toilet, crying.

For a moment, he couldn't breathe. Couldn't think. He'd ambled to the bathroom, half planning to join her in the shower, to pick up where they'd left off shortly before dawn. But she was just sitting there. His tough, fiery Gypsy was just sitting there, naked except for the towel wrapped around her.

Slowly she looked up at him, exposed him to eyes darkened by horror and rimmed with regret. Tears streaked her face, and her mouth swollen from the roughness of his passion.

The sight almost sent him to his knees.

He'd done this to her. He'd taken what he had no right to take. He'd known it at the time, had known it all along, but he hadn't been strong enough to walk away. Now the truth blasted him. In trying to help, in trying to heal, he'd only succeeded in hurting her more.

"Liam," she whispered, but he barely recognized her voice. It wasn't strong and vibrant, but small and vulnerable. Unsure. He wanted to go to her, touch her, fold her in his arms and hold her, promise her everything would be okay. That they were both alive and that he would never hurt her again.

But the way she was looking at him, lost and alone and broken, stood as an invisible barrier between them.

Frowning, he did the only thing he could. He turned from the bathroom and closed the door behind him.

The call came exactly an hour later. He'd just stepped out of the shower and finished drying when his cell phone started to ring. Through the foggy bathroom he reached for it and pushed the small button to answer. "Brooks, here."

"Lee, thank God," came Mariah's grim voice. "There's been another murder."

It was a med student this time. Constance Turner. She'd been on the fast track at Cornell Medical School, a young woman with an inquisitive mind and a bright future. Her professors had adored her, said she was the most promising researcher they'd seen in years.

Until last August when she'd vanished without a trace.

Her family, a hardworking couple from Queens whose world had been defined by their only child, had sworn they didn't know where she was. Her boyfriend had been investigated, but there were no signs of foul play. No history of arguments. Nothing stolen from her apartment. No body. Her credit cards had never been used again. It was as though she'd never even existed.

Until last night, when her body was found in upstate New York, at the scene of a single car accident.

The police reports made it sound simple. Constance had been driving too fast along a narrow, winding road, and she'd lost control of her car. There were skid marks leading up to the tree she'd wrapped around. She hadn't stood a chance.

Simple, routine, except for the postcard found on her body. Of a pastoral German farmhouse. Addressed to Liam.

Jerking on his jeans, he swore softly. Questions twisted through him. Who was Constance Turner and why was she dead? Why had she been driving so fast? Why had she had a postcard with her? What had she been trying to tell him?

The message was too smeared to know, Mariah had explained. His name and address were discernable, but the car had exploded, and the water used to put out the fire had smeared the scribbled note. Only three letters survived intact: ANT.

It meant nothing, Liam thought savagely, pulling a dark knit shirt over his head. Nothing.

But in truth, he feared it could mean everything.

He threw open the bathroom door and strode into his hotel room. He had to get to the local field office immediately and do some checking. Figure out what the hell ANT meant. That was all he could do for Danielle now. Find her son. Bring him home safely. Make sure Titan never touched either of them again.

The sight of her sitting in the wing chair by the window stopped him cold. He'd been staring out over the lake when she emerged from the bathroom thirty minutes before, and when he'd turned, he'd found her fumbling with the clothing he'd stripped from her body the night before.

He'd wanted to say something, do something, but knew he'd done enough. So he'd headed for the bathroom, sure that by the time he emerged, she would be gone.

But there she was, dressed now, but still sitting in the chair.

"I have to go." He slid his sockless feet into his loafers and reached for his gun and holster.

"I know." The words were simple, benign.

He turned and walked to the door, pulled it open but couldn't make himself walk out on her. Not without saying what had to be said.

Bracing himself, he twisted back toward her. "Don't blame yourself for last night."

She lifted her chin, the first sign of fire he'd seen since he'd extinguished it the night before, with a simple, dangerous question. *What do you need?*

"Who would you like me to blame? You?"

He winced, felt his jaw go tight. "This isn't what I wanted, Danielle." The words broke from deep inside. "Christ... none of this is what I wanted." To need and feel, to want. For so many years he'd kept the lines of his life pristinely clean and separate. When he'd gotten off the plane in Chicago, he'd never expected this would be the time he mangled everything. "I would walk out this door right now and never come back, if I could." Walk away, walk far. "But I can't do that, not until Alex is home safe and sound."

Her eyes went dark. "But then you will," she said, and the words lashed at his heart like a thin leather strip.

"Yes," he said. "Then I will."

Not wanting to look at her one second longer, not wanting to see the bed where they'd come together and come alive, where light had pushed aside the darkness, he did what he should have done last night. He turned from her and stepped into the long corridor lined by antique portraits of aristocrats long gone from this world, and closed the door behind him.

Danielle stared at the closed door for a long, long time.

The gravity of what she'd let happen stunned her. She didn't want to think of last night as a mistake, not when for the first time in years she'd felt alive, really alive. But the bright light of morning drove home everything she'd not let herself consider the night before. There'd been only the mindless need, the blinding desire to let down her guard and lean.

But she'd done far more than lean. She'd fallen.

And now regret slashed at her. What kind of mother was she? What kind of woman? Her son was missing, but there she'd been, in Liam's bed, giving herself to him in ways she hadn't even known possible.

She'd had sex before. Just with Ty, but they had been lovers. They'd shared laughter and pleasure. They'd created a son. But nothing that had passed between them compared to the force that had driven her into Liam's arms. She'd never known something as simple as a man's touch could cancel out every logical, rational thought. She'd never known a kiss could blind her to caution. She'd never known passion could be that urgent, as though if he hadn't touched her, hadn't loved her, she just might shatter.

Love her?

No. Not love. That wasn't what this was about. Need, that was all. Raw, primal, incessant.

Blinking back tears she refused to shed, Danielle glanced toward the window. Beyond, Lake Michigan sprawled as far as the eye could see. The hollowness inside of her was much the same, except it wasn't bright and blue and glistening beneath the sun. It was dark and dull and colder by the second.

And she hated it. She hated the stabbing sensation in her throat, the dull ache in her chest. Standing, she crossed to the bed and yanked at the covers, ripped them from the mattress. She wanted no evidence, no reminders. Not for her, not for Liam. After wadding the fine cotton sheets into a tight ball, she tossed them across the room and grabbed the key card to the room Mr. Mansfield had assigned to her, then abandoned the scene of the crime.

The phone rang fifteen minutes later. "Hello, Danielle."

It was a smooth voice, low and cultured, with the faintest trace of a continental accent. "Who is this?"

The man hesitated only a moment before answering. "You don't remember me?"

The hairs along the back of her neck bristled, and the chill inside, the dull chill left by Liam, turned sharp and punishing. Because she did remember. "The lobby," she said on a low breath. The elegant man with the salt-and-pepper hair. "You offered me a drink."

"And you should have accepted it," he said mildly. "Everything would have been so much simpler if you had." Laughter then, equally mild. "So tell me. What did you think of my little demonstration yesterday? Do I finally have your attention?"

Bastard! she wanted to shout. *Give me back my son!* But instinct told her to keep her cards close to her chest. "What do you want?"

"The same thing Brooks wants."

She stiffened. "Brooks?"

"You, my dear. I want you."

Horror flooded the gaping emptiness. It was hot and corrosive, boiling. Rage shouted through her. She wanted to crawl through the phone lines and hurt this man, hurt him bad. Hurt him as he'd hurt her. Instead, she forced her voice to remain calm and unaffected. "Tell me how, tell me when."

"Tonight," he answered politely, as though they were discussing dinner plans. "At the beach, just after sundown. You know the spot."

A cold resolve snaked in from the darkness. "I'll be there."

He let out another laugh, this one pleased. "And I will be eagerly waiting, my dear." A pause, this one short, charged by a blast of sinister energy. "Alone, Danielle. You're to come alone this time, or your son dies."

Or your son dies.

The insidious words stayed with Danielle long after the

man's deceptive voice died from her ears. She hung up the
phone and paced the small room, let her mind race with possibilities.

She would do anything. No price was too high. No risk
was too great. She would do anything to make sure her son
was safe. What happened to her in the process did not matter.

Staring out over the lake, she drew her hands to her stomach, much as she'd done during the nine months she'd carried
Alex. From the moment she'd learned of his conception, love
for the child growing within her had consumed her. She'd
treasured every kick, every swish, every hiccup. She'd even
treasured the pain of birth. She'd never forget her first sight
of him, his red skin all shriveled and covered by a white
paste, his body seemingly frail, his cry strong and hardy. The
doctor had placed him on her chest, and he'd taken to her
breast immediately and begun to suckle.

From that moment on, he'd owned her.

Emotion crowded her throat, and she let her fingers spread
wider against her abdomen. She and Liam had not used protection last night. She hadn't gone to his room with the in-
tention of making love, and instinctively she knew he was
not one of those men who carried condoms in his shaving
kit, just in case. Everything between them had happened so
fast, that even though she'd had the fleeting thought of birth
control, she hadn't cared. The need to feel him inside of her
had been too strong.

And now the thought of carrying his child almost made
her double over. She would love the child, just as she loved—

No.

There was only one choice left to her now, and no matter
how badly the thought of saying goodbye to Liam stung, she
really had no option. Not anymore.

Her hands shook. She stood at the window and clenched
the phone, swallowed to moisten her mouth. The phone rang
once, twice, and each time it did Danielle's heart stuttered.

A simple phone call shouldn't be so hard.

She closed her eyes, bringing the old fortune teller to mind. Her somber warning gave her all the strength she needed.

Those who walk alone are the first to fall.

Letting out a slow breath, she opened her eyes at the third ring and prayed the right person answered the phone. There was no logical reason why he would answer this private number that belonged to another, but with her brother, logic rarely entered the equation.

"H'lo," came the winded but achingly familiar voice, and Danielle's heart strummed low and hard.

"Liz."

"Dani!" her sister exclaimed. "Omigosh, this is such a wonderful surprise."

The sound of Elizabeth's voice, warm, buoyant, flowed through her like the forgotten strains of a lullaby. They exchanged pleasantries and preliminaries, Danielle listening patiently while Liz gave her the highlights of her and Anthony's latest adventures with Jeremy.

"Enough about me," Liz said abruptly. "Tell me about you. I've been worried."

Danielle stiffened. "Worried? Why?"

"I don't know," her sister said. "Just a feeling, I guess. I forget what day it was, but a few days ago I couldn't stop thinking about Alex."

"Alex?" Her son's name came out on a broken whisper.

"It was the strangest thing," Liz went on. "I was out shopping one afternoon and all of a sudden, right there in the middle of the crowded mall, I thought I heard him."

Danielle bit back a sob.

"I spun around, thinking maybe you'd come for a surprise visit—"

"—but I wasn't there," Danielle finished for her.

"No, you weren't. I was going to call you—" Liz's words broke off abruptly, followed by a sharp intake of breath. "My God, Dani, what's wrong?"

She closed her eyes and leaned back her head, drew in a slow breath, refused to let herself cry. Her sister didn't ask *if* something was wrong, because she knew. *She knew.* It had always been like that between the three of them.

The distance between them, the estrangement with her brother, was like losing a part of herself. "I need your help," she said, and her voice wobbled on the words.

"Anything," Liz said. "I can be at the airport in forty-five minutes. Just tell me where—"

"It's Alex." Danielle swallowed hard. "I have to do something, Liz. Something dangerous." She paused, worked hard to keep the fear out of her voice. "I need to know if anything happens to me, you'll be there for Alex."

Her sister gasped, and Danielle could almost see her standing there, all that spark and vitality frozen in place.

"Dani, you're scaring me."

"Please, Liz." The band around her throat, her heart, tightened. The thought of her precious little boy being swallowed by the foster care system, as she, Liz and Anthony had been, destroyed her. "Promise me. Promise me you'll be there for Alex if anything happens to me."

"Of course I will," her sister said, "but whatever it is you have to do, I'm not letting you do it alone. Just tell me what's going on and where you are, and I'll be on the next plane—"

Silently, her heart breaking, Danielle hung up the phone and moved on to the next phase of her plan.

ANT.

Three simple letters, but without the rest of the word, or the rest of the message, they meant nothing.

Liam strode through the glistening double doors of the Stirling Manor and toward the secluded elevator at the back of the lobby. On pure impulse his gaze slid to the front desk, where he'd first seen Danielle in what seemed like a long ago lifetime. She'd been so vibrant in those first moments, with that wild dark hair and flashing green eyes, like a sparkler come to life.

Then she'd gotten the phone call, and everything had changed.

Until last night. Last night she'd come back to life—

Liam shoved aside the thought, much as he'd done throughout the long hours of the afternoon, and continued toward the elevators.

ANT.

The postcard had been addressed to him, ready to mail except for the omission of a stamp. Had Constance Turner been heading to the post office? Had she been trying to warn him? Or was she just another of Titan's minions sent to mail yet another threat.

ANT.

Antique. Antiseptic. Ant…arctica. But none of the words made sense.

Antidote?

That word chilled.

Frowning, he jabbed the button for the elevator. He'd been out of pocket all afternoon, but knew he'd have to face Danielle soon. They needed to talk, to find some way to erase what had happened the night before.

"Brooks!"

Liam spun to see Derek Mansfield, owner of the Stirling Manor, former merchant marine, and one-time target of an intense FBI investigation, striding toward him. The man's face was hard and set, his dark eyes glinting, his hair pulled in an irreverent ponytail behind his neck. Dressed in black, he had the rogue pirate look down to an art form. "Mansfield."

"I've been waiting for you."

Vaguely Liam heard the elevator ding and the doors slide open. "I'm here now." Antidote. Could that be it? Had the med student been writing to Liam about a drug Benedict was developing? "What's going on?" he asked, turning toward Danielle's employer.

Mansfield pulled a long white envelope from inside his black suit coat. "Danielle asked me to give this to you."

Liam glanced at the four block letters that formed his name. Danielle had been upset the last time he'd seen her, but she'd written his name with obvious deliberation.

"Why didn't she give it to me herself?" he asked, using his foot to prevent the elevator doors from closing.

"Didn't say," Mansfield said. "I'd have to guess she didn't plan on seeing you herself."

The innocent statement landed with damning precision. No, Danielle probably didn't plan on seeing him again. Not after last night.

He looked at the note, felt a chill sweep through him. "Thanks," he said, taking the envelope and tucking it inside the folder. He stepped into the elevator and pushed the button for the fourteenth floor.

Mansfield's expression went hard, oddly protective. "Aren't you going to read it?" he asked. "It seemed important."

The gleaming stainless steel doors slid toward each other. "It was," Liam said quietly. *It was.*

At least it had been.

Too easily he could see her as she'd been the night before, and worse, the morning after—her tears, her desperation, the vulnerability he'd freed. Regret stabbed deep. He should never have left her alone in his hotel room, raw from the night of mindless, ill-advised lovemaking, teetering on the edge and hurting.

The doors jammed together, leaving Liam standing alone.

Whatever Danielle had to say in her Dear John letter, he'd read it in private.

Danielle stood alone, just as she had every night since Ty died. The sun sank beneath a horizon of skyscrapers, deepening the lavender shades of twilight as darkness swept across the lake. The breeze blew in off the water and whipped across the beach, carrying with it a misty spray.

Once, Danielle would have hurried for her car with the last light of day. Once, she would have refused to stand by herself on the isolated strip of windswept beach. Once, she would have refused to heed the voice inside.

Once, she'd let tragedy turn her into a coward.

Not anymore, she vowed silently, willing herself to ignore her deep-seated unease with wide-open spaces. She was done running when it was time to stand and fight. She was done hiding when it was time to confront. For more than twenty-five years she'd felt safe only when she had four walls to protect her—four walls, that was, *and* her brother and sister. *Those who walk alone are the first to fall.*

She didn't want to walk alone. For the first time in two years, she didn't want to face each sunrise, each sunset, every challenge, with no one standing by her side. For the first time in what felt like forever, she wanted—

That was just it. She wanted.

She wanted her son back. She wanted him safe. She wanted to hold him, see his smile. She wanted to give him his Spider-Man shoes. And, God help her, she wanted a man by her side. But not just any man. She wanted Liam.

And that was why she stood alone.

It was also why she'd covertly slipped the note to Derek Mansfield.

Night crept closer, shifting from hazy shades to sinister shadows.

Eight o'clock. She stared at her watch, then glanced at her mobile phone to be sure she had not missed a call.

She hadn't.

Derek had delivered the note. If he hadn't, he would have called her. That was the plan. And if he'd called, she would have aborted her plan. Because while she desperately wanted

Alex home, the whisper deep inside warned her not to walk into Titan's lair without backup.

Was he out there? Was he waiting in the shadows? Watching? Or had something gone horribly wrong?

The chill gripped her, despite the warmth of the early summer evening. The shiver started in the pit of her stomach and oozed to her extremities. After Ty's death, she'd trained herself to ignore the familiar sensation, the one she and Anthony and Liz had relied on for so many years. Their skills were more tangible, more quantifiable, but it was her gift of foresight, her Gypsy intuition, that stood as sentinel for them all. She'd always know when to push forward, when to retreat, and when to hide.

But that hadn't stopped Ty from dying.

She'd blamed herself for so long, but now realized the events of that horrible night, and the years of solitude that followed, had helped her become the woman she was destined to be. And that woman was not a coward. She was a fighter. She again trusted the whisperings deep inside, the intuition she'd lost faith in after Ty's death, the quiet awareness that enabled her to see the man beneath the aura of shadows swirling around Liam.

Now, the truth gave her strength. The ability to sense the future didn't translate into the ability to change destiny. At least not always. She *had* felt something dark and slippery that hot summer night. She *had* warned Anthony and Liz to be careful. But Ty hadn't been part of the plan. He wasn't supposed to be there. She hadn't known to warn him, too. And as a consequence, he'd died.

But that didn't mean she should slink off and ignore the gift she'd been born with. That didn't mean she should run and hide.

The movement was so slight, she sensed it more than she heard or felt it. Liam, she thought with a surge to her heart. The memory of the night on this very beach, when he'd followed her to the rendezvous, flared brightly. She'd felt his presence that night long before she'd seen the man.

Against the warm breeze, she braced herself, and waited.

The wind blew harder, and the last vestiges of evening dropped off into night. The darkness pulsed dark and deep, closing around her, slinking further within her. Because it was not Liam's presence that she felt.

"You came."

The voice was wrong. It was too plain, too reminiscent of the south side of Chicago. There wasn't a trace of European charisma to be heard.

She turned anyway. "Where's my son?"

The man was tall, balding, with a navy bandanna wrapped around his brow. "I don't know anything about a kid."

Panic backed up in her throat, much as it had the night she'd seen Ty show up unexpectedly. "Where's Titan?"

"Not here," the man said, then he lunged.

Danielle didn't try to run, as she had that night on the beach with Liam. She didn't reach for her gun. She didn't honor the scream that scalded her throat. Instead she let the dirty man grab her, pull her arms behind her back.

Shadows danced along the lakefront, dark, fleeting, concealing any evidence that her plan had worked. She searched anyway, looking for any sign that Derek had given the note to Liam. That Liam had read it. That he understood. That he'd made it in time.

Then the darkness came, not on the wings of nightfall, but courtesy of a blindfold crammed over her eyes.

And finally, at last, it was too late for second guessing.

Chapter 15

Darkness. So much darkness. It surrounded her like a living entity, warm and pulsing, crawling against her skin and sliding through her arms and legs, pressing against her mouth and her nose. Each breath burned like the fire that had swept through her garage and consumed her attic. And the smell, it was stale and dank, stagnant like rancid mud.

Danielle squirmed against the rope binding her ankles and wrists behind her back. The dirty bandanna around her eyes stung. Lying there in the fetal position and not putting up a fight went against every grain of common sense, but she was listening to her inner voice now, trusting that exiled place deep inside, praying she wasn't making the biggest mistake of her life.

A series of bumps jostled her, but with her hands and feet confined, she could do nothing to soften the blow. She could only plan, and count. So far she'd reached 1,893, which meant they'd been traveling around thirty minutes.

In Chicago, thirty minutes could take them almost anywhere.

The cramped space closed in on her, but didn't frighten her. Unlike her brother, she'd never been afraid of small crowded spaces. It was the wide-open spaces that got to her, the way she'd stood on that deserted beach, exposed from all sides, waiting for an attack she knew was imminent. An attack she welcomed, even as she prepared herself for the worst.

A sharp turn, then another thud of her body against something hard, then an abrupt cessation of movement. Danielle lay there, trying to breathe, praying she'd covered all her bases. Jeremy had trained her well. She'd been in tight spots before. She knew survival hinged upon keeping her wits and not letting the fear take over.

She welcomed the footsteps, the sound of metal scraping metal. A wave of air hit her, still warm and muggy, but no longer stifling and stale.

Hands grabbed at her, yanked her from the well of the dirty trunk where she'd been deposited. For safekeeping, they said. Whoever they were. The voices hadn't been fine and cultured like the one on the phone, but low and crude, heavy with southside accents. Locals. Hired guns.

"Where's my son?" she demanded through the rag cutting into her mouth.

"Don't you worry about your kid," one of the men said. "We got plans for you first."

Rage tightened every muscle in her body, but she let them lead her away from the car. The blindfold made it impossible to see where they were going, but she heard the sound of doors opening, felt the texture beneath her feet change. They were in a building, she knew, but no light leaked through the cotton strip covering her eyes. And it was warm inside. Still. Quiet.

Wherever she'd been taken, it was clearly deserted.

They stopped then, and she heard more metal against metal, the sound of another door. Light then, bright and glaring, flooding through the binding over her eyes. She staggered into the room, the sudden change in temperature momentarily disorienting her. Cold. So cold. And the smell, it was sharp now, almost sterile. Antiseptic.

The door behind her slammed shut.

"This must be the kid's mother," came a new voice, this one older, slightly more refined. But not the one from the hotel. Not Titan. "Get her ready."

The urge to fight was strong, but she resisted. "I want my son, damn it."

"No, you don't," the older voice said. Hands then, cold and rough on her body, guided her up onto a table. "Trust me, you don't want your kid to see this."

An insidious wave of panic tore through Danielle. She'd tried to consider every possibility, but doubts gnawed at her. There was always a loophole.

"What does Titan want with me?" The gag over her mouth slurred the question that nagged her and Liam.

No answer came. She was shoved onto her back, her shoulders and legs held against what felt like stainless steel. Instinctively she thrashed against the confinement.

"You're making a terrible mistake," she warned.

The men only laughed. "You'll hardly feel a thing," one promised. "And after that, you won't care."

Horror backed up in her throat. She'd been wrong in calculating her plan. Dear God, she'd been wrong.

Those who walk alone are the first to fall.

"Liam," she whispered, feeling the sharp sting of tears against her eyes. Somewhere along the line she'd miscalculated. She'd been so careful. Her note to Liam had been explicit. She'd been sure he would be at the beach, watching and waiting, ready to follow when Titan struck.

Now she could only pray Titan kept his end of the bargain, that in exchange for her, he would release her son. Liz would be a wonderful mother—

Darkness. Sudden, stark, complete darkness descended. There was no light straining against her blindfold now.

"What the hell?" one of the men barked.

"Get the door!" another shouted.

Danielle rolled upright, used her shoulder to push against the cloth tied around her eyes. But to no avail.

She heard footsteps then, running, drawing close. And the sound of clips sliding into place. Guns!

She rolled from the table and used it to shield her body seconds before the door blasted open. "Stand down," she heard Liam shout. "It's over. We've got you surrounded."

"Take him down," one of her captors barked.

Gunshots then, quick and precise.

Just as quickly as it began, the gunfire fell silent.

"Danielle!"

Her heart kicked hard. Adrenaline rushed through her. "Liam." Her feet were still bound, her hands still behind her back, but she staggered toward the voice. "Liam."

"Holy God," he swore, and then his arms were around her, drawing her to his body and holding tight. His body warmth flooded her as the overhead light hummed back on.

"You came," she whispered against his chest. "You came."

He pulled back and gently removed the blindfold from her eyes, the gag from her mouth. "Did you doubt that I would?"

Wordlessly she shook her head.

"Jesus, Danielle." Raggedly he cut through the rope binding her wrists behind her back. "Do you have any idea what your note did to me?"

She swallowed hard, fought the emotion screaming through her. She'd planned everything so carefully. It had been imperative for Titan to think she was working alone. If she'd tried to tell Liam what was going on, Titan would have known, and Alex would have paid the price.

"I was there," he said hoarsely. "At the beach, just like you wanted."

"I felt you," she whispered.

"I almost went out of my mind seeing you standing there,

wanting to follow you. Seeing Titan's men take you. Those men could have—''

"No, they couldn't have," she said. "Not with you there to cover my back."

Sickly, she looked around the sterile white room where she'd been taken. A gleaming stainless steel counter held various medical instruments, syringes and needles, vials, several scalpels. A huge lamp hung over the stainless steel table where she'd been placed.

And on the floor, three men lay still and unmoving. Two were dressed in black, one wore a white lab coat. Near his lifeless hand lay an empty syringe. None of them were the man with the graying goatee who'd approached her in the hotel lobby.

Titan remained at large.

The horror of it all clogged her throat. "I wouldn't have gone if I thought I was alone," she whispered, returning her gaze to Liam.

Mouth tight, he went down on one knee to slash at the rope around her ankles.

If Derek had called, she would have known Liam wouldn't be there to back her up, and she would have aborted her plan. "I would never have tried this without you."

He looked up at her, his eyes dark and somber but no longer overrun by the shadows and secrets that had once followed him everywhere. "'Those who walk alone are the first to fall.'"

Moisture flooded her eyes. "She was right," Danielle whispered. "The fortune teller was right."

Liam stood and lifted a hand to her face, swiped the tears from beneath her eyes. "You kill me, Danielle."

She sensed the newcomer to the room before she heard him, felt him before she saw him. She was already spinning around when his voice, young and exuberant and incredibly brave, washed through her.

"Mom!"

She saw him then, Alex, her son, in her boss's arms. Derek Mansfield lowered the child to the ground, and her little boy ran toward her. Barefoot.

She met him halfway. "Alex," she breathed, drawing him into the circle of her arms. Feverishly she ran her hands along his small body, inventorying every inch of him, assuring herself he wasn't hurt. Joy flooded her body, sang sweetly from her heart. And the tears flowed freely, unabashedly.

The risk had paid off. Her son was safe. "My sweet, big boy."

"Tell me I'm not dreaming."

Liam turned from the window overlooking Lake Michigan to find Danielle standing across the penthouse suite from him. Derek Mansfield had insisted she and her son stay in the Stirling's finest room until their house was restored or they bought a new one. Liam had escorted them upstairs, waited in the antique living room while Danielle tended to Alex.

The man Liam had been for the past three years told him to leave. Walk out the door and make a clean break, slip into the night before the lines between them vanished altogether.

But then there was the man he'd always wanted to be. The man he'd vowed to become all those years ago, when he'd watched his mother clear the table of a meal his father had never come home to eat, when he'd smelled the alcohol and cheap perfume on his father's clothes, when he'd stood outside his parents' bedroom and listened to her tears. That man refused to let Liam take one step toward the door, not when the sight of Danielle and little Alex together filled him with a warmth he'd never known.

Silently he'd watched her kneel in front of the bathtub and bathe her son. He'd heard the soft lilt to her voice, the infectious laughter. Then, after she'd tucked Alex in bed, he'd stood there in the shadows, listening to their hushed voices as she told her son how much she loved him. As they prayed.

"…and for Mr. Liam," Alex had said. "I think we should thank God for bringing Mr. Liam, too. He's cool, isn't he?"

Everything inside of Liam had gone still. Except his heart. It had slammed so hard he'd expected Danielle to twist around and catch him watching them.

"Yes, he is," she'd told her son. "And we should definitely thank God for bringing him into our lives."

Quietly Liam had turned and walked away.

Now he looked at her standing across the room from him. She'd showered, as well, changed into a pair of gold silk pajamas Mansfield's wife had dropped by. They fell gracefully from the curves of her body.

Moonlight trickled in from the windows and played against her damp hair. Even from a distance her eyes looked shockingly green, like a field of grass on a bright spring morning.

No, she wasn't dreaming, but he sure as hell was. Had been from the moment he'd first seen her.

It was time to say goodbye. His purpose for being in Danielle's life was over. He'd gathered enough evidence at the abandoned warehouse turned makeshift medical facility to convince his field director that further investigation into Titan was warranted. He wouldn't have to work alone anymore. He would have resources and backup, and he would not rest until he brought down the Titan Syndicate and made the man pay. Until then, he would make sure Danielle and her son were out of harm's way.

"It's over," he said, his throat painfully dry. Because it was over. Everything.

Frowning, he glanced at the glistening bar in the far corner of the room, where Mansfield kept an impressive collection of single-malt scotch. But for the first time in years, he had no desire to run his hands along one of the bottles. No desire to touch or taste. Not the scotch, anyway.

Only Danielle.

The shadow crossed her eyes so quickly he couldn't be sure he'd actually seen it. "I still don't understand, though," she said. "Why me? Why would the head of an international crime syndicate want me?"

The same reason any man would, Liam thought gruffly. But that was the man thinking, not the federal agent. Yes, any man would want Danielle Caldwell, but instinct warned that Titan's interest stemmed from a far more sinister place than blind lust.

He'd hoped to get information from the men who'd taken Danielle, but whereas he'd shot to maim, one of Titan's men had shot to kill, making sure no one was left alive to talk.

"One of Titan's trademarks is to strike randomly and without pattern. He moves from country to country, continent to continent, targeting disparate individuals. We've yet to discern any logic to his MO."

But he would, Liam added silently. If it was the last thing he did, he would crack the riddle behind Titan's plan and find out why he'd targeted Danielle. An intriguing possibility had been gnawing at him for days.

There Could Be More, he remembered seeing splashed across a grocery store tabloid several years before, when rumors of genetically engineered humans had been rampant. The government had quickly stamped out the whisperings, but now Liam had to wonder. Why had Gretchen and Jake heard Alex's cry in the dark? How was it that Violet had drawn pictures of him in captivity? Why did Gretchen and Danielle seem like they'd known each other forever? What had Titan hoped to gain by abducting Danielle and her son?

The questions defied logic, but the results of a simple blood test could provide the answers he needed.

"We've having the syringe analyzed," he added, "but it looks like the contents were injected into one of Titan's men before they were killed." The sight of all those glistening medical instruments still chilled his blood. "We found several other vials in the sink, but they were empty, too."

Danielle let out a slow breath. "How do I know he won't try again?"

"Because I won't let him," he said, and then he was doing what he'd told himself he wouldn't do, couldn't do. He was crossing to her, not stopping until he stood so close he could breathe in the clean scent of lavender soap and woman. Until he could feel the warmth radiating from her skin. Until he could touch.

But he didn't.

"So help me God, that bastard is never going to hurt you or Alex again."

Danielle lifted her eyes to his. "But you won't always be here, will you, Liam? You said it yourself this morning. Now that Alex is back—"

He acted without thinking. He acted without caution. He put his hands to her face and lowered his mouth to hers, drank in the sweet taste of her, absorbed the reality of her.

"Don't," she whispered, twisting from his arms, and when the moonlight swept over her face, the stricken look in her eyes gutted him. "Don't."

That was his cue to leave. To say goodbye and get on with his life. To continue his one-man crusade against Titan.

"I was wrong," he said. "What I said to you this morning, about not wanting this."

She frowned. "Liam—"

"Let me finish." He glanced toward the window across the room, where the reflection of the moon rode the waves of the lake, proof that light could emerge even through the darkest of nights. "I didn't think I could love again," he said, turning back toward Danielle. "I didn't think I wanted to love again." Didn't think he knew how. "But I was wrong."

The words cost him. She knew Liam well enough to see the toll register deep in his eyes. That wasn't all she saw, either. She hadn't expected to find him standing by the window after she'd tucked Alex in bed. She'd expected him to be well on his way to his next mission.

She looked at him now, standing so still and resolute, reminding her painfully of a small boy confessing his sins. But it wasn't the boy who stood before her. It was the man he'd become, the man who'd fallen and who'd hurt, but who'd picked himself up and dusted off the cobwebs, strode forward through life with purpose and compassion. The man who kept promises. The man who'd found a way to unlock that place deep inside her, the one she'd walled away two years before.

Silence stretched and pulsed between them. It filled the small moonlit room, drowning out all sound except the rapid-fire beating of her heart.

"Liam—"

"I can't walk away," he said, cutting her off, and then he was there, across the distance she'd put between them, taking her shoulders into his hands. The blast of heat was immediate. "Not when I can't imagine wanting anything more than I want you and Alex in my life. Not just today and tomorrow," he added. "But every day."

She barely recognized the small, choked sound coming from her own throat.

"I love you," he said, and suddenly his voice wasn't tight anymore, but low and warm and drenched with an emotion she'd never heard from him. "I love you so much I could barely see straight when I realized you were setting yourself up as bait. If that bastard had hurt you—"

"He didn't." The ache in her chest, the one she'd been fighting, denying, turned unbearably sweet. "Because I was wrong, too."

His eyes darkened. "Danielle—"

"I didn't want you in my life, either," she said. "I wanted to walk alone." She'd thought that would be the safest path, the one of least resistance. "I told myself we made love last night out of mutual need, a need that would dry up the second I saw Alex again, safe and sound."

"And then I would walk away," he said quietly.

"Yes." That was what she'd told herself. What she'd convinced herself she wanted. "Until I got that phone call earlier

today, and Titan told me to show up at the beach alone.''
The woman she'd been a few short days before would have
followed the instructions to the letter.

But the woman she'd become, the woman who'd been
touched by Liam, loved by Liam, no longer wanted to walk
alone. That woman had crafted the plan to make Titan think
she'd obeyed his command, while still making sure Liam
would be there to cover her back. "I couldn't do it," she
said. "I couldn't ignore what Magdalena said."

He lifted a hand to her face, fanned his fingers across her
cheek. "And now?"

"Alex is safe." Her voice broke on her words. "But the
need is still there." She pushed up on her toes and brushed
a kiss across his lips. "Stronger than before." More joyful,
brimming with light, not darkness.

"God have mercy," he muttered under his breath. Another
kiss, this one deeper, longer, slower. "I'd forgotten."

She drank in the feel and promise of his mouth, his body.
"It sure didn't seem that way to me," she said with a wicked
little smile.

He laughed. It was a bold sound, one she'd never heard
from him, deep and rich and almost playful. "Not that," he
grumbled. "A man never forgets how to show a woman how
much he loves her."

Heat flooded her. She'd tried to write off the passion between them as simple, primal sex, basic and natural, but now
she realized the truth. They'd been making love, even when
they were trying to keep each other at arm's length.

"Then what did you forget?" she asked with an equally
playful smile.

A fierce glitter moved into his eyes. "What it's like to feel
alive," he whispered roughly. "What it's like to *want* to feel
alive." He pulled her against him, made it very clear that he
was very alive. "What it's like to love."

His words flowed through her, as powerful and seductive
as his touch and his kiss, his promise. She'd sensed all along

that the aura of secrets and shadows that shrouded Liam concealed a passionate, honorable man, but she'd been scared to let herself believe. Let herself want.

There was no fear now, only a bone-deep belief and a soul-deep wanting, for this man, this love, the life she'd thought she could never have again but now knew that she could.

It was time to quit pretending. To quit denying the fierce longings of her heart. With Liam she could lean, but she knew he'd never let her fall. Just as she would never let him fall.

"Maybe we should get some practice in," she whispered, trailing her fingers down his chest, freeing the buttons of his shirt along the way. "Just in case."

"Good idea," he growled, and then his mouth was on hers, and his arms were around her, and suddenly she no longer stood but was swept up in his arms and well on her way to the rest of her life. And the voice inside of her, the one she quit listening to all those years before, sang loudly.

Those who walked alone *were* the first to fall.

But those who walked together stood tall and unbreakable forever.

Epilogue

Laughter danced on the late-afternoon breeze.

Gretchen Miller put down the pitcher of lemonade and glanced beyond the wooden deck to the play area she and Kurt had assembled that spring. She stood very still, listening, watching, her heart swelling with a mother's love.

Violet.

Alex.

She still couldn't believe it. The little boy she'd first seen in astonishingly detailed drawings on her daughter's art table was real. He wasn't a figment of Violet's imagination. Neither was his kidnapping.

"Fast friends, aren't they?" her brother Jake commented.

Gretchen turned to him and smiled. "You'd think they'd known each other all their lives."

"I've got a strange feeling about this," one of her other brothers, Marcus, put in. His voice was ominous, his gaze dark. A highly trained, decorated Navy SEAL, he'd learned, as they all had, to trust his instincts.

Gretchen settled into one of the lawn chairs and picked up a glass of lemonade. "So do I."

Jake scrubbed a hand over his face. "That day we heard the cry…that was the day little Alex was taken, wasn't it?"

"To the hour," Gretchen said.

Marcus stood. "Has anyone talked to Faith recently? Does she know how much longer until the tests are back?"

Gretchen gazed over the heavily treed backyard, where the children worked on a massive fortress in the sandbox. Danielle and Special Agent Liam Brooks had flown in earlier in the day. The second Gretchen had seen them emerge from the secure area of Logan International Airport, the familiar hum had started once again, deep, deep inside. It was the same buzzing she'd felt upon meeting each of her new siblings.

"At least another week," she said. Her sister, one of the finest medical scientists in the country, was running DNA tests to discover if the link they all felt toward Danielle extended beyond the psyche, to the blood.

"Triplets," Jake mused.

The gravity of the coincidence, if it was one, staggered. "Just like all of us," Gretchen murmured, wondering how it was possible.

"What about this leaf? Will it make a good flag?"

Alex Caldwell took the bright-green offering and speared it onto a twig. "Perfect."

Violet sat back on her heels and studied the little boy. He looked different in the sunlight, more real. His face was fuller, his eyes brighter.

Alex looked up and caught her staring. "Whatcha lookin' at?"

She chewed on her lip. "You," she said. "I'm glad you got your Spidaman shoes."

He glanced down at his feet and grinned. "Mom gave them to me just this morning."

Happiness swelled through Violet. "I still can't beweive you're weal. I thought you were only a dweam."

Alex reached for a pile of pebbles and lined them outside the moat. "Are you sure you weren't there?" He pressed the largest stone into the sand. "I mean, how else could we have seen each other like that?"

Violet dropped a few daisy petals among the stones. "My mom thinks we might be welated."

"Flowers don't grow in fortresses," Alex pointed out, brushing away the pretty white petals. "My mom said the same thing."

Violet waited until he'd turned to study his pile of sticks, then dropped three petals among the rocks. "Wouldn't that be cool?"

"Yeah," he said, "I always wanted cousins."

Violet grinned. She already had cousins, but with the exception of Hank they were all just babies. Alex was so much more interesting. And she could talk to him when he wasn't even around. "What about the bad man?" she asked.

Alex stabbed a twig into the fort. "Mr. Liam is going to make sure he doesn't come near us ever, ever again."

She glanced up to the deck, where the adults sat around in lawn chairs, drinking lemonade and talking about grown-up things. "Is he gonna be your new dad?"

"I think so," Alex said, scrunching up his face. "He showed me this ring...."

"Look at them," Danielle said from the doorway to Gretchen's shady backyard. "You'd never know they just met today."

Liam slid his arm around her waist. "Maybe they didn't."

The thought defied logic, but not the intuition the old fortune teller had told her to trust. Not the previously unheeded voice deep inside that had led her to Liam's arms—and his love.

"This is all so incredible...," she murmured, leaning into

him and absorbing the warmth of his body, the strength of his touch. "What happened with Alex…," she said, remembering the first phone call that chilling afternoon not so long ago. She'd felt as if the world had been yanked from beneath her feet.

But now a new world sprawled before her, a world populated by hope and promise, possibilities she'd never imagined. "Gretchen and her family…" she added, then gazed up at him. "You…"

His eyes, once dark and shrouded by shadows, gleamed like finely polished diamonds. "Maybe you'll quit pulling guns on me now."

The smile slipped from her heart and broke on her mouth. She loved seeing him like this, content and relaxed, the aura of darkness muted. The hunger for justice still burned within him, but there were other auras now, those of strength and courage, passion.

"Only if you behave," she teased, but then her smile changed, turned wicked. She rather liked it when Liam didn't behave. "On second thought—"

"There you two are!" Gretchen pushed her hair from her face and stood. "Come, sit." She extended an arm in welcome. "Join us."

The tight knot of emotion made no sense. Danielle gazed at the woman who'd welcomed her like a long-lost member of her family, then at Gretchen's two brothers, Jake, the polished, sophisticated financier, and Marcus, the rough-and-tumble military man, whose irreverence reminded her of her own brother, Anthony. Gretchen had other siblings, brothers Gideon and Connor, both technical wizards, and a sister, Faith, who'd drawn the blood that might explain the draw they all felt, why she and Alex—like they once had—had become targets.

Why they'd all heard her son's cry in the dark.

Liam reached for her hand and squeezed. "Don't be nervous," he said quietly.

She knew he was right. There was no reason to be nervous. And even if there was, with him by her side she knew she had nothing to worry about. It was okay to lean, because he would never, never let her fall. Too well she remembered that first day in the hotel, when she'd watched him sitting in the wing chair, pretending to read the newspaper. His eyes, she remembered. At the time she'd thought them the eyes of a man who saw everything but felt nothing.

Now she realized just how wrong she'd been. The aura of darkness had prevented her from seeing the truth. Liam Brooks, son of an abusive father, widower, FBI special agent, felt *everything*. Deeply. Passionately. Intensely. And because of that he'd been hurt. And he'd retreated.

But he was back now, alive and vital. He'd brought her back with him, taught her the full measure of what it was to love.

In a few hours they would travel to Brunhia, a remote island off the coast of Portugal. There, together, secluded and secure in the Millers' family compound, they could finish piecing together the mystery that had haunted him for years. And they would be out of Titan's reach. Liam wouldn't rest until he'd brought down the elusive criminal, she knew that, just as she knew Magdalena had been right.

Believe in yourself. Walk your own path. That is the only way you will rise above your enemies.

The intuition Danielle had denied for so long, the intuition that had once been the guiding force in her life, surged anew. She and Liam were on the right path, and together they *would* rise above their enemy. There was no more fear, no more denial, no more darkness. Only light and love.

"I'd love to," she said. Then, hand in hand with Liam, she took the first step toward the rest of her life.

*   *   *   *   *

Don't miss the next exciting story in the
FAMILY SECRETS:
THE NEXT GENERATION *continuity,*
IMMOVABLE OBJECTS
by Marie Ferrarella
and find out what happens
when danger finds Dani's sister,
Elizabeth Caldwell!

Coming in July 2004
Available wherever Silhouette Books are sold.

USA TODAY bestselling author

ERICA SPINDLER

Jane Killian has everything to live for. She's the toast of the Dallas art community, she and her husband, Ian, are completely in love—and overjoyed that Jane is pregnant.

Then her happiness shatters as her husband becomes the prime suspect in a murder investigation. Only Jane knows better. She knows that this is the work of the same man who stole her sense of security seventeen years ago, and now he's found her again... and he won't rest until he can *See Jane Die*...

SEE JANE DIE

"Creepy and compelling, *In Silence* is a real page-turner."
—*New Orleans Times-Picayune*

Available in June 2004 wherever books are sold.

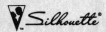

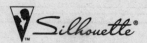
Silhouette®

COMING NEXT MONTH

#1303 RETRIBUTION—Ruth Langan
Devil's Cove

Had journalist Adam Morgan uncovered one too many secrets to stay alive? After witnessing a terrorist in action, he'd escaped to Devil's Cove to heal his battered body. He never expected to find solace in the arms of talented artist Sidney Brennan. Then the cold-blooded killer closed in on Adam's location. Could Adam protect Sidney against a madman bent on murder?

#1304 DEADLY EXPOSURE—Linda Turner
Turning Points

A picture is worth a thousand words, but the killer Lily Fitzgerald had unknowingly photographed only used four: *You're going to die.* Lily didn't want to depend on anyone for help—especially not pulse-stopping, green-eyed cop Tony Giovani. But now her only protection from the man who threatened her life was the man who threatened her heart.

#1305 IMMOVABLE OBJECTS—Marie Ferrarella
Family Secrets: The Next Generation

The secrets Elizabeth Caldwell harbored could turn sexy billionaire Cole Williams's hair gray. Although she'd kept her life as a vigilante secret, the skills she'd mastered were exactly the talents Cole needed to find his priceless statue and steal it back from his enemy's hands. When they uncovered its whereabouts, Cole wasn't prepared to let her go, but would learning the truth about her past tear them apart—or bring them closer together?

#1306 DANGEROUS DECEPTION—Kylie Brant
The Tremaine Tradition

Private investigator Tori Corbett was determined to help James Tremaine discover the truth behind his parents' fatal "accident," but working up-close-and-personal with the sexy tycoon was like playing with fire. And now there was evidence linking Tori's own father to the crime....

#1307 A GENTLEMAN AND A SOLDIER—Cindy Dees

Ten years ago, military specialist Mac Conlon broke Dr. Susan Monroe's heart…right before she nearly lost her life to an assassin's bullet. Now the murderer was determined to finish the job, and Mac was the only man she trusted to protect her from danger. Mac just hoped he could remain coolheaded enough in her enticing presence to do what he'd been trained to do: keep them both alive. Because Mac refused to lose Susan a second time.

#1308 THE MAKEOVER MISSION—Mary Buckham

"You look like a queen" sounded heavenly to small-town librarian Jane Richards—until Major Lucas McConneghy blindfolded her and whisked her away to an island kingdom. To safeguard the country's stability, he needed her to pretend to *be* the queen. But even with danger lurking in every palace corridor, Lucas's protection proved to be a greater threat to her heart than the assassin bent on ending the monarchy.